Sparrow Man

Sparrow Man Series

Book One

M. R. Pritchard

This is for all of my fellow townies who have ever had a dream and followed it.

And for Michelle, who rekindled my love for 80's music ;)

"A feather in the hand is better than a bird in the air."
    –Fortune Cookie

Faults and Feathers

"Tell us what happened," the man from the center of the desk-of-questioning says to me.

"It's in the report," I reply. "I wrote it down already."

My eyes flick from left to right. There are three of them sitting across the room from me; wearing dark robes, their aged faces placid and expectant, waiting to hear my story.

"We need to hear it from you," the man to the left says.

"Do you remember what happened?" the one on the right asks.

Like it was yesterday. You don't forget that shit.

"You said I could go," I remind them, pushing my sweaty palms across the legs of the maroon scrubs they gave me to wear, my Newcomer uniform. It seems I always wind up wearing these things, formless scrubs or jumpsuits.

"We've put out a notice," the one in the middle says, weaving his fingers together. "We can't let you free into the general population until someone comes to collect you."

I look away from the three men toward the corner, the wall, the floor, anything but them. I'm tired of looking at them. And yet, they are my last hope to find the one thing I want. Jim.

"When did it start?" the one on the left asks.

I let out a breath of air that I didn't realize I was holding. "When they came looking for guns."

"Who?" the one in the middle asks.

"Whoever the Governor hired." I look back at them. "All I know is it wasn't the local law enforcement."

"You knew them?" the one on the right asks, his thick white eyebrows migrating to the top of his forehead. Furry icebergs, that's what they look like.

"Yeah." I cross my arms over my stomach and sit up straighter. Everyone knew the local law enforcement, that's what you get in hickville.

"Go on," the one in the middle offers, waving an aged hand with his index finger extended. "Tell us the rest," he beckons.

"I was alone. Waiting for my fiancé to get home–"

"His name is Jim?" the one on the left asks. "Correct?"

I narrow my gaze on him. "Yeah, Jim Sullivan. If you know this already then why are you asking me?"

The one in the middle clears his throat and I swear I hear him kick the one on the left under the table. "Go on," he urges.

"I was waiting for my fiancé, Jim, to get home from work and the doorbell rang."

"Did you answer it?" the one on the right asks.

"No."

"Why not?"

"I could see them through the window." I shake my head a tiny bit. "They weren't good men."

"You could tell this just by looking at them?" the one on the left asks.

"Yes." They keep asking questions from each end of the

table, back and forth. The one in the middle is starting to look as annoyed as I feel.

"So you didn't let them in because they looked bad?" the one on the right asks.

"Because I was alone and pregnant." I look at the corner again. "There were seven of them. One of me."

"So you were outnumbered?"

I glare at the one on the right. "Men like that; you can see it written all over their faces. They were all hyped up from confiscating guns all day. Their trucks were blocking the street. None of the neighbors were outside." I shrug, tired of wondering why no one else came to help me. "Too afraid I guess. I told them to come back when Jim got home. I told them that I didn't know where the guns were."

"But you had to know," the one in the middle says.

"It doesn't matter. They weren't good men to begin with," I repeat. "I tried to stall them. Offered them sodas on the porch, but they wanted to search the house."

"But you knew where the guns were," the one on the left says.

"Of course I did!"

"Please, Meg, don't yell." The one in the center raises his palms toward me, placating-like. "These walls aren't sound-proof. We don't want to disrupt the others."

There is a moment of awkward silence as the three men wait for me to continue.

"They broke down the door. I guess it was best that Jim wasn't there after what happened, after what they did to me. It's best he didn't see that." I shake my head, pick at my nails. The one in the middle squirms in his seat. Yeah, they read my report.

"Why didn't Jim stay when he found you?" The one on the right asks.

"I told him to go. When he found me and what I did... I

told him that I would find him later when it all blew over. We had a place set up to meet in case of an emergency. Jim was always prepared for an emergency."

"So he left you?"

"He had to. After what I did I knew there'd be trouble. The guns were illegal. Hell, it wasn't just the guns. Those were twenty-five round magazines. State law says you can only load a max of five rounds per magazine. And there were more of them. Those were felonies, each magazine, and there were a lot."

"So he left you there with all those injuries?" The man in the center asks with a frown.

"I told him to," I reply. "Argued that the state would show leniency to me after what those men did. They would have locked Jim up forever if he had taken the blame."

"How much time did you get?"

I roll my eyes. "Here, let me tally up the charges for you. For seven men breaking into my house and raping me, tossing me down the stairs, killing my unborn child and threatening to kill my fiancé, I got seven months in the county jail, which includes the hysterectomy and three blood transfusions."

The man's face pales to a stark white.

"You think I got what I deserved?" I ask.

"Well…" The one on the left clears his throat. "You did kill them all."

I glare at him. "Wouldn't you?"

"What happened next?" the one on the left asks.

"Went to the Hospital. Then county lockup."

"But you didn't serve all of your time. You escaped?" the one on the left asks. "How?"

"Have you ever seen Shawshank Redemption?"

"That's how you got out? With a spoon?" the one in the middle asks.

I guess Canada does have a slight affiliation with great American movies. I nod yes to him.

"What did you eat? You were there for months."

"Rats from the walls." I control a shudder, remembering that. I could handle the walking dead. I could handle the shuffling and the moaning. It was the biting into the flesh of a warm rodent that made my skin crawl.

The men look at each other.

"We find it hard to believe you made it out alone," the one in the center says.

I shrug. "Call it an act of God then. There was no one left but me. The rest had all turned."

"So you believe in God?" the one on the left asks. His eyes rise in an almost hopeful expression.

This is what they're looking for here, believers. Well, they won't find one in me. "No," I tell them firmly.

"But you just said—"

"It's a phrase." I lean forward, pressing my elbows into my thighs. "That's all."

"So when you got out, where did you go?" the one in the middle asks.

"Where I knew I'd find guns to protect myself," I reply. "The local drug dealers."

"So you used to do drugs?" the one on the right asks. His expression turns into one of concern.

"No, Chuckles," I say out of extreme annoyance. "I went to high school with them. We all grew up together. Tiny town. Remember?"

They shuffle papers and murmur to each other.

The man from the center of the desk-of-questioning looks at me. "You still haven't cleared up our questions. Why did those men target you and Jim?"

"I don't know." I shrug my shoulders.

"Look, Meg, we want to let you in. We think you would

make an excellent addition to the community. You could help us here. But if you want to see your fiancé, answer the questions."

"I have." The reply comes out as a sigh. I'm tired of this.

"Why did you come all the way here?" he continues. "Why didn't you just give up and find one of the Safe Houses near where you were?"

"Jim had a plan. We were to meet in Kingston. I just want my home, with him. I wanted to get home again. That's why I'm here now. I just want Jim back."

"But you can't truly go home. You came here," the one on the left points out.

"I'll be home when I find Jim. Home is where he is." And as the words leave my lips, for a split second I wonder where Sparrow is and what he's doing.

"Isn't that what the army men used to say?"

"I don't know," I reply.

"Can't you see," the one on the right starts, "you're just like them? We need someone like that here, especially a woman. That would be great for recruitment."

"No, I'm not army." I shake my head and straighten in my uncomfortable chair.

"I think so," the man on the right argues.

"I don't care what you think." Agitated and tense, I'm ready to launch from this stupid chair. "I'm not military. Just a country girl from a small town."

"You sure? You talk like them, like those men. You have that look in your eyes," the one on the left says.

"What look is that?" I ask.

"Like you've almost lost all hope."

Never have six words ever hit me so hard. Not even all the crap daddy used to say to me. I sit up a little straighter. "Like I said. I'm not military." I glare at them, all three of them. "I never went away to war. I never saw the travesties of third world countries. I only witnessed what happened here." I point at the floor.

"Shouldn't..." the man in the middle rubs the stubble on his chin, "shouldn't you be more... emotional?"

"You want me to cry or something?" I shout. "Fuck off!"

"Ms. Clark!" he stands, his robes swaying. "The others will hear you."

"I don't care." I stand, tipping over the lone chair that they gave me to sit in and head for the door. "I'm done with this."

"We did not dismiss you."

I bang on the door with my fist. "You don't need to. My free will tells me that we're done here. I can dismiss myself."

"You're in a Safe House now, Meg," he continues. "Your free will is something you're going to have to get used to giving up."

"Bullshit," I mutter as the door opens.

"This will impact our final decision," he warns.

"I hope it does," I reply, just out of earshot.

...

"THIRD DAY IS ALWAYS THE HARDEST," my Parole Officer, Deacon, says as he escorts me to my cell.

Parole officers used to be the ones to watch over criminals, keep track of them and where they are. Now they're used to help assimilate Newcomers to the Safe Houses. They are our guides; they help in the research and the admission process. If there is a family member or friend who might be in the community or another one nearby, the Parole Officer is responsible for finding them and helping them claim us. People like me who aren't a walking corpse... yet.

"Lots of emotion rolling around for the last overnight in the cell," Deacon continues.

"The last night in the cell?" I ask, my steps echoing on the metal platform we walk across.

"Yeah."

"Doesn't everyone spend the night in a cell here? The only difference is if they are with someone that they love, family or friends."

He doesn't answer, just moves one thick hand to his collar and adjusts the white band there before stopping and opening the door.

"Did you find Jim?" I ask as I step into my cell.

"You know I can't tell you that," Deacon says as he reaches for the door and slides it closed, locking me inside. "If we find him, he'll claim you. Until then you should use this time to reflect on what you've done with your life." Deacon tips his head and gives me a stern nod before walking down the elevated platform, hopefully to find Jim.

Needing to cool down from the questioning, I head for the shower. That's the one nice thing about these Safe Houses; they may be jails and prisons used to lock the survivors inside, but there's fresh water, food and safety and something that my last jail cell never had: a shower.

Stripping off the maroon scrubs they gave me to wear, I turn the water on hot. I scrub my skin and wash my hair. Stepping out of the shower, I take the small towel off the sink and dry myself. I reach for my clothes, the ones I wore here and cleaned in the sink, a pair of worn jeans and a light blue top with a wide neck. They don't like this shirt here. It shows my tattoos. Deacon already told me to stop wearing it three times. He said the people here don't like women with tattoos.

Turning to the mirror, I comb my hair with my fingers, thankful it's just above my shoulders and easy to take care of. It's straight and black and a few days without a shower don't show so easy. After almost a week with my hair like this, I don't even miss my old hair. Long hair got me nothing but trouble. Men like long hair and it's easy to grab onto. Sparrow Man helped me cut it. I don't think I'll ever have long hair again.

The summer tan that once darkened my skin is already starting to fade, leaving behind a spattering of freckles over my nose and under my eyes. I'll be back to pale as a ghost in no time being indoors like this, and all it took was a few days. I adjust my shirt across my shoulders. I like this shirt. Makes my eyes look a brighter blue, and yes, the tattoo shows, the image of a black quill across my right collarbone. Maybe that's why Sparrow Man helped me so much–he has a thing for feathers.

I should tell them that there are more tattoos under the shirt, a spattering of tiny stars across my left shoulder, a heart on my right hip, and an anchor on my ribcage. They would probably kick me out if they knew all that.

"Dinner!" a voice shouts from outside the cell door.

I leave the bathroom.

"Nothing funny," the chick with my plate of food warns as she twists a key, opening my cell. She tosses the tray on my bed, tipping over the glass of milk and wetting the bedspread with it. She smirks as she locks the cell door before leaving.

"You're an ass," I tell her.

"And you're not supposed to be wearing that shirt." She smirks again. "Makes you look like the sinner you are."

"I hope you wake up with a third eye." I mime an unkind gesture in her direction.

"Third eye'd be nothing compared to what your third day's gonna be like." She laughs and walks away.

That delivery chick is a bitch. If I have to stay here much longer, I might kill her. All she had to do was set the tray down. She didn't even have to step in the cell. I pick up the tray, placing in on the table that's next to the door, and pull the bedspread off the bed. If the milk soaks through this place will reek all night. I don't know what it is about unpasteurized milk, but it smells terrible after a few hours of being soaked into the linens.

I was hoping Deacon would say something to her, if we all complained enough, but no one else on containment wants to risk being thrown out. I guess I shouldn't risk it either, since this is my last hope of finding Jim.

I eat the stew. At least, I think it's a stew. I can see what looks like tiny chunks of potato and carrot, but the meat... yeah, the meat. I try not to think about it.

When I'm done eating, I pull on my clean pair of socks and my shoes, tying them in double knots. Reaching for my bag, I pack my other things inside of it; the scrubs they gave me and a package of crackers that came with the stew. I set the bag next to my bed. Just in case. You always have to be ready to run these days.

Lying on the bed, I stretch out, hands behind my head, feet crossed. Tomorrow, I tell myself. Tomorrow this will be done. Jim will come to collect me and then I can live out the rest of this life with him, just as we planned. And I will finally be home.

Days Ago...

The first place I ran to when I spooned my way out of the county jail was my house. It was stupid really. Never go back to the scene of the crime. Everyone knows that. Too many memories. Paralyzing memories. But I couldn't help myself. I had nothing; no supplies, no clothes, no weapons, and I needed all of that stuff. I couldn't be running around in this bright orange jumpsuit. That just screams criminal. And it makes me more visible. I need dark clothes, layers of clothes for these northern nights. I need food, if I can find any. And I need weapons, because while I was in that jail cell something strange happened to the rest of the world. I thought what happened when the men came for the guns was a nightmare. I was wrong, this is much worse.

The great part about small towns is that everything is close by; the stores, the houses, and the county jail. So when I got out of that cell, when I broke through the crumbled cement with my worn out spoon and climbed my way through the space in between the walls, I made it to the basement. There was a way out in the basement of the county jail. I knew this because that's what happens in tiny towns with no money and old buildings. The county jail has a basement with a sewer cap, and if you get to that sewer cap and open it, you can walk the sewers to anywhere in town.

I knew this because Jim had done it before, when he was a kid. His dad was the county Sheriff in Gouverneur, so Jim knew lots of tricks and facts. Like the fact that his dad didn't want him around me. I was nothing but trouble and trash. I knew what the people here thought of me. They thought the same thing when I was here growing up, when I left, and when I came back.

I would have never come back if it weren't for Jim. If I hadn't run into him at college downstate, things would be a lot different right now. But all it took was a few drinks, a few sweet words from a local boy on a lonely night, some willing sperm, and one of my stupid little eggs. And the deal was done. Jim dragged me back to this godforsaken town before I could get an abortion, brought me to meet his Dad and declared that we would be married. Just like a small town love story.

Barf.

I wanted Jim. That was all I wanted. I wanted Jim because he was the only one who had ever wanted me, and I wanted to run away from this place. I never wanted this town. There was too much here, too many memories of a past that I wanted to forget.

But Jim's dad knew that stuff already. He told me so, right after he told me to get the hell away from his son and get the abortion like I wanted. He told me he knew all about my trashy family drama and he didn't want none of that ruining his pristine bloodline.

By the time I got done reminiscing about my sad little life story, I had made it to the manhole in front of our house.

Now I know what you're thinking–*house?*–they don't

have houses up there. They have trailers and dentures. Nope, I had a real house, bought with the money from my mother's estate. Daddy held it until I was eighteen. Then it was enough for four years of college and a new start elsewhere. Instead I used it to buy this, a real brick and mortar colonial with the big front porch and oak tree in the back, picket fence and all.

I climbed out of that sewer and ran into the house. There wasn't a door to close behind me. That was gone, kicked in and never replaced by those men.

I pause in the living room, smelling the stink of rotting food and empty house. There are cats in here now, probably feasting on the mice which were cleaning out the cupboards. I wait to hear noise in the house, the sound of another person or one of *them*, those things that used to be human. Now they are nothing more than walking rot.

I glance around the living room. All my furniture is still here, the pictures still on the wall, the coats still hanging by the door. I make my way to the stairs, ascending slowly. I step over the dried blood on the carpet. There's more blood upstairs, on the bed and in the bathroom. I know this because I was here. I have the scars to prove it.

I try not to remember what they did to me in my own home. How men could do something like that to a pregnant woman on American soil, I just don't understand it. Our nation was changing—no—it had changed. Jim and I were prepared for this. He may have been full of pretty-boy hopes and dreams, but he was also a planner and a thinker, and Jim was making sure we were ready to get out of here when the shit hit the fan. Something bad was brewing in our country. You could taste it in the water, smell it in the air, see it on the faces of the locals around town. I just didn't expect it to be *this*, the dead walking the streets, ready to eat your face off.

Stepping over another dried pool of blood, I remember

my plan. Kingston. That's where we were to meet. Kingston, Ontario. We had our passports, we had our stories, and Jim even had a small cabin in the woods up there that we bought with my leftover money. All I had to do was make it the eighty miles, then I'd be safe, then I'd find Jim, then I'd be home, then I could put this all behind me.

Reaching the top of the stairs I take a left, headed for the bedroom. Hearing the creaking of the floorboards behind me, I turn quickly, only to find one of the cats has followed me. I close the bedroom door and push a chair under the door handle. It won't do much to keep them out, but at least it could give me a head start. I pull open my dresser drawers. Finding all of my clothes still here fills me with a tiny bit of glee. I strip off the orange uniform and throw it on the floor. No one will be searching for me, not now; everyone else is too busy trying to save their own ass.

I change, savoring the feel of my own underwear, a real bra, my worn jeans and old soft shirt. I use the bathroom and take a handful of ponytail holders, twisting my hair up with one and shoving the rest in my pocket.

Next, I crouch under the bed to find the black backpack Jim had stashed in case of an emergency. It's all I have, since the guns are gone. How do I know they took all the guns? They read a long list of everything they confiscated at my bedside hearing. Brought the courtroom to my hospital room. I guess they felt bad wheeling me into court after all that had happened. And I'm sure the Governor didn't want this in the news. It was all very hush-hush.

They may have taken the guns, but I was pretty damn happy to find that they thought nothing of a dusty backpack under the bed. I pull it out and unzip it. Yes! Everything is still there: a Swiss Army knife, one of those survival bracelets with a few feet worth of paracord, reflective blankets, empty water bottles with filters, dinner kits, and a few toiletry items. I stand and put a change of clothes and extra socks and underwear into the bag. The backpack has one diagonal strap that goes across the chest. Jim always said it was so it could be unclipped and left behind in an emergency. I adjust the strap and put the bag on.

Next I get my shoes; a pair of those boots that look like sneakers, already worn in from the few hikes Jim took me on in the mountains until I was too pregnant to walk more than a mile.

Standing by the door, I listen for any movement. Hearing none, I move the chair and open the bedroom door. The cat that followed me up the stairs meows at me. I pay no attention to it. Instead, I stare straight ahead at the closed door at the end of the hallway. There's a nursery behind that door, painted all light yellows and greens. Something inside me wants to walk down that hallway, open that door and run my fingers over all the soft baby clothes and blankets.

Stop it! I had more than enough time to think about that loss as I laid in my hospital bed for all those weeks, and then in my cell.

It's strange really, just when I got it in my head that I wanted that baby, that I really wanted it and got excited about it and started thinking about our future as a family, it was taken away from me. Funny how life works like that. Usually trash like me has five kids by the age of twenty-four. That's what we get up here in the North Country; a rap sheet, five kids, a trailer in the country, and then our incisors and ten-year molars rot out.

At least I tried to be different, and even though I knew they all called me trash, at least I was changing. I went to college, bought a real house, buried my rap sheet. Hell, I still have all of my teeth. Didn't matter to Jim's dad though. Didn't matter to my dad either, not that I have spoken to him much since I packed my single suitcase and left that broken down trailer I grew up in.

I walk past the cat and make my way downstairs, headed for the kitchen. Cats scatter as I walk through the small dining room. I hold my breath. The stench of rotting food is enough to make me gag. Searching the cupboards, I find a few packages of crackers and some stale soda. I pack them in the bag and then circle the kitchen and dining room.

I need a plan. I know where I have to go and how to get there. God knows we discussed it about a million times. Kingston. I look out the back window at the garage. There's nothing but heavy equipment in there, shovels and axes that would slow me down and make my arms tired. I look under the window and notice Jim's baseball bat. This could work. I grip it in my hand and swing it around.

Satisfied with the meager weapon, I take a step, getting ready to leave, but hearing a deep moaning sound, I spin myself around and see one of those things schlepping-it across my backyard.

"What the fuck," I mumble to myself.

The backyard is totally enclosed by white picket fencing. And I have no idea how that walking meat sack got back there. I take it as my cue to get the hell out of here.

"Bye bye, kitties," I whisper to the cats that currently inhabit my house and run out the door.

Running down the street, I don't stop until I'm three blocks away. I need to find weapons–a gun and bullets. But ever since the raids I'm sure it's going to be hard to find anything.

Stupid government, I think to myself. They raided all the law-abiding citizens, those of us with a few registered firearms and permits, but you know the places they never hit: the criminals.

That gives me an idea and I think I know where to start

looking; the local drug dealer's house. And I know the best one. Noah Cooper. My old flame and half the reason for all the trouble I got into. I run down the street, turning left on Main Street, then running for three more blocks until I reach Gleason. It's just a bit further to Birchwood. I slow when I get to the elementary school. Small town drug dealers, they always live across the street from a school.

I pause at a tree, taking in my surroundings and wiping the sweat from my forehead. Noah's house is right in front of me. A big brick Victorian he inherited from his grandmother. It has a huge basement, with no windows, and that's exactly where he grew his weed.

Now the windows of Noah's house are boarded up, but the front door looks the same, a metal knocker and red paint. I make my way to the front steps, hoping to hell that his cache of guns is still in that root cellar off the main basement. Not that he needed guns here. He had no competition being this far north, but Noah had some gangster idea in his head that he needed those guns to protect his weed.

When I reach the front door, I hold my hand up, ready to knock. But before I can make a move the door whips open and someone grabs my wrist, hard, dragging me into the house. I drop the baseball bat as I'm twisted and shoved face-first up against a wall, an arm pressed to my back and a gun to my chin.

"What the fuck is wrong with you?" a voice whispers harshly into my ear. "You don't just wander up to the front door and knock like you're selling fucking Girl Scout cookies."

It's this moment that I realize, *yup, Noah's got guns*. I can feel one being pressed to my jaw as this douche spits in my ear. Someone clicks on a dim light. My eyes focus on the face in front of me; it's some Asian kid I've never seen in this town before.

"Would you like to answer me, you dumb bit–"

"Whoa. Whoa. Whoa!" I hear a familiar voice. "If you ain't a sight for sore eyes."

I focus behind the Asian kid and find Noah standing across the room, arms crossed, blonde hair a bit too long and looking like the lady-killer that he thinks he is. "Let her go, Rick." Noah must be speaking to the Asian kid because he pulls away from me and holsters his weapon in his belt.

"Rick?" I raise my eyebrows at the Asian kid. I've never heard an Asian be called such a redneck American name before.

"Shut up, dumbass." He flicks a finger across his nose. "You could have gotten us killed pulling that crap."

Noah walks closer. "Keep it down. We don't want them finding us here. Plus, my lady Meg here just got out of jail. I'm bettin' she doesn't even know what's going on now."

"Better give her a lesson then." Rick peers out of a narrow crack between the window boards.

I feel Noah wrap an arm around my shoulders, and my entire body stiffens. "Sorry." He releases his arm from around me. "Almost forgot that about you."

Most people don't expect it; it's kind of unnatural, not wanting to be touched. I can't remember when it started, all I know is it that it's worse now than it ever was.

"Come on, Meg." He leads me away from the door, down the hall, to the kitchen and through the door that I know leads to the basement.

I stop dead in my tracks. The last time I was led to a set of stairs, it turned out very badly for me. Noah must sense this because he stops and gives me a concerned look. I'm sure he heard what happened to me. News like that makes it across town before you're out of the operating room.

"I'm not going to hurt you, Meg. We just need to go somewhere safe."

I turn to look at him. This is my first interaction with real live people in weeks–no, months. "Noah?" I ask. His name sounds strange exiting my lips at this moment.

His brown eyes soften as he smiles. They're like chocolate, light milk chocolate. God what I wouldn't give for a piece of chocolate right now.

"It's okay." Noah steps in front of me. "I'll go first."

He walks down the stairs, flicking the stairwell light on along the way. I hear people talking when he reaches the bottom.

"What happened?" someone asks.

Noah turns and holds his hand out, waiting for me to descend. I grip the backpack strap and placing one foot in front of the other I step down into the basement.

There are people here and the shelves Noah once used to dry and package marijuana are now stocked with canned food and supplies. I look around at the six faces that are down here with him, four other guys and two girls. I notice one face is missing, Noah's older brother, Jack.

"Where's Jack?" I ask him.

"Not here. Come on." In all the years I've known Noah, the tone of his voice tells me not to ask about Jack. Noah pulls on the sleeve of my shirt, leading me to a table in the corner of the basement. "We need to talk."

I sit across from him at a rickety card table.

"Thought you were doing time?" Noah asks.

"Got my get out of jail free card today," I reply.

"They just let you out?"

I shrug and unclip my backpack, letting it fall to the floor at my side.

"How did you get out, Meg? Last I knew you were in County, getting your three meals a day and free cable. Actually..." He taps his finger on his chin. "How did you get to go to County for killing seven men?"

"Must be Governor of the state grew a heart or something." Noah's eyebrows rise. "I'm guessing he didn't want the Times publishing a story about how a poor trashy pregnant white girl got assaulted and almost killed by the goons he hired for his gun raids."

"I thought you were supposed to go to the federal prison—"

"So were you, Noah. I'm not an idiot. I read the papers when I was in the hospital. You got caught with a lot of weed and locked up for possession, sent to state prison down in Auburn. They just let you out?"

He laughs. "Kicked us out, actually. Nobody wants a bunch of criminals hanging around with this stuff."

"Must be nice."

"They didn't let you out."

I shake my head.

"How did you get out?" he asks, tipping his head to the side.

"Shawshank Redemption style."

He thinks for a minute. "A spoon?"

"Well, that got me through the wall. You know what a piece of shit County is. And you know those rumors about the sewer drains?" Noah nods his head. "They're true."

"You went through the sewer?" He snorts. "Thought you smelled kinda bad."

"Screw you, pretty boy." I look him up and down. He doesn't have that fucked-up aura that the others who come out of prison do, the one that tells you they went through something terrible and are truly sorry for the sins that sent them there. "You never made it to the state pen, did you?"

He shakes his head no.

"How'd you get out?"

"They pulled the bus over on our way there." He looks

at his hands. "Unlocked the cuffs, kicked us off the bus, and sped away to save their own asses."

I stare at him for a long moment, everything swirling in my head. "How is this happening?" I finally ask. "Do people get bitten or something?"

"This isn't like them zombie movies everyone used to watch. Nobody get's bitten, they just wake up that way."

"What do you mean they wake up that way?"

"Just like I said, they go to bed all normal and fine, and wake up a walking bag of dead flesh. That's why they kicked us out of the jails. The others, they lock themselves up at night. Guessing that's what happened to you. Guards locked everyone up at bedtime, and the ones in charge woke up in that state. Strange, you were the only one to survive."

"That's so fucked up…"

"Sure is. But, it sure gets people saying their bedtime prayers."

"Why would they say prayers?"

Noah leans forward, his knuckles shifting closer to my hand on the table as he speaks. "I know it's been a while since you last visited a church, but that's what people used to do at night; say their prayers, apologize for their sins, pray to God that they survive the night and don't die in their sleep. You must be saying your prayers each night to have survived on your own this long."

"I don't pray. I don't believe in God."

How could I believe in a God that would let my mother die in childbirth and let that man raise me? If he could even be considered a man. I haven't even thought about him since I left for college. Actually, deep down I hoped he was one of the first ones to change.

Noah raises an eyebrow at me. "Might want to start," he suggests.

"No," I tell him. "You know me better than that, Noah."

He smiles, showing a row of perfectly white teeth, lady-killer teeth. "I do know you pretty well, inside and–"

"Shut it," I warn him.

Noah looks away, at the group of people sitting on the other side of the basement. There are couches and cots. Two of the guys are playing cards, one's sleeping and another stands against the wall.

"Why did you come here, Meg?" he finally asks.

"I need a gun and bullets. Just enough to make it to Kingston."

"What's in Kingston?"

"Jim."

He clicks his tongue and leans back in his chair. "Good 'ole Jim boy, huh?"

"What?" I ask, narrowing my eyes at him.

"They got a Safe House up there in Kingston, good one I hear. They got hot water and everything. Pretty safe place if you can get through all their qualifiers."

"Qualifiers?"

"Yeah, they test you, question you, quarantine you for a few days to make sure you're not a walking sack 'o death in disguise."

"Sounds awesome," I tell him flatly.

"Okay, I'll help you. But to tell you the truth, Meg, I don't care who Jim was to you. Any man who leaves his woman behind after all of that, he ought to be smacked in the head with a shovel."

I feel the toe of his boot rub against mine.

"Stop it, Noah. You know you're like a brother to me now."

He cringes, exaggeratedly. "I really hate it when you say that."

"It's the truth." I push my chair back a few inches, far enough away so that his wandering toes can't reach my foot anymore. "When are you going to see that? You got me into way too much trouble a while back. I'm not going to relive all of that. Besides, it's the end of the world, isn't it? I'm sure all the townies are throwing themselves at your feet. I bet some of them even have teeth left." The leggy brunette across the room scowls at me. "See," I tell him. My eyes scan the room, stopping on the guy standing against the far wall. "Who's that?" I ask Noah.

"Oh, that there's Sparrow Man. Don't mind him. Harmless."

I try not to stare in the dim light, but it is hard not to. Sparrow Man is tall, almost the tallest person I have ever seen. And since my father is just over six feet, this probably puts Sparrow at almost six and a half feet. He has brown tousled hair and eyes as green as I would expect the fresh Ireland grass to be. He's wearing a trench coat that should have hit at the shin on a normal person, but it hits at his thigh. The coat is buttoned so tightly, all the way to his neck, that only his black boots and jeans are visible.

"What's his deal?" I ask.

"A bit cracked in the head." Noah taps the side of his skull and makes a face.

I stare longer than I should at a stranger. Sparrow Man's shoulders twitch, his eyes dart, his right hand shoves in his pocket. As he scans the room, his eyes suddenly flick to mine. Too shocked to look away, I hold his gaze as he pulls his hand out of his pocket and twirls a black feather in front of his face.

"What's up with the feather?" I ask Noah out of the corner of my mouth, unable to break my stare.

"He's got some obsession with feathers. Sings lots of Bon Jovi too."

"He's not from around here," I tell Noah. "He's not a local. Where'd he come from?"

"Just showed up one day. Stopped one of those meat sacks from chewing on my head down by the local pharmacy."

"Nice of him."

"Sure was."

"You trust him?" I ask.

"He's saved my ass ten times already. I trust him more than these other chuckleheads." Noah waves a hand at the others in the room.

I lift my backpack off the floor, holding it to my stomach.

"Meg?" Noah tips his head at me. "You okay? You know, after everything?"

"I'll live," I tell him, gripping my bag tighter to my chest.

...

NOAH INTRODUCES me to the others. I don't care what their names are but I do nod when he tells me. I'm only staying here for the night, and then I'm gone. I grip my bag as they wave when Noah introduces them. One of the guys tries to shake my hand. I just stare at his open palm.

"Don't take it wrong," Noah tells him. "Meg doesn't like to be touched."

Nope, Meg doesn't like to be touched. Noah's hand slaps down on my shoulder. I can handle Noah's touch, only sometimes, because I know him. I know how he thinks. I know what his touch feels like. Under that pretty boy face, he's harmless.

After feeding me a small dinner of rice and canned

pears, Noah gives up his bed for the night. And instead of finding another spot to sleep, he leans his back against the side of the bed and lets his head fall back.

Across the room I hear a low voice start humming a tune.

"Jesus Christ," one of the guys on the couch mumbles.

"Ah," Noah chuckles. "Told you, Bon Jovi."

I listen as Sparrow hums quietly. It's not long before I recognize the tune, *Livin' on a Prayer*.

"How appropriate," I whisper to Noah.

He laughs, louder this time. "Last night it was *Dead or Alive*."

I laugh for a second then stop short, unable to remember the last time I actually laughed. "Noah?"

"What?"

"Thanks for letting me stay the night."

"Least I could do for a local and the first girl I ever kissed."

I wrap my arms around myself and force my eyes to close. This will be the first time in a long time I get to sleep in a room without bars, without decaying arms reaching through the bars for me, and without the dead moaning at me.

It's not long at all before I manage to fall asleep.

...

FEELING THE COT GIVE, I jolt out of bed.

"Noah?" I ask.

The room is dark and after a second I remember that I'm in Noah's basement.

"Shhhh," a voice whispers.

I feel something cool and metallic press against my neck and a body molds itself to mine.

"Noah?" I whisper.

"Shut up," I hear his voice in my ear.

It's Noah's, but it's different than it was earlier. He runs his hand across my ass. I let out a whimper.

"You like that?" He squeezes one jean-clad cheek. "See, you still nothin' but trash," he whispers in my ear. "Just like they all said. Now that your mamma's money is used up and you ain't got that jackhole Jim around anymore."

I don't understand how he smells this bad, like he's rotting. He still has some of his sense, and strength. This is how it must work–they wake up rotting, turned already, and get progressively worse.

"Noah?" I whisper. "Stop this!"

His nails dig into my arms.

"Help!" I call for the others.

He jerks my shoulders a bit, silencing me. "When they wake up they'll be the same as me. It's their time."

I yank my shoulders hard enough for him to lose his grasp and reach for my bag. Just before I get there I feel a hard tug on my hair. I fall back. Noah, or what's left of him, grasps my hair, twisting it around his arm like a rope and digging his fingers into the base of my ponytail.

"Pretty hair," he says. "Just like I remember." He leans forward and sniffs it.

Oh God!

Just before trying to yank myself away from him again, I feel his grip slacken. Twisting around I find Sparrow standing there, a machete in his hand and Noah, holding up a stump of an arm.

"Holy shit," I breathe out.

"Get your bag," Sparrow says, his green eyes flick to me in the dim light. "Hurry now, Meg, before the others wake up without their souls and then we'll be in a load of trouble."

I scramble, running for my bag. Picking it up, I turn and pull a few jars and packs of food off the shelf.

"Meg!" I hear Sparrow's voice.

"Guns," I tell him. "I have to get the guns."

"Don't need guns."

I hear a strange sound. I imagine it's what a butcher sounds like when they're hacking away at a cow. Noah's corpse groans. I run for the root cellar. Pushing open the creaky door, I find his cache. I take two handguns and boxes of bullets, loading down my bag.

"Meg!" Sparrow shouts.

I run for the stairs. Passing Sparrow, I notice Noah's body crumpled on the floor, his head missing. "What the fuck."

"Go!" Sparrow shoves my shoulder and we run up the stairs.

When we reach the kitchen, he slams the door closed and locks it. I stand against the kitchen table, trying to catch my breath. Sparrow walks toward me, his face set, reaching for me. I lean back.

"Get away from me!" I twist from him.

I feel him in my hair, just like Noah's corpse, his hand pulling. He stops as I reach the kitchen sink.

"What the hell is wrong with you people?" I shout, turning to face Sparrow.

When my eyes focus on him I notice he's just standing there, his lips pressed together and Noah's severed hand in his grasp.

"Would you rather walk around all day with this in your hair?" he asks.

"Holy shit," I exhale. "That is disgusting!"

Sparrow drops the hand on the floor. He tips his head,

looking around the kitchen. "Let's go," he says, stepping toward the back door.

"Wait, where are we going?"

"North," he shoves a hand in his pocket and pulls out a feather. "I need more feathers."

Oh yeah, he's crazy. Just like Noah warned. But at least he was lucid enough for five minutes to save my life.

"Why north?" I ask.

He turns to me and blinks. "You need to go to Kingston and I need the feathers of a snowy owl." He says it so plainly, so flat, like we're speaking about pizza toppings.

Sparrow is cracked in his head.

I look out the window. "But it's night."

"Best time to travel." He walks to the door and reaches for the handle. "While they're sleeping, before they wake up a rotting bag of meat." He twists the door handle and pulls the door open. "You coming?"

"Shit," I mumble to myself. "Yeah, I'm coming."

I step around Noah's hand on the floor and walk out the door, following Sparrow.

...

I ADJUST the backpack across my shoulders. Now filled with the boxes of bullets and a few jars of food, it's heavy and weighing me down. I skip a few steps to catch up with Sparrow.

"What route are we taking?" I ask. "Eleven?"

"No." He shakes his head.

"But you said you were taking me to Kingston."

"And I said I needed the feathers of a snowy owl."

"Okay…" I look around us. There is just the sliver of a moon lighting the street for us.

"We head north. Take Oxbow to Route 37, to Route 12, then we'll be at Wellesley Island crossing."

"Sounds like you have the route all mapped out."

"There's an old barn on 37 with a snowy owl."

"I see." I look around, noticing the cars parked on the street. "Do people still drive cars, Sparrow?"

"Hmm?" he walks fast, obviously excited to get this snowy owl.

"Hey!"

"Shh!"

I grab his sleeve and Sparrow stops dead in his tracks. He looks at my hand on his arm, his eyes turn a little darker. I pull my hand back.

"Sorry, I was just asking if people still drive cars."

He shrugs his shoulders. "Of course they do."

"So then why don't we get one?"

"Noise. Cars make noise, noise brings the dead."

"Oh." I adjust the backpack again.

"You brought too much," Sparrow points at my shoulder. "And…" His hand reaches forward as he focuses on something below my chin. "You're bleeding." He flicks my neck.

I take two steps away from him.

"Don't touch me," I warn.

He holds his finger out with a smear of blood on it. Noah must have cut me when he held the knife to my neck.

"You touched me first." He wipes the blood on his coat and starts walking. "How about you don't touch me."

I follow him, not even the least bit interested in starting a conversation about who touched whom first.

After months in that county jail cell without exercise, my legs are already burning by the time we cross the Main

Street bridge. We head out of town, taking Johnstown Street, which I know eventually turns into Oxbow once we get to the state parks.

I notice Sparrow slowing his speed to wait for me. "You're slow," he says as we pass the old veterinary clinic.

"You're, like, so fucking observant."

He stops and turns, facing me. "That's not very ladylike."

I try to catch my breath as I speak. "I never... I never said I was a lady."

Sparrow smirks, his eyes focus on my shoulder where the heavy backpack presses down, and then his eyes glide down my entire body.

"What do you think you're doing?" I ask.

"What?"

"I'm not blind. You were just checking me out."

"Like you did to me in the basement when Noah was telling you how crazy I am?" He reaches into his pocket, pulls out a feather, and holds it in front of his face.

Maybe it's the lack of real human interaction from the last few months, but my filter is gone. "What's up with the feathers?"

"I need them."

"What do you need them for?"

"I just do."

"Why do they call you Sparrow?"

"Because it's my name." He turns sharply and starts walking again. Slower this time, so I don't have to try so hard to keep up with him.

When the sun starts to rise, Sparrow stops and looks around.

"What?" I ask him.

"We need to find shelter. Last night was a bad one. Lots of them will be waking up dead."

"Great," I grumble, recognizing that we are barely on the outskirts of town. Walking like this, it's going to take me forever to get to Kingston, if I don't wake up dead beforehand.

Sparrow turns sharp, down an old gravel road I recognize as the Halstead's farm.

"Are we going to stay here?" I ask.

"Yup."

"Good, I hear they have a really nice house." I imagine myself sprawled on their king-size bed.

"Have a nice barn too." Sparrow pulls me from my thoughts.

"What?"

"B-a-r-n," he enunciates each letter. "We can't stay in the house, houses hold meat sacks."

"And barns don't?"

"Barns have lofts, with ladders. Meat sacks can't climb."

I follow Sparrow to the large barn. We can hear the cows whining before we get to the doors.

"Get up in the loft," he tells me. "I'll let the heifers loose."

"Why would you let them loose?"

Sparrow takes a deep breath and closes his eyes. "And they say I'm the crazy one," he mumbles.

"Hey!" I yell at him. "I just spooned my way out of county lockup, so excuse me if I have no fucking idea what the hell is going on here."

Sparrow smiles—he freaking smiles at me—and dear Lord in heaven it's the most beautiful smile I've ever seen. His teeth are straight and white, his green eyes crinkle in the corners, and a deep dimple appears on each of his cheeks underneath the beard stubble.

I think I stop breathing when he does it.

"Sorry," he says. "I forgot about all of that."

Shocked, I take three steps away from him. "Why are you smiling?"

"Because you were angry." He turns his head to the side. "And now you're not."

He turns away from me and heads for the barn. Pulling the door open with ease, he whistles at the cows and they stampede out. When the last cow trickles out of the barn, Sparrow turns to me. "Halstead's will be waking up a little..."

"Dead?"

"Yeah."

"So you just saved their cows from a slow starvation in the barn?"

"Yeah."

"That's awfully nice of you."

Strangely, he scowls at me. "You shouldn't patronize."

"Sparrow, I'm from the North Country and patronize is a big word." I laugh at my own pathetic joke.

Sparrow stops and turns to face me, his eyebrows drawn together. "You should know it. Let's go." He jogs down the center of the barn and I follow him, until we reach a tall ladder that stretches through a square cut into the ceiling. Sparrow grasps the ladder and steps to the side.

"Ladies first." He swipes his hand at me.

"I'm not a lady," I snap. As I begin climbing the ladder, I think I hear him laughing lightly behind me.

When I make it through the ceiling cutaway, I move to the side so Sparrow can get through. And then I watch as he grasps the ladder with two hands, and twisting and jerking it, he lets it fall to the floor below.

"You said they can't climb."

"Better safe than sorry."

I move near a window and sit, watching as Sparrow inspects the loft space. He stops, looking up into one of the rafters, and reaching up with one long arm he picks some-thing up.

"Ah," he says. "Barn Swallow, I don't have any of your feathers yet." He holds a small bird in his hand, spreads its wing and pulls hard on its feathers.

"Sparrow! What are you doing?" I stand and reach for his arm, but he opens his palm and sets the bird back in the rafters before I get to him.

"You'll kill it, stop!"

He turns and blinks at me. "It's just a few flight feathers. They'll grow back." He holds up two blue-hued feathers.

"What?"

"I only pulled out two flight feathers. They can still fly. The feathers will grow back."

"But... I thought... I thought you were going to kill it."

Sparrow blinks rapidly at me. "What kind of a man do you think I am, Meg?"

"I... I don't know. I don't know you." And I don't. I know nothing of this man oddly named Sparrow. The few men that I have had in my life have gotten me nothing but trouble and pain, except for Jim. Jim was good. Jim took care of me. Jim loved me like none of the others ever did.

Sparrow presses his lips together and turns away from me, moving to check on each of the windows. I return to my bag on the floor, sitting and unzipping the backpack.

"How long are we going to be here?" I ask.

"At least for the day, until you're rested and ready to walk."

I feel my shoulders drop. Getting to Kingston is going to take forever.

"You should eat and sleep," Sparrow suggests. "And your bag is too heavy."

I don't want to admit it, but Sparrow is right; the bag is too heavy. I pull out the jars I took from Noah's house. It looks like corn and tomatoes packed in them. Since I never knew Noah to be a canner, I can only assume he learned or got this from someone else. I twist the jars open and search my bag for the dining kit that I know is there.

"You want some?" I ask Sparrow, holding out my extra fork for him.

He looks at the fork as though it's some strange object. "No thanks," he tells me glancing at the jars.

"Don't you eat?"

"No."

"That's not possible," I tell him. "You have to eat something."

"I don't need to eat. I get my energy from the sunlight."

I stare at him, holding in what I really want to say. He *is* crazy.

"What were you in jail for?" he asks, watching me eat.

"Didn't Noah tell you?"

"Nope, didn't speak much to those guys." Sparrow sits not far from me.

"Something happened," I tell him, chewing on a forkful of the corn.

"Did you do something bad?" he crosses his legs and leans back on his hands.

"Are you worried I'm going to wake up like them," I motion out the window toward the Halstead house, "because of my terrible sins?"

"Nope," he tells me.

I set the jar and fork down and run my hand over my hair, remembering dead-Noah's hand gripped there. My neck tingles; it's that tingle you get when you think about bugs crawling on you. It doesn't stop. I pull my hair out of the ponytail holder and search the backpack for the Swiss Army knife.

"What are you doing?" Sparrow asks.

"Something," I reply as I open the knife, searching for the scissor attachment. This hair has gotten me into trouble before. Men like to pull on hair, and earlier it was nothing but a tether to control where I was going. It has got to go. I pull a handful of hair in front of my face and start cutting.

Sparrow frowns. "Why are you doing that?" he asks.

"Because," I sigh, "it causes too much trouble."

"I like your hair." Sparrow sits up, coming out of his relaxed position.

"That's exactly why I'm cutting it."

He watches, his gaze a strange, sort of *entertained* look.

"What?" I finally ask.

"Would you like some help?"

"Are you a hairdresser?"

"Nope." He reaches behind his back. "But I have a really sharp knife." The machete I saw him with earlier must be strapped to his back.

I stop cutting and look at him through the hair in front of my face. "Are you serious?"

"Yeah." He moves to stand. "How short do you want it?"

I pull my hair pack, holding it between my fingers just above the nape of my neck. "Like this."

I feel his hand wrap around my hair. "Let go," he tells me.

I release my hand, pressing it to my neck as though it might protect me if he changes his mind about killing me. I feel a slight pull and hear a strange sound, like a slice from a paper cutter.

"Done."

I turn around to see Sparrow holding the long length of my dark hair. He starts walking toward one of the loft windows.

"What are you doing?" I ask.

He pushes the window open and I notice there's a pine tree outside this particular window. He flicks his arm and throws the hair up into the tree branches.

"What are you doing?" I repeat.

"Nesting material for the birds. They like hair too."

I run my hand across my now bare neck. "Oh."

I think of Jim, of seeing him again. Of him seeing me like this. He doesn't like me with short hair. I always kept it long for him. Now I wonder what he'll say when he sees me.

"You should get some sleep," Sparrow suggests, wiping his hands on his coat.

"I have to eat this first." I shovel the corn mix into my mouth. The kernels burst like overripe grapes as I bite down on them.

When I'm done, I dig through my backpack until I find the reflective blankets. "I have an extra blanket," I offer Sparrow.

He waves it away. "I don't sleep."

"So you don't eat and you don't sleep."

"That's right."

Sparrow walks to the front of the barn and sits down near the window. From where I'm sitting, I can see the roof of the main house. He's chosen a good lookout point.

"That doesn't really make you human then," I tell him, spreading the blanket on the floor and wrapping it around myself.

"I'm just as human as I need to be."

"Sparrow Man?"

"What?" his voice sounds amused.

"If I close my eyes and fall asleep," I ask him. "Can I trust that I won't wake up with you holding a knife to my throat like Noah did?"

"You can trust me." He nods and runs his fingers over the feather in his hand.

And for some reason, I do trust him.

...

I WAKE up to the worst alarm clock ever: the sound of moaning and shuffling feet. And for a moment I panic, thinking I'm back inside my cell with all the dead reaching through the bars at me.

A dark figure drops by my side and I scream.

"Shh!" A hand claps over my mouth. I try to pry it off, screaming and kicking my feet. "Meg!" the voice is a harsh whisper. "It's me, Sparrow."

Holy shit. I stop freaking out and he takes his hand off my mouth.

"Oh my God, you scared the shit out of me!" I tell him, trying to catch my breath.

"You need to wake up," he tells me.

I sit up and look around, noticing that it's night again.

"I slept the whole day?" I ask, running my hand through my hair, it feels strange when I reach the back of my bare neck.

"You must've been tired." Sparrow stands. "Sorry I touched you."

"What?"

"I touched your face." He turns to face me. "You told me not to touch you before."

"Oh, um, thanks." I stand, feeling the tight muscles in my legs stretch from our earlier walk. "Are the dead down there?" I ask hearing soft thuds and moans below us.

"Yeah." He walks over to the opening cut in the floor that we climbed through, and looks down. "They'll be asleep soon. In a big heap of rot on the floor. Then we'll get out of here."

"Okay," I reply as I fold the blanket and tuck it into my backpack.

"Did you want to eat again?" Sparrow asks me as he bends down to get a good look at what's below us.

I open my backpack and find the sleeve of crackers and old soda. My stomach growls. I don't think I'll ever be able to fill the hungry void. Not out in the boondocks like this. I need a Wal-Mart or an IGA or a gas station convenience store. I need to load up on snack cakes and soda and candy bars, all the things you can't buy with food stamps. All the things you can't find within the walls of the county jail. My stomach growls again.

"No," I tell Sparrow. "I'll eat at our next stop."

I decide to distract myself and, reaching into my bag, I pull out the two handguns and boxes of bullets. I load them. The sound of the smooth metal of the bullets sliding against the metal of the magazine is strangely soothing to me, like sharpening a knife on a stone. When I open the last box, four fully loaded magazines instead of rows of bullets rest inside.

Thanks Noah, even though you tried to eat my face.

Sparrow spins on his heels, in his crouched position, viewing the commotion below us. "What's with you and guns?" he asks.

"Protection," I tell him as I check the safety on each gun and wrap them in my spare T-shirt.

"Guns can't help us now, Meg."

"I don't care," I tell him. "I'll never live another moment of my life unable to protect myself."

"You think you'll do that with guns?" he asks, blinking at me.

"You bet your ass, Sparrow Man."

Sparrow makes a noise as he slides against the wall, sitting next to the hole we climbed into the loft through. Every few moments he leans over and looks below us.

"How long until they're sleeping?" I ask him.

His hand moves in his pocket, and although I can't see it, I know he's running his fingers along the smooth feathers in there. "When the moon rises above the trees, the dead sleep."

Remembering that Noah seemed to turn in the middle of the night and wake up causes me to ask, "Why didn't Noah wake up as a corpse? It was the middle of the night when he turned and attacked me."

"What time of the day do you think it was when you arrived at Noah's house?" Sparrow asks. He removes his hands from his pockets and taps his fingers on one knee.

I try to think back. I finished breaking the hole in my cell wall not long after I woke up. And those meat sacks in the jail were moaning and reaching through the bars as soon as the sun lit the sky. It couldn't have taken me more than a few hours to make it to the sewer cap and to the front of my house. Then less than an hour to change and get the bag. Nothing more than a few minutes to run to Noah's house.

"I think, maybe early afternoon," I tell Sparrow.

He nods. "Noah and them slept during the day, Meg. They knew the same thing I know; the dead wander in the daylight, they sleep when the moon rises over the treetops. You ate and you slept. It was dark in that windowless basement, but it wasn't dark outside. Noah and the others changed at the end of the day, when they woke up. It was almost perfect timing too because if it were any earlier, we would have had a hard time getting out of town with a trail of the dead following behind us."

"Jesus Christ," I mumble to myself, staring at the backpack in my hands.

"You have quite the mouth on you," Sparrow quips as he leans to the side again.

"I like beer and cigarettes too," I tell him. "I'm sure Noah and his pals told you that as soon as I stepped foot on his porch." I don't want Sparrow to be disillusioned, thinking I'm some prissy working-class princess. Not even close. The working class don't grow up in a busted down trailer with a kerosene heater in the living room for the cold northern nights.

"You're weird," Sparrow tells me after a long pause.

"I'm not weird." I find it odd that a crazy man who collects feathers and sings Bon Jovi each night thinks I'm weird. "I've just come to terms with what I am."

"What are you, Meg?"

"Trash, through and through–"

There is a sound below us, like someone dropped a huge sack of laundry on the floor. Sparrow's lip tips up. "They're out," he says, leaning to the side and looking below us.

"Just like that?" I ask. "They all drop like a sack of shit at the same time?"

"Yup."

Sparrow stands and adjusts his coat. I watch as he bends, grasps the side of the cut out in the floor, and swings himself down.

I stand, taking my bag with me and run over to where he just was. Peering through the hole, I see Sparrow's face as he looks up at me.

"You coming?" he asks. "These things reek."

I toss him my bag down, and trying the same technique as him, I grasp the hole in the floor across from me and jump, swinging myself down. But I never let go. I'm not exactly short and not exactly tall, but I can tell the drop is too far and I'll injure myself. So I hang there, swinging like deer bait.

"Uh, Sparrow?" I ask, digging my fingers into the wood floor of the loft.

"Yeah?"

"Can you help me?"

"To help you, I'd have to touch you..." he starts.

I catch a whiff of the mound of flesh bags piled on the floor near us. It's worse than rotting garbage. My stomach churns at a rate I've never experienced before. It's either from the smell or the canned food I ate earlier. I panic.

"Just grab my goddamned legs, Sparrow!" I shout.

I feel his arms wrap around my knees. "Jeez," he says as I let go and he bends to set my feet on the floor. I grab my bag off the floor and run out of the barn as fast as I can. Standing in the moonlight, taking deep breaths of the crisp northern air, I wait for Sparrow to waltz out of the barn.

"I'm sorry," I tell him as he gets closer. "It's just... I spent months in county with those fuckers clawing at me and the smell of them..." I shiver.

Sparrow just nods at me and starts walking down the driveway toward the barely lit road.

...

WALKING in the pitch black of night, in the boonies, with a crazy man by my side, is an odd feeling. It's better than spending a few months locked in a jail cell with the dead grabbing at me through the bars, but it's still... odd. Every so often as we're walking, the clouds cover the moon and I can't see a thing, I can only judge where I am based on the sound of Sparrow's footsteps next to me. For a moment I wonder if we'll trip over any of the sleeping dead.

Since there's not much space in a jail cell when there's

three foot of rotting arms stretching toward you, this is the most physical exertion I've seen in a while. It's not long before my thighs burn from the walking and it doesn't take long for exhaustion to set in.

"Can't we get a car?" I ask Sparrow, interrupting the night calm.

"I told you, cars make noise, noise brings meat sacks."

"You also told me that they sleep at night. So what does it matter?"

"...I guess you're right."

"If we had a car we could be to the border in a few hours."

"Doesn't matter."

"Why?"

"Because I don't drive and I don't have a car."

"We could steal one," I offer. "It's pretty easy. Noah taught me how to hotwire one when we were sixteen. We snuck off to Six Flags down in Rochester for the day. Didn't have much money, just enough for gas and admission. Sheriff picked us up just as we pulled onto route eleven near Antwerp later that night... I'm not sure why I just told you all that." My admission doesn't seem to faze him; he doesn't even bother to look back at me.

"Sounds like cars get you in trouble. Walking is good for us."

"But I'm tired as shit already." I adjust the backpack across my shoulder and bend to rub my thighs.

"Garbage burns for a long time, you'll be fine."

I jerk upright and scowl. "What in the hell is that supposed to mean?"

"It means we walk." He hooks his thumbs on the pockets of his jacket and continues on into the night.

Sure, I'll walk for now, but the first car I come across I'm going to wire that sucker up and drive off into the sunset headed for the Canadian border, whether Sparrow likes it or not.

...

AFTER A FEW HOURS I recognize the area we've made it to; soon this road we're on will loop around just south of Yellow Lake State Forest, then we'll be in Oxbow—a tiny little hamlet which is really nothing but a blink on the highway—before it loops north.

"Who's Jim?" Sparrow asks as we walk down the dark country road.

"Jim is my fiancé."

"Why is he not with you then?"

"Because I was in county lockup," I reply.

"And he went to Kingston?"

"Yeah, he went to Kingston."

"That's not very nice," Sparrow points out. "Leaving you behind like that."

Suddenly I am filled with a strong need to defend Jim. "I told him to go," I inform Sparrow. "I told him to go to Kingston and I would meet him there."

"Did he visit you in jail?"

"No." I grip the strap of my backpack, annoyed.

"Then how did you tell him this?"

"I told him before I went to jail."

"*Did you tell him that when you were bleeding on the floor and half-dead?*"

I stop and turn to Sparrow. "What the hell did you just say?" I ask.

"I asked, when did you tell him?" Sparrow blinks at me. "Are you okay?"

"I could have sworn you asked me something else."

"Nope," he answers so innocently, his green eyes glistening in the moonlight.

We start walking again. What the hell? I decide to tell Sparrow a little bit of the truth. "I told Jim to meet me in Kingston after I was attacked in our home."

"Who attacked you?"

"The men that the Governor sent around town during the gun raids."

"Noah had guns," Sparrow seems to drift off topic. "No one took his."

"Noah also never registered his guns," I point out.

"But..." Sparrow tips his head to the side. "That doesn't make much sense."

"I know this already," I tell him.

"So the men attacked you."

"Yes."

"Did it hurt?"

"Yeah," I hear my voice lower. Hurt like hell, worse than any of the smacks my daddy ever laid on my trouble-making ass.

"Did Jim save you?"

"No. Jim showed up afterwards."

"Oh." I watch as Sparrow rotates his arm up and plucks a leaf from a tree that we pass under.

"Let's talk about something else," I suggest.

We walk for a while, our footsteps echoing off the blacktop in the night. I find myself savoring the smell of the fresh air and the feeling of being out in the open, not locked in a twelve by twelve cell.

Sparrow interrupts the darkness. "What's your favorite bird?" he asks.

"I don't think I have one," I tell him.

"That's preposterous, Meg." He sounds thoroughly

appalled at me. "I'm sure you have a favorite food, a favorite drink, why not a favorite bird?"

"Yeah, I do have a favorite drink." A few actually. Ice cold Diet Pepsi and lime flavored beer. My stomach growls at the thought of it all and on a night as calm and quiet as this, I'm pretty sure Sparrow hears it. Still, he doesn't say anything.

"I think my favorite bird is the loon," I tell him.

"The loon?" he asks.

"Yeah, they make that sound on the water."

"Like this?" I hear Sparrow take in a breath and replicate the sound into the night air. An echoing tremolo. And I swear that I'm sitting on the lake in the misty morning with a cup of coffee in my hand.

"Yeah, I like that," I tell him.

He stops making the noise and we are back to listening to our hollow footsteps.

"I like owls," he tells me.

"That's nice." I'm not making any owl sounds for him. "Can we stop soon?"

"Yeah," his hands flutter in his pockets. "There's a barn up here just a ways."

"How do you know?"

"Just do."

"How? I don't understand. I've never seen you around this area before and here you are, knowing things about this road and perfect places to stay. How is that?"

"When the shit hits the fan, people migrate. I've been through here before," he tells me, suddenly stopping and turning. He walks to the edge of the road. "We're here."

I look ahead of him, in the direction of his gaze. "Great." Maybe this was a barn at some time, but right now, it's not really looking like a barn, more like a haunted dilapidated building. There's not much of a roof visible in the early morning light, but the moss stringing across the open space tells me there has to be some roof left. I can see spider webs gleaming with dew and stringing across the holes in the walls.

We step through a hole in the door. The inside of the structure is nothing more than a shell of a barn filled with forest. I look up, seeing broken and dry rotten slats of wood.

"We have to get up there." Sparrow turns and looks toward the door. "Sun's coming up."

It's all the warning I need to move. I know what comes next. I search for a ladder and come up with nothing. The only things I see are ferns and saplings and squirrels running across the rafters.

"Over here."

I follow the sound of Sparrow's voice and find him standing along one wall of the barn that doesn't have a hole in it. There isn't a ladder, just a haphazard pile of wood next to the wall. Sparrow reaches down and picks up a long board. He shifts it, leaning it on the rafters above us. Stepping one booted foot on the board and stomping on it, he tests its strength.

"Come on." Sparrow holds a hand out, waving for me to get moving.

I walk, mostly stumbling on my weary legs, to where he's standing. Needing no instruction, I begin climbing the ramp. When I get to the top I see that he's set the board against what looks like the only section of the second story that remains covered by a roof. I kick the loose twigs and piles of leaves off the space.

Sitting, I open my bag and pull out the package of crackers and one of the sodas. "Want some crackers?" I ask Sparrow.

"I'm good." He wanders along the edge of the loft, stomping in a few places, testing its strength.

"If I fall through this floor while you're doing that," I tell him as I rip open the package of crackers, "I'll never forgive you."

"I wouldn't let you fall." He wanders back to where I'm sitting, stopping a few times to inspect holes in the floor.

"Of course you wouldn't."

"I wouldn't," Sparrow promises.

Pausing, it strikes me that I believe him. I eat the crackers, telling myself the entire time to only eat half of the package, but by the time I slow down I see that I've already gone through three-quarters of it. I chug the soda and jiggle the can just to make sure it's empty. My stomach growls as I tuck the last of the crackers into my bag and pull out one of the survival blankets.

"I need some more food," I tell Sparrow as I lie down.

"I think there's a country store down the road."

"Does that mean we can stop there?"

"That means we'll take a look."

"You're pretty bossy for a crazy guy," I tell him between yawns.

"Get some rest, Meg. Tomorrow we've got a lot of walking to do."

"I'm stopping at that store." I close my eyes. "I need some water too," I tell him. "I can't live off sunlight like you."

"Sure."

"Sparrow?"

"What?" he sounds slightly annoyed. Maybe I shouldn't have mocked where he gets his nutrition from.

I open my eyes to look at him in the morning light. "Why are you crazy?"

He looks away, seemingly ashamed. "I can't remember."

"Anything?"

"Every now and then I get a few bits and pieces of memories, but for the most part it's nothing."

"Why do you wear that coat all the time?"

"Don't worry about it. Close your eyes and go to sleep."

I hear the boards underneath us creak as he moves and then his deep voice starts to hum, *Hey God*.

...

Tonight the air is cool. I feel a shiver run through me as soon as I wake up. Reaching for my backpack, I pull out a thin sweatshirt that I had stashed in there. Sparrow seems antsy, pacing the loft and trying to peek out of the barn through the holes in the walls.

"You ready?" he asks as I sit up and pull the sweatshirt on.

"Sure." I stand and stretch, before securing my backpack and following him down the ramp.

Walking out of the overgrown path, we reach the stretch of road that we left off on and start walking toward Oxbow.

"The Country Store is up here," I remind Sparrow as I notice a curve in the road ahead of us.

"Okay," he replies. He seems edgy and I wonder if it's because he's gone over twenty-four hours without adding to his feather collection or if something else is going on with him. Remembering how quickly Noah changed, I keep my distance from Sparrow, leaving a few yards between us in case I need a head start at running.

We follow the road to a four way stop. Dark traffic lights hang over the intersection and in the middle of the road there is a visible mound of... something.

"What's that?" I ask, pointing at the dark object in the middle of the road.

"I think..." Sparrow walks a little faster, headed straight for it. "It's a crow."

"Is it alive?"

"No," he crouches down. "It's dead."

Turning away from him as he inspects the bird, I notice the County Store to my left, and begin walking for it.

"I'm going to the store," I holler back to Sparrow.

I hear him mumble something as I walk away, the lure of food almost too strong to contain. As I get closer, I notice that boards are secured across the front door glass and the windows. I reach for the handle, my mouth salivating at the thought of warm soda and sugary treats. As I pull the door open I am not only greeted with the stench of stale air and sweaty humans, I'm greeted with a shotgun pointed directly at my face.

"What the hell you doin' here, girl?" a rough voice asks.

I back away. Hands up, just like the troopers asked me every time I got arrested. "I don't mean no trouble," I tell the shotgun, since I can't really see a figure behind it. "Just looking for food. That's all."

"Yer lookin' in the wrong place." The voice seems to change a bit with recognition. "I know you." I hear a step as the gun moves closer to me. "Yer' that little tramp that robbed me of all those candy bars and condoms few years back."

"Okay, mister." I keep walking backward, far into the street where I left Sparrow with his dead crow. "I'm leaving now."

"Good," the rough voice responds. "Don't need no more trash 'round here like you."

"Meg?" I turn to see Sparrow is standing not too far

from me; he holds eight violet-black feathers in his hand. He must've pillaged that dead bird.

The gun releases a shot and I turn, grabbing Sparrow's sleeve and running as fast as I can.

...

RUNNING, we head away from the Yellow Lake Forest area, turn onto Rossie-Oxbow Road and don't stop. When I start thinking we've run at least five miles, faster than I've ever run in my life, I slow to a jog.

We are in the middle of the Pleasant Lake State Forest. And I know what's here. Nothing. No stores, no houses, no nothing for miles, until we reach Route 37, where I know there are a few farmhouses. I think of all those delicious snack cakes that could've been in that County Store. Maybe it's best I didn't get any, they'd probably just rot my teeth. Still, the thought doesn't stop my stomach from growling.

"I'm really hungry," I tell Sparrow, feeling the pull of my leg muscles from the running and the ache in my dry throat. I follow that up with, "I'm thirsty too."

Sparrow kicks at a rock in the road. "I know, Meg. We'll find something for you."

"How can you be so sure?" I ask. "There's nothing out here. We are in the middle of nowhere."

"Just am."

As the full moon lights the highway, we stop, hearing movement in the forest. Rustling and snapping of dried undergrowth. The hair on the back of my bare neck rises.

"Sparrow, is that–" All I can think is that the dead are up and walking early.

"Shh!" he silences me, holding a hand up.

The rustling continues, pauses, and then four deer waltz out of the underbrush and begin crossing the road. My fluttering heart settles. I'll take a deer any day over a walking sack of rot.

"You like deer?" Sparrow asks.

"Ah, they're okay." I shrug. "Pretty harmless I think…"

Sparrow drops to one knee and reaching behind his back, he pulls something out. I see the glint of a knife as he raises his arm over his head and flings it at the small herd of deer. As they begin stomping off into the forest, one pauses, then drops to the ground with Sparrow's knife sticking out of its neck.

"Holy shit, Sparrow!" I breathe out.

He walks to the deer and, reaching down, he pulls the knife from its throat and starts cutting.

"What are you doing?" I ask.

"Getting this ready for cooking."

"What?"

"You're hungry." He gives me a cold look, like I'm an idiot for asking, then turns around and glances at the forest. "Go get some wood for a fire."

I leave Sparrow and head for the side of the road, collecting sticks and twigs and dried leaves to start the fire. I drop them in the middle of the highway, right on the double solid yellow line. Digging through my backpack, I find the lighter Jim placed on one of the inside pockets and light the fire.

Sparrow walks to me, carrying a slab of meat that looks like it's still attached to the bone. He moves the sticks around and settles the bone in the middle of the small fire. In the light from the flames, I can see the blood dripping off his hands. He turns, looking crazy and dangerous with his coat and bloody hands and bloody knife. I'm pretty sure I gasp and lean away from him.

Sparrow holds a gory hand out to me. "Give me your water bottles. I'll go fill them."

"Where?"

"There's a stream, not far from here."

"How do you know?"

He presses his lips together before answering, takes a calming breath that does nothing to cool his current mood. "I can hear it," he practically growls.

I tilt my head to the side and listen. I hear nothing. "Are you sure?" I ask, reaching into my backpack.

He swipes the water bottles out of my hand and walks away, into the dark forest at the edge of the road.

"What a dick," I mutter to myself and wonder if maybe it was the act of killing the deer that has him on edge.

I wait, warming my hands by the fire and trying to stop the shivers from rolling up and down my back. I can hear Sparrow walking through the forest as he returns to me. He doesn't even attempt to be quiet. He sets the water bottles next to me with clean hands and sits, not quite on the other side of the fire from me.

We watch the flames, my mouth watering from the smell of the meat.

"Thank you," I force out.

He nods, his forehead wrinkled in a scowl.

"You didn't have to kill the deer if it was going to upset you this much."

"Couldn't do anything different." Finally, he turns to me. "You're human. You needed something to eat."

"And what does that make you?"

"Doesn't matter." He shakes his head.

We both turn to the fire and let the silence settle between us.

After a long while of staring into the glowing embers,

the mood seems to lighten a bit. Sparrow asks out of the blue, "What is your deepest, darkest secret?"

My back straightens at the question. I can't tell what kind of a moment he's having right now, crazy or lucid. I stare up at the night sky, watching the smoke rise, deciding how to respond.

What the hell, no one will believe what I tell a crazy man who collects feathers. And it's not like we have anything else to talk about out here. I start with the worst secret I have. "I killed my mother."

"Unpossible," he dismisses the confession immediately.

"What? That's not even a real word."

"It is in my book." He pokes at the fire with a stick, the end of it burning red hot. "You didn't kill your mother. Don't believe it."

"Yes I did," I argue. "Pulled her placenta right off as I busted through the birth canal. She bled out and died before daddy could even call 911."

"That's not your fault."

"Daddy thought it was, made me pay for it too. Every single day of my life."

"What do you mean?" he stops poking the burning twigs and squints at me.

"I mean every morning I woke up in our crappy trailer and my daddy didn't say good morning or ask how I slept. He started my day by saying, *you killed her and don't you forget that.*"

Sparrow looks at me with his mouth hanging open. He sets his stick in the road and stands.

"Where are you going?" I ask.

Sparrow walks to the edge of the road. With the full moon illuminating everything in a yellow hue, he bends and picks something off the ground.

"Here," he says as he walks to me, holding his hand out.

I hold my open palm up to him and he drops a tiny white flower into my hand. "What's this?" I ask.

"Nothing." He sits down near me and continues poking the fire with his stick.

Now, I've seen a lot of nothing in my short time on this earth, but a guy giving me a flower, that has to be something. Jim never even did that.

"I hate cats," Sparrow says as he pushes at the deer meat with a stick.

"Oh really?"

"Did you know when cats came to America they decimated the wild bird population?"

"Had no idea about that," I reply. "Who brought them, Columbus?"

"Spanish. Before Columbus. In South America. Didn't you pay attention to your history?"

"I'm pretty sure we never learned that in history class. Not that I ever showed up much for history class."

"Hmm."

"What's your obsession with birds, Sparrow?" I ask.

He shrugs. "What's your obsession with sins, Meg?"

I stare at the roaring fire in front of us, the smell of the roasting meat making my stomach growl louder. It seems neither of us is going to answer the questions we have asked each other. Sparrow stands and pulls a stick from the fire with steaming meat on the end of it. He hands me the end of the stick and I wait for it to cool before devouring it.

Now I've had deer before, usually in stews and stuff, but this has got to be the best deer I've ever tasted. Maybe it's because I'm so hungry. I clean the bone, eating until my stomach is full, bursting at the seams with roast deer. It's not what I really wanted to eat, but it's better than raw rat.

When the sky starts to brighten and the songbirds chirp

high in the pines, Sparrow stands and starts stomping out the fire. "We need to move."

"But," I start. "We never slept." My voice sounds whiny.

"You ate, Meg. You got fresh water. We are in the middle of a state park, no better place to walk during the day. Shouldn't be many people–alive or dead–for miles." Sparrow starts stomping on the fire and breaking up the burning sticks.

I stare at the deer carcass. "Do we just leave that in the road?"

"Yeah. There's a turkey vulture down there," he points behind us. "He's been scouting that deer carcass for hours now."

"Oh." I look behind us and see movement on the side of the road. "Are you going to pluck some of its feathers?"

Sparrow laughs. "No. Turkey vultures are huge and mean and we really, really need to get walking." He looks around. "Walking during the day, we'll need to move fast."

Standing, I adjust my bag and start following Sparrow.

As we walk in broad daylight, the machete that Sparrow used to chop off Noah's head is gripped tightly in his hand. It seems that this is the first time I've seen it since we started this little journey, besides when he cut my hair. And I wonder if he does have one of those leather things to strap it to his back and maybe that's why he wears that coat.

...

We walk fast and quiet, just like Sparrow suggested. No chatter about birds or feathers or sins. He said that the meat sacks would come and they do. We can hear them moaning behind us, moving slower than icebergs, dragging their feet until the moon rises. Then Sparrow holds up his hand so we could hear them all drop asleep in the road with a collective *thud*.

Now, walking in the dark again, I'm too tired to talk. Sparrow must notice this. He slows himself considerably so I don't trail too far behind him. Eventually, we reach a portion of the road where there is forest on one side and steep, rocky cliff ledge on the other, stained with mineral deposits.

"Want to sleep outside today?" Sparrow spins a stick in his hand as we walk down the middle of the road.

"How could we manage that?" I ask, my voice thick with exhaustion.

Sparrow points the stick up. I follow it and see a flat grassy area jutting out of the cliff above us. "Meat sacks can't climb."

I sigh, not looking forward to climbing. "Sure."

"Come on. It's not that far up," he replies cheerfully.

I follow Sparrow, walking along a rocky incline before it turns into a cliff with crevices and hollows perfectly spaced for us to climb.

"One time," I start to tell him as we climb. "We had this neighbor in the trailer park and her husband had this collection of remote control helicopters. I think I was like twelve or something. Anyways, we were pretty poor, especially since my mom left all of her money to me and not a penny to daddy. That pissed him off real good cause I couldn't touch it until I was eighteen. I never had many toys, but I wanted to play with one of those helicopters real bad. So Noah and me, we snuck into the house and stole one, played with it all day long until Noah crashed it into the side of another trailer in the trailer park. Got both of us two weeks in juvy. Didn't realize that helicopter cost over five grand." I'm not really sure why I tell him this, but ever since he asked me to tell him my sins I've had a verbal catharsis.

"That's quite the expensive toy."

"Yeah. When I got released, daddy surprised me by emptying my room of all of my possessions. Everything except for my clothes and a mattress on the floor."

"What did he do with it all?"

"Not sure. I think he sold it to pay for my restitution."

"I think that's one of the worst stories I've ever heard." Sparrow's hand slips and a small waterfall of rocks plummets to the road below us.

We continue our climb in the dim morning light, and sure enough, as the sun comes up, the meat sacks come out. Gimping down the road, moaning like injured cows. A few of them stop and wander around the base of the cliff. Sometimes, when we push off the rock to boost ourselves higher, the loose rocks tumble down the cliff and hit the walking dead. They moan and stare, too stupid to look up.

When we finally reach the flat outcropping that juts off the cliff, the sun is pouring down on us. The sky is light blue, not a cloud visible and I have the sudden uncontrollable urge to sunbathe.

"Do you have a problem with skin, Sparrow?" I ask, reaching for the hem of my shirt. White trash like me has no problem walking around in a bra and shorts that barely cover our ass cheeks.

"Why would I have a problem with skin?" He sits and leans over the side of the cliff to see what's going on below us.

I pull off my shirt, my boots, my socks, my jeans. And as I dig for my blanket to lie on the ground, standing there in nothing but my underwear, I catch a glimpse of Sparrow's red-cheeked face out of the corner of my eye.

Stomach still full from the deer, I forget about eating

anything as I lay on my back, close my eyes, and start soaking the rays into my skin. The warm sun combined with the exhaustion of walking so much has a calming effect.

"What is that scar from?" I hear Sparrow ask.

Groggy, I open my eyes to find Sparrow gazing at me. I look down, seeing the straight scar across my lower abdomen. "That's where they took my uterus out."

"Why did they take your uterus out?"

"I was pregnant once and something bad happened."

"Was it because of those men?"

"Yeah." I roll over to hide the scar and tan my backside. "Can we talk about something else?"

"Why do you have tattoos all over?"

My father said it was because I was stupid, a waste of life and his time. That's what he said, but I don't tell Sparrow that. "Because I'm bad, Sparrow, a bad, bad sinner," I tell him as I rest my cheek on my folded hands.

"Are you bad to the bone?" Sparrow asks and I can hear the hint of amusement in his voice.

I laugh. "Yeah, I guess so. Are you afraid I'll wake up a walking meat sack now?"

"Nope," he replies.

I hear him move.

"You hungry today?" I ask, smiling to myself.

"Always hungry."

Remembering that he told me he gets his energy from the sunlight I ask, "Gonna take off that coat and soak up the rays?"

"Don't need to."

Turning to look at him I say, "You are strange, Sparrow."

His eyes narrow on me. "You are strange, Meg."

He looks away, closing his eyes and facing the sun, and starts to hum, *Never Say Goodbye*.

Somewhere between the third and the fifth verse, I fall asleep.

...

Sinners don't dream but we do always wake with a startle, afraid that our wrongdoings have finally caught up with us as we slept and might surprise us with a reprimand. Today is different. I wake up, slowly, to witness an amazing sunset. There's not a cloud in the sky and it's all light pink and orange and so beautiful, like I've never seen in my life. My hand still resting on my cheek; I feel something covering my back. I turn, finding that I've been covered with my spare blanket.

"You seeing this, Sparrow?" I ask. Sitting up and looking around, I notice that Sparrow is no longer next to me.

"Oh, my God," I mumble scrambling to the edge of the cliff to see if he fell off. There's nothing on the ground, just two of those meat sacks milling about.

I rush to put my clothes on, and feeling the ache of sunburn on my shoulders, I think that maybe I should have left my clothes on to sleep. Bending to pack the blanket, something hits me in the back. I turn and look up to find Sparrow climbing down from the rock above us. When he gets close enough, he jumps down beside me.

"Sparrow?"

"What?" He asks with an accomplished grin.

"I thought you fell off... I thought you left."

"Nope, just had to get these." He holds his hand up with two huge gray-brown feathers between his fingers.

"Where did you get those?" I ask.

He points up. I look, focusing on the rock above us.

"Eagle's nest," he says with exhilaration in his voice that I've never heard before. He rubs the feather across his cheek and closes his eyes.

I squint and see that jutting from the side of the cliff is a collection of twigs. Before I can take a breath, a giant bald eagle lifts off the cliff and flies away.

"See?" Sparrow asks, tucking the feathers into his coat pocket. "Told you. Eagle nest."

"Jesus Christ, Sparrow, could you tell me next time you do something like that?"

He tips his head to the side. "You thought I left you behind?"

"Kind of," I reply. "Or, I thought you became meat sack surprise." I point to the bodies milling about below us.

He leans over the side of the cliff, looking down, and I notice for the first time how his long lashes brush his cheeks and his hair curls up at the nape of his neck.

A crazy man shouldn't have those features.

I throw myself on the ground and search my bag for something to eat. I polish off the rest of my crackers and drink the last flat soda.

When the sun is gone and the moon is almost straight above us, Sparrow stands up and begins to descend off our perch. I strap my backpack on and follow him.

...

WE WALK DOWN OXBOW LANE. Eventually, in what feels like a hundred miles ahead of us, we will come to the road where Sparrow will find his snowy owl.

It's not long before the effect of the previous day's walk

and sunburn catch up with me. Before it's even close to dawn my feet are dragging.

"Sparrow?" I ask.

"Meg?" He twirls a stick in his hand.

"I'm really tired," I confess to him.

"I can tell." He taps the stick on the pavement.

"Can we stop soon?"

He points his stick ahead of us, down the road. "Just around this bend there's another flat spot in the cliffs. We can stop there."

I follow him, barely able to keep up. While we climb the rock face that rises above the highway, I don't confess any sins to him this time. And as I lay down on the flat area he's designated our camp for the night, I don't even hear what song he starts humming before I fall asleep.

...

I wake to a loud thud and Sparrow making some strange grunting noise. No, he's gurgling! I scramble to my feet.

"Sparrow!" I scream at him as one of the walking dead grips a decaying hand around his throat. "You said they couldn't climb!"

His eyes flick to the wall of stone above us. "I think," he chokes out. "I think this one fell."

I look up. Dear God, maybe it was a camper who turned in his sleep. Maybe he was camping up there away from the dead like we've been doing. Either way, he's dead now, and I have to get his rotting ass away from Sparrow.

Near his feet I see a metallic gleam. I bend and pick up the machete I've seen Sparrow use, and grasping it in my hand I slice at the dead man. The machete thumps into his back. It doesn't slice, it doesn't cut, it doesn't do anything but hit the dead man like a blunt spoon.

"What the hell is wrong with your weapon?" I shout.

"It doesn't like you," Sparrow chokes out as he pushes at the dead man's face.

"What the shit is that supposed to mean? Your machete has feelings?" The corpse turns around and hisses at me. "Holy fuck, Sparrow!"

I bend down, my fingers fumbling as I unzip my bag and pull out the handgun I took from Noah's basement. I aim it at the dead man's head and fire. Just like a rotten cantaloupe it explodes and Sparrow and I are covered in rotting, putrid debris.

Sparrow shoves the corpse off him and we watch as it tumbles down the rocky cliff.

"I think," I choke on my breath. "I think I'm going to puke," I tell Sparrow, clicking the safety on the handgun.

Sparrow stares at me, shocked, sweat dripping down his face and panting like the other night when we ran five miles from that crazy man in the Country Store with the shotgun.

"It will be night soon," Sparrow tells me between breaths and standing very still. "We'll find a pond or a waterfall or something before the dead wake up and get this washed off."

I look down at the gun in my hand and a violent shudder, one that I can barely contain, runs through me. The last time I shot a gun it was aimed at seven men who had just got done doing some very, very bad things to me.

Sparrow's image before me blurs, turns to white, and for some reason I no longer see him. Instead, I see those men busting through my front door and I feel the baby kicking in my belly as I run away from them. I can hear their heavy footfalls as they chase me up the stairs, the sound of them kicking in the bedroom door. Screaming. Running.

Shit.

"Meg?" I hear a familiar voice. "Meg?" It's just a tad bit louder.

The image of Sparrow comes back into focus before me and I see that his face is pale as a sheet, his eyes wide with worry. When I glance down, I see why—I'm pointing the handgun at his chest, with my finger on the trigger and the safety off.

"Meg?" he asks again as he reaches out, placing his pale hand on the barrel of the gun.

"Sparrow?" I whisper, my voice faltering.

"It's okay." His green eyes bore into mine and I wonder what the hell am I doing and what the hell has happened around me.

I click the safety on and drop my arms. "Shit."

"It's okay," Sparrow tells me as I wrap the handgun up in the shirt it was in.

I zip my backpack and fall to my knees. "I'm so sorry," I tell him, unable to meet his eyes, knowing that I could have shot him. I could have killed him on this little cliff, just like I killed those men in my house.

As we wait for the moon to rise, an awkward silence vibrates around us and Sparrow starts to hum, *Letting You Go*. Angered with myself, I want to tell him to shut up, but with the realization that I almost killed the one man who's been nothing but nice to me, I can't seem to find words.

...

As we walk, with the stench of the rotting dead wafting off us, I notice a road sign in the threatening glow of morning. Split-Rock Road, it says. This gives me a glimmer of hope. Just past Split-Rock Road is a house with a fenced in yard and a pool. I used to have a friend that lived there. They had one of those huge kidney shaped pools and a pool house and everything. I know this because I seduced my friend's boyfriend in that pool house the summer before I left for college and she walked in on us.

"There's a place up here," I tell Sparrow. "A house with a big pool."

"You sure?" he asks.

"Yeah." I spare him the details of how I know.

We walk, stopping at the end of the gravel driveway.

Sparrow tilts his head to the side as though he's listening to something far away. With a quick movement he rights himself and starts walking toward the house.

"Are there people here?" I ask.

"Nope, empty."

We stroll up to the sprawling McMansion that sits in a clearing off the end of the driveway. I remember this place and the riches inside of it. Sara Shepard lived here, a pretty girl with blonde hair who never wanted a day in her life. She had everything I didn't: a mother, parents that loved her, money in her pocket, a closet filled with the most stylish clothes money could buy from the nearby shopping malls. Sara didn't know how lucky she had it. She didn't even notice when I took things from her room like a shirt here, a pair of designer jeans there. I was the worst type of friend. She found that out the moment she walked in on me and her boyfriend. That's what kind of friend I was—a bad one— just like daddy said.

I was bad at everything; friendships, life, school.

Sparrow tries the front door to the house. "Locked." He leans around the porch, getting a good look at the huge brick fence that surrounds the back yard.

"Oh!" I hold up my finger, remembering that there was

always a spare key kept under the flower pot near the steps. I turn and tip the pot on its side, finding a silver key underneath. As I unlock the door and push my way inside, we are accosted by the smell of rot.

"Ugh!" I cover my face. "I thought you said this place was empty?"

"It is." Sparrow walks in behind me and looks around. He points at a dog leash. "Pets?"

It doesn't take more than a second for me to get him. The humans left, the pets stayed, and without someone to care for them, they most likely died here. Then I remember, "Hey, they used to have canaries here, in the sunroom upstairs."

I see an eyebrow rise on Sparrow's face. The kind of excitement you see on a kid's face on Christmas morning. He takes one step toward the stairs before stopping, turning, and locking the front door.

"I have to clean up," I tell him. "Meet you out back when you're done."

We split up. Sparrow, unable to control himself with the hopes of pillaging those yellow canaries, runs up the stairs two at a time. I walk down the center hall, headed for the kitchen, where I know there is a sliding door that leads to the pool and patio.

The house looks the same as it did the last time I was here; high ceilings, stone floors, and earth tones on the walls. This place is definitely out of the norm for the types of houses we have up here in the North Country.

When I reach the kitchen, I find it's still magnificent with high cupboards, a chandelier over a huge granite topped island. I feel out of place here. Our entire trailer could have fit in this kitchen, and the nice little house I bought is smaller than their garage.

I find the sliding glass door, open it and walk through.

The back yard is overgrown, but the pool and the pool house are here, along with the huge privacy fence. I'm not sure what they needed a fence like this for, being in the middle of nowhere upstate New York. I walk to the edge of the pool, which is pretty clear with the exception of a few spots of algae on the liner. They must have doused the pool with chlorine not long before all of this happened.

Unable to take the smell of myself anymore, I unclip my backpack and jump into the pool, clothes and all. The water is cool, refreshing. I dunk my head, running my hands over my face and hair, trying to get the decaying splatter off me. When I can no longer smell the rot on my face, I start peeling away my clothes. First my boots, which I wish I had taken off before I jumped in. They'll probably still be damp by the time we need to walk again. Next are the socks, jeans, and shirt. I scrub the clothes in the pool water, trying to get the splatter off, and then lay them out on the surrounding cement to dry in the morning sun. Looking down at myself in my underwear I figure what the hell, and unclip my bra and take off the underwear and scrub them clean in the water as well.

Just as I'm stretching the clothes out to dry, Sparrow walks through the sliding glass doors with a handful of bright yellow feathers clutched in his hand and a huge smile on his face. The smile drops as soon as he catches the sight of me in the pool. He takes one look at my clothes on the patio and spins around, retreating into the huge house.

I chuckle to myself. He should have expected this from me.

Holding onto the side of the pool, I turn to the pool house, hoping that it's still the same in there. There was a bathroom, a couch, and a queen-sized bed. Sleeping in a real bed right now, the thought of it is enough to make me lift myself out of this pool and run over there naked to find out. I grip the side of the pool and kick my feet in the water.

"Here," Sparrow's voice startles me out of my daydream of sleeping on pillow-top luxury. A gust of air brushes by my face as he drops a stack of towels next to me and a mostly used bottle of shampoo. He turns, refusing to look in my direction.

"What's wrong, Sparrow Man? Afraid to see me dry off in the sun, naked as the day I was born?" I tease.

Seems like Sparrow is having a rough day today, first I almost shoot him and then he gets to see me like this. I guess the thought of seeing me naked is enough to spoil his feather orgasm.

"I'll go check out the pool house," he mutters, walking away from me.

I wash with the shampoo and then lift myself out of the pool and wrap myself in a towel. Seems Sparrow has good taste and selected the huge beach towels from the cupboard. They're musty smelling but clean. I move my clothes to the dusty patio furniture and lay them out to dry for the day. As I walk to retrieve my backpack, Sparrow exits the pool house and looks right at me.

"See you're decent again." He looks down the length of me. With the towel that reaches my knees there really isn't much for him to see. "Have you no dignity?" he scoffs.

I shrug and toss the bottle of shampoo at him. "Want to freshen up? I won't peek," I promise.

He sets the bottle down on a patio table and motions to the pool house. "Doesn't smell like dead animals in there." He looks around. "You could probably sleep in there for the day."

I walk past him into the pool house, backpack in hand. Yeah, it's just the same as it was before. Staring at the queen size bed, using the last bits of control left in me to not run, jump, and roll around in it naked, I remind myself to get dressed.

Emptying my bag, I find a tank top, an oversized flannel shirt, and a pair of almost-too-short jean shorts. I wish I had paid closer attention when I grabbed the change of clothes from my dresser drawer at home. The summer nights here are cool and a second pair of pants would have been ideal. I could go into the house and search Sara's closet, wouldn't be the first time I stole her clothes. But, I took enough from her and right now I can't muster the strength to go in there. I only hope that my jeans are dry by the time we need to move again. I put the clothes on and start pulling back the blankets on the bed.

Sparrow walks through the door I never closed. He's carrying a package of dry pasta and a can of beer.

"Is that for you?" I ask, my mouth salivating at the sight of the beer. I guess you can take the girl out of the trailer but you can't take the trailer out of the girl. Soon I'll be smoking cigarettes and walking around in my bra.

"I told you." He tosses the beer and pasta at me. "Sunlight, that's all I need."

I catch the items, opening the beer as fast as I can, not even caring that it's warm. "Almost forgot. Thanks." I give him a quick smile and take a long drink. "God, I hope this doesn't get me wasted." I take another long swallow. "I haven't had beer in so long." I open the bag of pasta and crunch on a dry noodle. It's not fine Italian dining, but it will have to do for now. "Sure you don't want some? This beer isn't going to last." I down the rest of it, squeezing my eyes from the carbonation burn in the back of my throat.

"Nope." Sparrow moves around the pillows on the couch near the door and sits down.

I set the empty beer can on the glass-top wicker nightstand and roll up the bag of pasta. Leaning back on the pillows, running my fingers across the thickly padded mattress, I think for a second that I could share this little luxury with Sparrow, and then I remember all the bad things I put him through today. I'm surprised he's even staying in the same room with me. Just as I pull the covers over myself and lay down, I hear him start to hum, *Never Say Goodbye*.

"Sparrow?"

He stops mid-hum. "Yeah."

"I'm sorry I almost shot you."

"Worse things have happened."

"Spar–"

"Go to sleep, Meg."

Normally, being bossed around would piss me off, but for some reason–maybe it was the beer or the exhaustion or the cool bath–I close my eyes and drift off as he continues his humming.

...

As soon as I wake up, I can tell what Sparrow has done and a fury burns deep in my chest. I was slightly confused by these feelings as I watched him, his hair damp. Sparrow had cleaned himself up and it was more than just a splash in a birdbath. He took a bath in that pool while I was sleeping. His clothes are changed too, the jeans clean and a shade darker than the last pair he had on. I wonder if he found something in the house to wear? Sara did have an older brother.

I kick the shampoo bottle when we walk by it, empty. I don't know why it bothers me so much that he refuses to take that coat off in front of me and that he refuses to get cleaned up while I'm awake.

"Hell, I'd stripped down to my bare skin with him walking around," I grumble to myself as I collect my dry clothes and tie my boots on.

One beer never resulted in a hangover before, but for some reason I'm having a hell of an attitude problem today. I blame it on the beer and continue to glare at the back of Sparrow's glistening wet hair in the moonlight as we walk.

Maybe he doesn't trust me; maybe that's what his problem is, even though I saved his life yesterday when that sack of skin had its hands around Sparrow's throat. That was me who blasted that rotting piece of meat off the mountain, and then...shit... I had held a gun to him. Almost shot him, remembering all that crap that happened. No wonder he doesn't trust me.

Doesn't matter, I tell myself. Maybe going on this adventure with a crazy man was a bad idea, but it has gotten me a whole hell of a lot closer to the border. Soon I will have Jim and Sparrow will be on his way to wherever crazy men go. I actually can barely believe that I've stuck with him for this long.

We take a left onto Route 37, the anticipation growing stronger inside me. We're close to the border and all I can think about is finding Jim.

"This is the barn." Sparrow's deep voice breaks the night calm.

"The one with the snowy owl?" I ask.

Sparrow takes a deep breath, puffs his chest out a bit. "Yup," he starts walking at a fast pace toward a decrepit barn. "This is the place."

"How can you be so sure?" I ask, following him.

"Just know. Can feel it in my bones. This is the place."

Standing still, watching as he searches the barn for an opening, I look around, noting the summer grass and leaves and I wonder what the hell a snowy owl would be doing in this area at this time of the year.

"Sparrow?" I shout.

"Shh!"

"Sparrow, you're not going to find a snowy owl here."

"Yes. She lives here. I can feel it."

"She?" I walk closer to him. "Sparrow, snowy owls only come here in the winter. It is early summer. You're not going to find one."

"You have little faith in me, Meg." He looks around, eyes focused on the ground, and crouching, his hand reaches out lightning fast and I see that he has plucked a mouse from the tall grass. He holds it in his hand in front of my face.

"What would you like to be?" he asks me. "The bait or the feather remover?"

"Is there an option for neither?" The mouse squeaks and pedals its legs in the air.

"I need extra hands, Meg." He smiles at me. "You owe me, anyways."

"No, I don't." I take a step closer to him. "You saved me. I saved you. We're even."

"Yeah, but I got you that beer. So you still owe me."

"What?"

He smiles again, saying nothing.

"You found that beer. And... and I think it made me sick!"

"You're fine." He jiggles the mouse, it arches back, trying to claw at him and get free. "What's it going to be?" I stare at the mouse. Sparrow widens his eyes in a begging motion. "I suggest you be the bait."

"Fine!" I hold my fingers out to pinch the mouse tail. "But I'm telling you this is pointless. Snowy owls don't frequent these parts in the summer months."

"Ye of little faith." He points to an open clearing behind

me. "Can you stand right over there? In the full moon light?"

I scowl at him.

"Please," he adds.

"Where will you stand?"

"In the shadows," he whispers and fans the fingers of his left hand like a magician.

Sparrow starts walking backward to the barn. I move to the spot he pointed to and hold my hand out, the mouse squirming, its tail wiggling between my fingers. I stick out my hip and make a face for Sparrow to see. I can't judge his reaction to my attitude, though, because I can't see him anywhere. There is nothing but stars and moon and night air brushing around me. Then, I hear strange noises coming from the shadows, a screeching hoot, strange dark whistling, a hiss.

"This is pointless," I mutter to myself.

Just as I'm ready to drop the mouse and stomp off, I catch movement in the upper levels of the barn. A white head peeks through a hole in the siding, followed by a neck and the entire body of a snowy owl.

"Holy shit," I whisper.

The sounds made by Sparrow turn into a deep hooting. The owl opens its wings and lifts itself into the night sky. Circling over my head once, twice, it descends and flies straight for me, its flapping wings moving my hair as it lands on my arm. I stiffen and every muscle in my body turns tight and rigid. I wasn't expecting the owl to be so heavy. The owl blinks at me and I can almost see my reflection in its huge golden eyes.

"Ah, my beautiful, beautiful snowbird." Sparrow leaves the shadows and stalks up behind the creature as it cocks its head to the side, looking at me first and then the mouse in my hand.

I stare at the owl, transfixed in its beauty; the moonlight glowing off its white feathers speckled with brown, the catlike eyes that seem to be judging me. Its claws dig into the skin under my plaid shirt.

Out of my periphery I see Sparrow walking quietly, inching closer, murmuring words to the owl of how beautiful it is. I blink, focusing on my reflection in the owl's eyes. Sparrow's words are much like what a man would say to a woman he loves. I don't think I've ever heard words like this with my own ears. Words like this have never been spoken to me, not even by Jim.

Sparrow moves slowly, murmuring his soft pillow talk the entire way until he is just behind the owl. He reaches both hands out on either side of the owl, his fingers ready to pinch.

"My sweet, sweet, magical creature," Sparrow's voice is soft and deep. He reaches up, grasping a feather on each side of the owl's wings and pulls, hard.

The owl's eyes widen as it screeches in my face just before lifting off. I feel its claws dig even deeper into my arm and I drop the mouse.

"Holy fuck!" I breathe out, realizing that I hadn't taken a breath that entire time.

I turn to Sparrow who holds two large white feathers, spotted with brown at the tips. His eyes are gleaming and excited. And as I watch him, something inside me starts to feel strange. Remembering his cooing at the owl and the realization that I have never had anyone talk to me like that, something catches in my chest and I'm not sure what to do about it. As a result, I conclude, the only reasonable option at this moment: I think it's my time to leave Sparrow.

This is what I tell myself over the span of three seconds. I don't need him for the rest of my trip and I'm so close to the border now. He has his owl feathers and I'm pretty sure my arm needs stitches from the owl scratching it during lift off. I back away into the shadows, just as Sparrow did. He doesn't even notice as he stares at his prized feathers, the feathers he's been searching so long for already.

Well, I've been searching for something too–for someone. And after listening to Sparrow murmur to that owl, I can't wait one second longer to make it to Kingston and find Jim.

As Sparrow is distracted with his feathers, I turn and run.

...

I RUN AWAY from the barn, stumbling into the forest. The sensation of my heart beating fast and seeming to burn at the same time slows me until I reach the pavement of the highway. Then I run until I can't remember those things Sparrow murmured to that owl. And I try to remember the things Jim would say to me, the things that made me agree to marry him, but I can't think of one thing.

I run until the sky turns pink and the sun peeks over the tops of the treetops and then realize what a stupid idea it was to run at this time. I slow, the sound of my footsteps replaced with the sound of moaning and shuffling feet. Then I look around, searching, trying to find a safe place to hide. There are no cliffs or gated yards here. There are only pavement and trees. I look to my left, seeing a large oak and wonder if that's my only option right now.

Focusing in front of me, they're moving closer, the dead waking and shuffling down the road. Screw it. I run for the tree, wrapping my hands around the lower branches and walking up the trunk. I fit my left foot in a deep crevice and move my hands until I'm upright. The moaning gets louder. I reach for a branch above me and climb higher as the meat sacks collect at the base of the tree.

Shit.

I sit on a narrow branch, out of breath, arms wobbly. This is a great mess I've gotten myself into, stuck in a tree with no way of making it down. I sit, leaning my head against the trunk, reminding myself that I can't fall asleep up here because that will only result in my death from a quick fall to the ground. The smell of rot wafts up, my stomach churns. I check my arm and find that it's not bleeding; the scratches from the owl barely broke the skin. And I can't get the sound of Sparrow's voice out of my head, no matter how hard I try.

This is where I sit for the entire day, with the rough bark of the tree digging into the backs of my thighs and my butt going numb from not moving. When the moon rises over the treetops, the walking dead below me drop to the ground, leaving a pile twenty bodies deep or more below me.

Listening, just to make sure the dead are all out for the night, I attempt to climb down. Off in the distance I hear someone humming.

"Sparrow!" I shout into the darkness.

Whoever it is, they don't answer. The humming gets closer along with footsteps. And I know I should be scared, stuck in a tree in the middle of the night, not knowing who's walking in my direction, but these past few days I've come to know that humming voice. It's Sparrow.

"Sparrow!" I shout again and looking down, between my legs and the branches I sit on, I see him standing not far from the base of the tree and the pile of bodies.

"Hey, Meg." He waves at me like I never ran away and abandoned him in the middle of last night.

"What took you so long?"

His hand pats his side. "Hit the jackpot in that barn. You should've seen it. Nests everywhere." He splays his fingers, opens his palms and arms wide like he's imitating fireworks. "Swallows and chickadees and mourning doves and a ton of pigeons. Even found a Grouse, almost stepped on the sucker. Even though they don't really fly I still got a feather from a nest near the barn." He holds up a small brown and white feather for me to see.

"Sparrow! I've been trapped in this goddamn tree for an entire day."

He quirks his lip and tucks the feather into his chest pocket, patting it like a pocket watch. "You're the one who left me, Meg." He tips his head to the side. "Why did you run away like that?"

"I... I don't know." I stutter, real pathetic-like.

But I know exactly why, I just don't want to tell him. I couldn't take the sweet murmurings he spoke to that owl. I look at the pile of rotting bodies below me. "How do I get down?"

"Jump."

I climb down to the lowest branch and focus on a small patch of grass between the bodies. I jump, landing hard, my backpack slapping against my back, almost falling forward into the rot as something squishy and crunchy explodes under my foot. I look down to find a meat sack without a hand; the goopy mess is under my boot. My stomach lurches.

Sparrow starts for the road. "Come on, Meg. I bet we've got one more night until we make it to the border."

I run after him, wiping the bottom of my boot off in the pine needles and roadside gravel along the way.

...

One more day, that's all we have left for walking. Just like Sparrow said. He whistles while we walk, pointing out the mansions and old hotels near the bay. He doesn't ask me again why I ran away from him last night, and his ignoring what happened makes me feel even more like a jerk.

"Bet this place will be busting at the seams with meat sacks come morning," Sparrow says a little too jubilant.

"Great," I mutter as I crunch on the rest of the dried pasta Sparrow found for me the other night.

We make good time as we walk down Route Twelve toward the highway that connects the mainland to Wellesley Island. My hopes are high, and the excitement from thoughts of seeing Jim again make the deep parts of my stomach tingle.

"What do you think Jim will say when you see him?" Sparrow breaks the silence between us.

"I'm not sure," I tell him between popping the dried noodles into my mouth like super crunchy popcorn.

I think for a minute. I would hope he would run for me and pull me into his arms, maybe spin me around in a circle like they do in the movies, or talk to me with the admiration and adoration as Sparrow had for that white owl. I still can't remember a time when Jim spoke to me like that. Maybe when I see him tomorrow, maybe then he will have missed me so much that those words will come spilling out of his mouth. He'll call me precious, and baby, and beautiful, and squeeze me between his strong arms because he's missed me so much. That's what I wish will happen.

Just in time for the sunrise we find a small yard all enclosed with a high fence to keep the dead out. I think it was some type of animal pen, maybe a small goat enclosure or a dog sitting business. Either way it is clean now, no sign of any animals living in it for a while and the nearby house is empty. I fall asleep, wrapped in survival blankets, dreaming of what it will be like when I find Jim tomorrow.

I wake up in the middle of the day to find Sparrow lying in the tall grass next to me with his eyes closed, his face slack and relaxed. He's out cold.

Liar, I think to myself.

I crawl to him, silent as a mouse in church, and stare. For the first time I get a really good look at him. If he shaved that stubble off and trimmed his unruly brown hair, he could be very good looking. Even better looking than Jim is. The pit of my stomach seems to quiver a bit at this realization and I'm not sure why.

My gaze wanders down the length of him. I know he's tall, really tall, with a big frame. But it's hard to tell what his body really looks like with his pockets stuffed with feathers. I reach for the top button of his coat, wanting to see what's under there so bad before we part ways. I flick the button and frown; it's just a button-down shirt, dark blue and checkered, buttoned up to his neck. I reach for the next button on his coat and as my finger tips the button up to flick it open, Sparrow's hand is on mine in an instant. I breathe in and look to his face. His green eyes are dark and wild. He moves faster than I've ever seen his crazy ass move, pushing me away and standing, backing far away from me.

"You're not supposed to touch me," he says as he buttons the coat back up to his neck. "We have an understanding. I don't touch you, you don't touch me." He shoves his hand through his tousled brown hair.

"I'm sorry," I tell him, sitting back on my heels. "It's just... just..."

"What?" he shouts.

"You've been hiding yourself under that coat all this

time. I just wanted to see you." And this may be my last time to find out what's under there.

"What the fuck does it matter to you, Meg? You hide in plain sight all the time." He whips his hands in the air real crazy-like. "With every step you take, every move you make, everything you do, you're just hiding yourself in plain sight. You might think that no one notices but I do!" He takes a few more steps away from me. "How about you go the fuck to sleep, Meg, and keep your hands to yourself?"

I stop moving, stop breathing, my gut drops and a lump rises in my throat. In all of Sparrow's crazy quirks I've never heard him drop an f-bomb. I've never seen him this angry before and for some reason–I'm not sure why–but I flinch away from him.

Sparrow stops, stills, and taking one last look at me he turns, walking to the far edge of the enclosed field and stands facing the fence.

I wait for him to turn around and sit next to me, to hum some Bon Jovi song like he does for me each morning, but he doesn't. He stands still, his back straight, his coat stretched tight over his shoulders. I can see the bulge of something under the coat, whatever it is he's hiding under there.

I lay down on the warm grass with my backpack tucked under my head. And just like a true sinner, I fall asleep without feeling a hint of remorse for what I just did to him. Something inside of me really wants to see what lies underneath that coat.

...

"When do you think we'll make it to the border?" I ask Sparrow. He's refused to look at me since I got up. I get the sense that he's still mad.

"Few hours," is all he says.

I get a good look at him as he goes to open the fence so we can leave. His coat bulges with all of the feathers he has in there, some even stick out of the tops of his pockets on the outside of his coat.

As we walk I start to feel a little bit guilty for trying to sneak a peek at whatever he hides under his coat. Even though I'm not sure why he has to keep it such a secret; I've pretty much told him all of mine since this journey began.

He doesn't talk to me. He doesn't ask me any questions. His face is set hard, his tall body stiff as he walks down the road in the moonlight. When we reach the last few miles to the border, I can't take it any longer. I can't leave him like this as I move on to find Jim, never having apologized for my actions.

"I'm sorry," I tell him. As the words come out of my mouth, I realize this is the first time I've ever actually apologized to anyone, ever, in my life.

He stops in the road. "Sorry only works when you mean it, Meg."

I step in front of him so I can face him, remembering all he's done for me these past few days. I shove my hand in my pocket and find the flower he picked for me when I told him how my father greeted me each morning. I look down myself at the short shorts and flannel shirt that's unbuttoned just a little too far and I notice in the crook of my arm where the snowy owl landed there is a tiny white feather stuck to my shirt. I grasp it between my fingers and hold it out to him.

"I'm sorry," I say. "I mean it."

Sparrow's eyes focus on the object in my hand.

"I'm sorry," I repeat. "I won't ever try to look under your coat again. It was wrong of me to try."

He stares at the tiny feather and I'm not even sure he's heard what I said until he responds with, "No one has ever given me a feather before."

"Really?" I ask.

"Really."

He takes the feather from between my fingers and tucks it into his chest pocket, repeating his pocket watch pat.

"Better?" I ask.

He nods. "Better."

As we walk, Sparrow whistles a tune that I recognize as *Have a Nice Day*. It seems my offering has improved his current disposition. It's strange how something as simple as a tiny feather can do that.

...

JUST AS THE sun starts to rise, I squint at the view in front of me and recognize the border crossing a few miles ahead of us.

"Jesus, Sparrow, look!" I point. "We've made it and just in time for daylight!"

I take off running and I can hear his steps right behind me as he follows. As I get closer I notice that the gates, the ones that you used to be able to pull up to and flash your I.D. and they would let you pass with just a few questions then let you drive on in to Canada, they're locked. It's all gated, locked up, and topped with barbed wire. As we get closer I see movement, a guard steps out of one of the huts you used to be able to drive past.

"Hey!" I shout at the guard. "Hey!" I wave my arms. "Let us in!"

He meanders over, taking his sweet time, chewing on something.

"Well, well, well," he glances between us. "So there are some of you that are still alive in there."

"Let us in, please?"

"Afraid I can't do that." He shakes his head.

"What? Why?" I ask. "Oh, wait a sec!" I shift my bag and dig through it, pulling out my passport. "I have dual citizenship!" I hold up the passport for him to see.

"Doesn't matter, lady." He shakes his head. "Under strict orders not to let you filthy Americans in."

"What?" I feel my shoulders drop in defeat. "But we've come so far..." I turn to Sparrow but he's looking away, his gaze locked in the treetops across the bridge where I can see some dark birds fluttering about.

"Listen," the officer starts. "I feel bad for you two, seeing you're alive and all and you look like you've traveled a mighty long way. Look over there."

I follow the direction of his hand. There is a dam, with water pouring out of it into the nearby river.

"That's the only location around here without gates. And it's for a good reason. That water pumps through there faster than a jet plane at top speed. Those meat sacks can't climb that, but if you and that crazy man can scale that, you're in. I won't even call it in to report you until a day after."

"What makes you think he's crazy?" I scowl at the man.

His eyebrows rise.

"Okay." I look at the dam and then back at Sparrow who now stares down at me. "Okay," I tell the officer. "Thanks."

"Oh, miss," the officer starts, pointing in the direction

of the dam. "Those walking dead creatures, eh, they're at the bottom of that river, milling about like piranhas. Those suckers can't swim or climb, but they can hold their breath for a mighty long time."

"Thanks for the warning." I nod at him. "Come on, Sparrow."

...

I stand on the bridge that once stretched over the dam. It's busted now. Looks like someone blew up the middle of it so no one could cross. We have to climb down, across, and then up. I watch the water and see the walking bags of flesh under the surface.

"How deep do you think that is?" I ask Sparrow.

He looks down, leaning a little too close to me. "Looks deep enough," he replies.

I turn to look at him and he smiles. I kind of love it when Sparrow Man smiles, his perfectly straight teeth all white and gleaming at me. His green eyes twinkle a little. I smile back at him.

"This is going to suck, isn't it?" I ask through gritted teeth.

"Most likely," he replies, still smiling, his green eyes still twinkling.

Crazy men shouldn't be able to make faces that look so innocent.

...

THE ROCK and crumbling cement are cold and wet. On top of that, it's slippery and hard to hold onto. Sparrow follows me. Every few moments I catch him leaning over my shoulder to look in the direction that we are going. Being daytime, I can see the meat sacks milling about in the water and it's just like the officer said; piranhas.

I grip the rock at my side, my fingers numb from the cold spray of water, and slip a little. I stand still and take a deep breath. I need to stop thinking about those bodies in the water. I need to focus on the task. Or maybe I just need a distraction.

"What's on the playlist for today, Sparrow?"

"Bon Jovi," he says.

"It's always Bon Jovi. What song?"

He takes a thoughtful breath. "*Dead or alive?*"

I stumble a little. "Please, don't sing that."

"*Blaze of Glory?*"

"Hell no."

"*Bed of Roses?*"

I think for a moment. I can deal with *Bed of Roses*. It has nothing to do with death, or dying, or heaven or hell. "That's good. Sing that."

We continue our climb down as Sparrow starts to hum.

...

AS WE REACH the bottom of the dam I can see the dead, and they must sense us because they've congregated right below the area where we are climbing. It's hard judging the depth of the water, but it looks like it's a few feet above their heads. This is good, because we have to pass a few steps of the broken dam that are just under the water.

Stepping down, I settle my foot on a piece of water-covered rock, I grasp a rock to steady myself and as I move my other foot, I slip.

"Oh shit!" I mutter, trying to steady myself, waving my arm as I dip backward. My heart thumps so hard I think it's going to pop out of my chest. I feel something brush my boot and realize there isn't a few feet of water above those dead people, there's just a few inches! The next thing I feel is a tight grip on my arm. Sparrow's lean body jumps down next to me, and just as he lands he grunts and shoves me up and away from him, across the slippery water-covered dam to the other side.

I grip the rock and press my face to the cold stone, taking deep breaths. That was close. I turn, reaching for Sparrow and...dear God those dead things have a hold of his trench coat as it dips in the water. I reach out for him.

"Sparrow!" I shout.

He doesn't look at me, instead he lets go of the rock and grips his coat with both hands, standing on the slippery submerged piece and struggling to pull his coat away from them. The fabric starts to tear, and I see a handful of feathers fall out of his inside pockets and flutter toward the water.

"No!" I yell at Sparrow. "Stop!" I scream at him.

"My feathers!" he says with a panicked voice.

"Sparrow!"

"Can't, can't lose them..."

Another dead hand reaches for his coat, pulling it harder, ripping the corner of his coat and the pocket of feathers off him. I see one of the large white feathers of the snowy owl drift away from us.

"My feathers!" Sparrow leans forward like he's going to dive in after them. "My feathers!" he shouts, panicked.

"Sparrow!" I scream at him until he turns to face me.

I hold my hand out to him. "You can't risk your life for a pocket full of feathers."

"They... they aren't just feathers."

"Sparrow!" I scream louder. "You will die!"

"My feathers," he whispers, his green eyes wide, his hand reaching as they flow downstream.

"I will find you more feathers!"

His eyes flit to mine; he reaches further, bends his knees to jump.

"SPARROW!" I scream at the top of my lungs. "NO!" He stands up straight. "I will find you more feathers! Don't jump in that water, please, dear God, don't do it!"

He stills and looks at me. "You promise?"

"Yes!"

"A promise is a promise, Meg." I don't miss when his eyes flit downstream, toward the feathers that are floating away.

"I promise!" I reach for him, the spray of the water soaking my sleeve. "Let's go!"

Sparrow reaches out with one long arm, his hand wrapping tight around mine, and I use every bit of strength I have to pull him up onto the rock where I am.

We stand on the broken dam ledge, one of Sparrow's arms across my shoulders and gripping damp rock on the other side of me. For this moment I don't mind that he's touching me or that his chest is pressed against my back or that he's so close I can feel his heart beating and his rapid breaths. I am just thankful that I didn't watch as Sparrow was pulled into the water by those things.

"Are you okay?" I ask when I catch my breath.

"I don't know," he replies, his voice vacant.

"Let's get out of here."

We climb up to the top of the dam to freedom, to safety. I could care less that I am coated in a thick sheen of sweat and dirty water as I realize that I'm one step closer to home, to Jim.

...

We walk down a two-lane highway with signs pointing to Lansdowne, Gananoque, and Seeley's Bay. We follow the sign pointing to Kingston, Sparrow clutching his torn coat tight to his body. He makes a strange sound deep in his throat. I stop, reaching my hand out to stop him too.

"Sparrow?" I ask.

He blinks at me.

"Are you okay?"

He makes the sound again, and for a second I think he might be crying deep inside his chest, although no tears fall from his eyes. I know he's crazy, but he has his moments, and we saved each other back there on that dam. But remembering the look on his face when those feathers washed downstream, I think it cracked him a bit more, and watching him kind of broke my heart a little.

"Can I touch you?" I ask him.

He nods, biting his lip.

I step forward, hesitant at first. We have had an understanding: no touching...well, unless we're saving the other's life. I open my arms and reaching up on my toes, I wrap my arms around his shoulders, pressing my face to his bony clavicle. It takes a minute before I feel his arms wrap around my back. I squeeze him tighter and rub my hands across his shoulders, trying to soothe him. He shudders a little and presses his face into my neck.

We stand like this for a long time, two crazies in the road, hugging and crying. But we made it this far together, and after all that's happened we are so close. I'm almost home. I'm almost to Jim.

Sparrow seems to collect himself in the moments that I'm thinking. "You promise," he starts, his voice cracking. He clears his throat. "You promise you'll help me find more feathers?"

"I promise," I tell him. Then I remember that we just spent days searching for those damn feathers and now I'm hours away from Jim. My heart sinks a little for Sparrow because I think I just lied to him.

...

We resume our walk down the long stretch of highway. Every few minutes a car passes us heading in either direction. We stop at a bus stop, a real bus stop. Sparrow points to a piece of paper hanging on the window.

Wait here for Safe House Shuttle, it says in bold ink.

We sit and wait and before long I see a city bus driving down the road. The bus pulls to a stop in front of us. The door opens and an old lady leans out.

"Which one you headed to?" she asks.

"Kingston," I tell her.

"This is your ride then." She leans back in her seat and adjusts her seatbelt. "Hop on kids."

Sparrow and I both stand.

"Ladies first," he whispers, moving to the side so I can get on the bus ahead of him.

I roll my eyes. "Still not a lady."

We take an awkward walk down the bus aisle. I stop in the middle and move to sit down, pressing myself against the window.

"Sit with me?" I ask Sparrow—no, I beg him.

He sits next to me, hovering on the edge of the seat so our shoulders don't touch.

"Next stop, Kingston Safe House," the bus driver says over the loudspeaker.

"This is weird," I say to Sparrow. "We are the only ones on this bus."

"Doesn't matter," Sparrow says as he drums his fingers on his knees. "You will have your Jim back soon."

"And then who will you have?"

He shrugs.

"Will you go to the Safe House with me?" I ask him.

"Meg." He turns to me. "Maybe your adventure is over, but mine isn't. I still have things to do."

"Like what?"

"Feathers," he whispers as his green eyes flick to my lips.

Just this one second, when he looks at me like this, I am filled with so much hope of seeing Jim again, but at the same time I'm filled with this almost unbearable sadness at the fact that I may never see Sparrow Man again. I don't think I've ever felt so thoroughly torn in opposite directions in my entire life.

...

THE KINGSTON SAFE House is just as Noah described it: nothing but a huge prison. There are miles of chain link fence topped with barbed wire. Guards pace the lookout points with weapons in hand. As we get off the bus, a man walks toward the gate, keys jingling on his belt. I walk to the gate, my heart in my throat, barely able to breathe, barely able to believe that I am here right now.

The man with the keys looks at me and then Sparrow. He clears his throat. "Miss? We can take you but not him." He nods at Sparrow.

I turn. "Why not?"

"His kind can't cross these grounds."

I narrow my eyes on the man with the keys. "His kind?"

"It's okay," Sparrow interrupts. "I don't need this place, you do."

A bit confused, I settle my eyes on Sparrow. "Where will you go?" I ask.

"Don't worry about it," he replies with a smile.

"Goodbye, Sparrow," I tell him, feeling mighty sad.

"Goodbye, Meg." He gives my shoulder an awkward pat. As I walk away from him through the gates of the prison, he says something strange. "I hope you find the answers you're looking for."

I notice the bus is already gone as he walks to the dusty parking lot, a gray feather sticking out of his pocket. I turn away from him and follow the man down the fenced entryway and into the large prison.

Qualifiers and Quarantine

THE FIRST THING they did when I walked into the Safe House was search my backpack. They took the two hand-guns, didn't even ask me about them, they just took them and the bullets. The second thing they did was hand me two pieces of paper and a pen. The first sheet of paper was just like my college admission forms. I wrote my name at the top, my date of birth, my age, every personally identifying tidbit about myself. The second page had two questions: *Are you searching for someone?* Followed by *What is your greatest sin?*

Noah warned me about this part, how they lock everyone up at night because they think it's their sins turning them into the walking dead. I guess they want to know up front what to expect.

I sit there, tapping the pen on the paper, thinking real hard about all of the bad shit I did and trouble I got into. I'm sure they want to know my juvy record and the fact that I was knocked up before getting married. Gosh, when I sit down and think about it, there's a lot I've done wrong with my life. But my worst... Well, my worst has got to be killing those seven men. Killing is wrong, that's what they all say, even if it was in self-defense. I write down my story and hand it to the man who escorted me in.

Then I wait.

It's not long before a man in a black suit with a white Roman collar tucked into the neck of his shirt arrives. He nods at me.

"Meg?" he holds a hand out. I stare at it. "My name's Deacon, it's nice to meet you."

"I don't touch people," is my response.

"Okay, then." He clasps his hands together and sits across from me. Staring. Like a creeper. He has a plain face with light brown hair and thin eyebrows and I think if I saw him in public I'd probably look right past him.

My eyes settle on the Roman collar. I may not go to church but I know enough that a Deacon holds some religious status. "Is your name really Deacon or are you a Deacon?" I ask.

"It's my name, my title. So you're looking for your fiancé?" he asks.

"Yes, Jim. Jim Sullivan. He's supposed to be here. We had an agreement if anything ever happened that we would meet in Kingston." I reach into my bag and pull out my passport. "Look, I have dual citizenship."

He holds his hand up, waving away the passport. "That's okay. Are you familiar with the Qualifiers and Quarantine process?"

All I know is what they did when I got sent to county lockup: fingerprints, pictures, body cavity searches. "No," I tell him, hoping that the process isn't the same here.

"Well, I will be your Parole Officer." He taps his fingers on the table as though he's bored. "I will be responsible for locating your loved one and helping you through the Quarantine process. The first part was the test you filled out."

"I didn't realize that was a test."

"Well, you certainly wrote some colorful things on there."

"I thought you wanted to know the worst?"

"Yes, we do and we appreciate your honesty. So the next step is for me to show you to your cell and then the interview process starts. It takes three days and we can't release you into the general population until someone comes to claim you."

"Jim," I remind him. "Until Jim comes to claim me. My fiancé."

"Yes." He folds his hands and smiles.

"So, are you ready to be shown to your cell?"

I sigh. Another cell. "Sure."

I get up when Deacon does and follow him, my backpack strapped across my shoulder. We trail behind a man who unlocks and relocks gates as we walk down long corridors with barred cells. Some are empty, others decorated with pictures and colorful blankets, just like someone's house would be. We walk down some stairwells and across some catwalks, until we come to a row of cells where there are no personal items on the beds or taped to the walls. This must be Quarantine.

Deacon stops and steps aside.

"This is your cell." He points to the bed at a set of maroon scrubs. "Those are Newcomer uniforms. You will wear them to the interviews so the decision will not be impacted by your clothing or... other things."

His eyes settle on the tattoo across my collarbone. I pull at my shirt to cover it, annoyed that he can stand here and judge me based on how I look. What a dick.

"Would you like something to eat before the interview begins?" he asks, his face completely complacent.

"That would be nice, thank you."

He waves at me to go into the cell and I do. But as I hear

the metal door slide across its track and the turn of his keys, I am filled with a sense of dread.

...

Three days later.

I HAD this last day of questioning to make it through and it went pretty much the same as the others: they asked me what happened, they asked me what I did, and they asked me why those men targeted my house. I gave them the same answers as I have the last three days. I have no idea.

They wanted me to tell them something I didn't know. I think they were just killing time, making me wait the extra day in Quarantine, to see if my tattoos would make me wake up a walking dead person.

Then that bitch threw my milk on my bed again. I refrained from punching her in the face. Instead, I sang her a little tune I had thought up last night:

> *As I lay me down to sleep,*
> *I hope you turn into a creep,*
> *I hope your guts rot and twist,*
> *I hope you get punched with a fist.*

SHE SLAMMED THE CELL DOOR, locked it, and whispered to me, "That shit only happens to sinners like you. Not good Catholic school girls like me."

I told her to fuck off. I'm not a poet, or anyone remotely artistic, but I thought it was good; it rhymed and shit.

I shower, just like I did after the other questioning sessions. It's not that I was sweating or anything, just pissed off and angry and... and... I just wanted to be home. I wanted Jim to come get me just like he did when I was at college and I called him to tell him that I was pregnant and that I wasn't going to keep the baby but I thought he should know.

That night, my last night of waiting for my fiancé to collect me, I slept in my borrowed cot that smelled of unpasteurized milk, again, and I dreamt of Sparrow Man, and it was hot.

He took off that stupid coat and whatever else he wore under there and he was all pale skin and hard muscle. He had shaved the stubble and trimmed his hair, and I swear to God he looked like he stepped out of the pages of a magazine. And he smelled so good, like... like... I don't know, just really, really good. When he walked to me, all naked and gleaming, I didn't step away. Holy hell no, I stood there, eyes wide, holding my breath. I let him strip off every piece of clothing I was wearing. He did it so slow, like he was unwrapping a gift, so slow I thought I was going to die before he finished. I let him run his lips over my skin, every scar, every mark of ink. He mumbled sweet things in my ear, he licked my neck and when I turned my face to meet his, I finally took a breath, and... yeah, he smelled like heaven, like Christmas and New Years and cake batter. My stomach quivered. I let him lay me down on my borrowed cot. I let him press himself to me and I could feel him on my leg. He was hard and I was achy. His hands trailed all over, touching every inch of me. I moved my legs apart, ready for him, ready for this. Sparrow pulled back, his green, green eyes looking into mine, and he smiled that smile he only ever gave me. I felt his hips move and–

I WOKE up all sweaty and panting and I'm pretty sure I had the female equivalent of a boner. Part of me felt dirty, dreaming that way about a poor demented man. A sinner? Yeah, I am a sinner. Only a sinner could have a dream like that while she was waiting for her one true love to come claim her. Maybe my daddy was right; maybe I am nothing but a trashy whore. I'd be surprised if I didn't wake up a walking meat sack by sunrise.

...

IN THE MORNING, Deacon collects me from my cell. He walks me to the visiting room. "We've put out a notice. But we can't let you leave until someone comes to collect you."

I sit at a table. There are three of us here, me and two men. I sit there all day and watch as each of the men leave with someone else. By evening I am the last one left. And that's when it hits me: that pain that reverberates through your chest like ripples from a stone tossed in a pond. The one that hurts too much to bring tears even when you try. You feel it over and over, each time it gets stronger and stronger, until your heart swells and your chest caves at the same time, pulling and twisting your lungs in the wrong direction. I realize, sitting here alone that he's not coming for me. Jim's not coming for me.

...

Deacon doesn't come to bring me back to my cell. Instead the man whom I recognize from the center of the desk-of-questioning, the middle man, walks into the room, his robes flowing around his feet like ocean waves. His face is set, grim.

"Sorry about this," he tells me.

For an instant I hope he's telling me that Jim is on his way, that maybe he was busy or lost or something.

I close my eyes and take a deep breath, grip the backpack that's across my shoulder. "He's not coming?" I ask.

The man shakes his head no.

"Okay." I stand to leave, and there is a strong sensation in my gut that I recognize as the need to vomit.

"We can still use you here," the man starts. "There's not many women. We can keep you here. You'll be safe and maybe, in time, we can locate your Jim, maybe he'll come around."

From the sound of his voice it sounds like they've already found Jim and the news is not good.

"No thank you," I tell him.

"You'll be safe here," he offers again. "Safer than you will be out there."

"I'll be a prisoner. If Jim were here for me that would be one thing. But I've spent enough time locked in a jail cell. I'm not going to live my life like this; locked up, waiting for my sins to turn me into one of those things. And I'm not going to hang around here so I can make a bunch of men happy."

"Very well then." The man tips his head. "This guard will show you out." As I pass him he reaches out to stop me. I weave away from his touch. "You need to be careful who you trust out there," he warns me. "Things are not what they seem."

"They never are."

I walk away from him, recognizing the guard that appears at the door as the same one who let me in. I follow as he leads me out of the prison, down the fenced walkway. I can feel the eyes of the people here watching me as I leave.

"Too bad," the guard starts speaking as he unlocks the gate. "Hear you don't have the baby making parts any longer. Men here could make you very happy. Baby making isn't allowed with the fertile ones."

"Shut up," I tell the guard. "I want my guns back," I demand, remembering the two handguns they took from me when I got here.

He shakes his head from side to side. "Can't do that."

"What the hell is it with people taking my guns?"

"Guns can't help you here." He shrugs. "Looks like you have a visitor." The guard tips his head. "Looks like he's still breathing too."

I raise my head and find Sparrow sitting on a cement block in the parking lot. I walk to him. He smiles, tilting his head to face the sun.

"Sparrow?" I ask. "What are you doing here?"

"Would you like to come with me?" he asks.

"Where?"

"On an adventure."

"An adventure?"

"Yes, I still have things to find."

"Like what?"

"Feathers." He turns away from the sun and looks at me. Something in the center of my chest warms as I stare at his face and his green eyes. God, how I missed Sparrow while I was waiting in that cell. It's all I can do to tear my eyes away from him to look around at the desolate space around us.

"You promised you would get me more feathers," he reminds me.

"Sure, Sparrow." I have nothing else to do. No one else to look for. When I really think about it, I missed Sparrow more these past three days than I did Jim. That means something, right?

"Great!" Sparrow jumps down from the cement block, dirt wisps up at his feet.

"Where are we going?"

"I have to find feathers."

I sigh. Noticing the corner of his lip quirk up I ask, "What kind of feathers?"

He looks up to the sky, then turns. "Flamingo."

"We are in Canada. Flamingoes aren't native to this area, Sparrow. There are none anywhere near here."

"Yes there are. At the zoo, just across the border."

I stop in my tracks. "You want to go back across the border? After all it took to get here?"

"Look around, Meg, they've got the same problem here as we do in the states. That fence at the border isn't helping them at all."

I turn around and look at the Safe House I just left. It seems, even though we haven't seen any of the dead walking during the day, they must have the same problem here, or they wouldn't be locking themselves up in prisons at night and praying that they wake up in the morning.

…

We walk down the same highway we showed up on, headed for the American border. It feels strange, walking during the daytime, instead of waiting for night to travel.

Sparrow doesn't seem to notice the difference. He walks next to me, his hands in the pockets of his ripped coat.

After we've walked for a few hours, I hear the sound I recognize as a city bus. It stops next to us.

"You kids headed in the wrong direction," the same old lady who drove us to Kingston shouts out the window at us. "Didn't find what you were looking for?"

"Nope!" Sparrow tells her. "No flamingoes here."

I burst out laughing.

The bus driver's chest hits the steering wheel as she slams on the brakes.

Sparrow laughs.

"Whelp." She grins. "Want a lift?"

I turn to Sparrow. "I've gotten enough sun for the day," he tells me like a man walking away from a buffet table.

"Sure," I tell the lady as we walk around the bus to board.

She drops us off at the same bus stop where she picked us up from three days ago. As we approach the giant fence that keeps Canada and America separate, I notice that it looks a lot less intimidating from this side. The same guard steps out of the observation shack as we get close.

"Thought you two wanted in?" he asks as we approach him.

"Didn't find what I was looking for," I tell him.

The officer looks at Sparrow and twists his face. I feel a sudden need to defend Sparrow, even though this man isn't saying anything I can tell what he's thinking.

"Leave him alone," I tell the officer.

"Didn't say a thing," he replies with a chuckle.

"You don't need to."

The officer grunts and tugs at his belt. "Guess you want to go back to your filthy America?"

"At least we'll be free there."

"Until your sins catch up with you," he says as he reaches for a keychain in his hip. "It's kind of weird, huh?"

"What?" I ask as he twists the key in the gate lock.

"You guys used to keep your borders all locked tight, didn't want to let the immigrants into your free country. Now look at you all, fighting to get out of there with nowhere else to go."

"Whatever," I mutter. "I didn't vote for those assholes that locked up the border."

"Yeah," the officer laughs. "You don't look like the voting type."

The officer opens a narrow door and waits for us to walk through.

"Safe travels," he says with a smile as we walk through.

"Thanks for nothing," I snap at him. "Fucking Canadians."

The officer slams the gate behind us, locking it up tight.

We walk across the bridge to America. I feel defeated and renewed all at the same time. It's a strange feeling, losing Jim but having Sparrow Man back. The only downside is now I'm not really sure what to do with myself. But, I did promise Sparrow that I would help him find more feathers. I guess now that is just what I will do.

...

"There's a castle down the road here." Sparrow points ahead of us. "We could stay there for a bit, no rush now that you don't have a place to go."

There is a severe burning behind my eyes. I know he doesn't mean it, telling me I don't have a place to go. I only wanted to go home, find the home I had with Jim, but it seems he either doesn't want me anymore or he's gone.

"What do you think?" Sparrow presses.

I think I want to punch him in his neck for the insensitive words he just spoke to me. But, I'm sure physical violence–especially toward a crazy person–because you don't like the words coming out of his mouth is definitely not ladylike.

"Sure," I tell him. And instead of punching him in the neck I shove my hands deep in my pockets. "Staying in a castle sounds like it might be fun."

Sparrow smiles and we walk, him with his hands in his pockets, me with my arms swinging at my sides once the urge to physically harm him has passed, my tattoos hanging out of the wide neck of my shirt. I don't bother to cover them up like Deacon suggested at the Safe House.

We walk Route 81, following Ely Drive all the way to Blue Heron Drive and then a tiny gravel road to the end. There, sitting on the lake, is a small castle, all stone and arches and a narrow moat like something out of the middle ages and not much bigger than one of those McMansions like my old friend Sara had.

"What do you think?" Sparrow asks.

"Looks nice."

I follow him around the side of the building to find a long deck that ends at the lake.

"Can you fish?" he asks. "Sunrise is the best time to fish."

"But we don't have any fishing poles," I tell him.

"Maybe you have something in your backpack?"

I unclip the bag from my shoulder and search through it. I pull out the dining kit, the survival bracelet, the Swiss army knife and two self-filtering water bottles. "There's not much more in here besides clothes."

Sparrow walks to me with two sticks in his hand. He bends down, picking up the bracelet and the knife. "This should do." He unwinds the bracelet and attaches the long string to each of the sticks. I watch his deft fingers as he ties knots and unhooks the clasp to use as hooks. He hands me a stick. "Done. Let's fish."

We sit on the end of the deck, which extends just over the water. With the blunt clip of the bracelet and the lack of bait, I suspect that we won't catch much, but I'm surprised when Sparrow pulls up four fish. I, on the other hand, catch nothing. I dip my water bottles in the water and fill them in order to feel some type of accomplishment for the day.

"Okay." He stands and looks over at the rocky shoreline. "Let's get some firewood."

I follow him, simply watching as he bends and collects a handful twigs from the shore. I cross my arms and stare out over the lake, trying to figure out what the hell just happened at the Safe House in Kingston and why the hell I am still hanging out with a crazy man.

"Hey, Meg!" I hear Sparrow's excited whisper.

"What?"

"Look." I follow his arm as he points over the water at a dark colored bird. It takes me a moment to realize it's a loon. And just like when I told Sparrow that my favorite bird was the loon, Sparrow calls to the creature with an eerie tremolo. The loon calls back over the water. Sparrow looks to me, smiling, his arms filled with sticks and eyes gleaming.

"That's fucking amazing," I reply dryly. "Are you going to pluck its wings now?"

Sparrow frowns and twists his face. I feel a pang of guilt for acting like an ass when all he's trying to do is help me.

"Sorry," I frown back at him and shove my hands in my jean pockets.

"You know, Meg," Sparrow starts as he hands me a bundle of sticks to start a fire. "You shouldn't swear."

"Why?"

"It's not very ladylike."

"I've told you before, Sparrow, I'm not a lady."

I'm nothing but trailer trash, just like my Daddy and the rest of those town people told me my whole life. But, I still have my teeth. I run my tongue across them all, just to make sure.

"You could be," he suggests as he turns away and waltzes to the shoreline to collect some of the larger pieces of driftwood. "You could prove everyone wrong about you." Sparrow walks along the rocky shoreline, picking up sticks. "Okay," he says as he grabs the line of fish and looks to the sky. The morning is getting brighter. "Time to hide."

We cross the bridge into the little castle. I don't tell Sparrow, but I see the moat water stir as the dead under there awaken. I shudder, remembering how we crossed that dam and they almost pulled Sparrow in. We lift the drawbridge and close the door, locking the heavy latches. I follow Sparrow as he chooses a room to accommodate us both for the day and protect us in case any of the dead get in.

We stop at a bedroom on the second floor that has a fireplace and a private bathroom. I drop the bundle of sticks in the hearth and turn to help Sparrow lock the door and move some heavy furniture in front of it.

As I light the fire, Sparrow prepares the fish, skewering them on a thin stick and laying them across the fire. I take a drink from my freshly filled water bottles and stare at the huge four-poster bed on the other side of the room. I'm going to make snow angels in that bed later. I'm going to stretch out my arms and legs as far as they go. It's going to be amazing. I look around the room and notice the only other piece of furniture is a wingback chair. Sparrow works diligently making my dinner and I know that even though he says he doesn't sleep, he can't sit up all day in that chair. It looks like I will be curled up on my side, sharing that bed with my crazy companion.

After I've eaten the fish and drank my fill, I head for the bed. I catch Sparrow settling himself into the chair.

"Come on, Sparrow." His eyes flick to me and an apprehensive look appears on his face. "You're not resting in that chair. This bed is big enough for the both of us."

"I don't need to sleep," he reminds me.

I could tell him that he's a liar. I caught him sleeping in that yard when I tried to look under his coat. "You need to rest and relax and you can't do it in that chair."

I lie down and pretend to ignore him as he walks to the other side of the bed and kicks his boots off.

We each hover on opposite edges of the bed, a large open space of mattress between us. Maybe if we didn't both share the same issue of not wanting to be touched we could use up some of that space and be more comfortable. I wait, taking shallow breaths, until I hear Sparrow start to hum. Tonight it's, *We Weren't Born to Follow*. I fall asleep listening to his voice and realizing how much I missed it those three days I was in that prison.

...

As my eyes flutter open, I find that I am curled up on my opposite side from which I fell asleep and dangerously close to Sparrow. He stares at the ceiling, eyes open, hands folded across his stomach. He must sense that I'm awake, even though he never looks at me. Not long after my eyes open he rolls to the side and stands in one quiet movement.

As he walks across the room his hands flutter over his coat, checking the buttons, ensuring that they are secure. I frown to myself, realizing that he doesn't trust me—still—to not look at what he hides under that coat.

"I didn't look," I tell him trying to control the defensive tone of my voice.

"I know that."

"Then why were you checking your buttons?"

Sparrow shrugs. "Habit I guess." He walks to the window and looks out. I can see the fading light of day from where I sit. Soon it will be night, and we'll be on the move again. I run my hands over the sheets of the bed, knowing that actually finding a bed and not a hard floor or rotting barn to sleep in is one of the few luxuries we have left right now.

...

"Which zoo are you headed for?" I ask Sparrow as we walk down Route 81, headed south, away from the border. The roadside is mostly bare with just a few cars littering the side of the road.

"There's one in Syracuse," he responds, scanning the sides of the highway.

"Jeez, that's like almost a hundred miles from here," I tell him. "It will take us a week or more to get there."

"We'll get there and look," he points to a road sign. "It's only ninety-six miles from here, not a hundred."

I let out a frustrated breath, not looking forward to another long walk, into a large city nonetheless. And then, in the shadows under the highway sign, I notice a red Jeep Wrangler parked on the side of the road, just calling my name.

"Meg," Sparrow warns as I skip to the vehicle. "We aren't driving," he says from the middle of the highway.

"Why not?" I reach for the door handle and open the driver's side door.

"I told you, it's too much noise." He makes no attempt to walk to me.

I open the door and lean inside. Something glints at me from behind the steering wheel. "They even left the keys!"

"Don't–"

"Come on, Sparrow." I turn to face him. "We could be there in less than two hours." I turn back around and turn the key. The Jeep engine turns over and rumbles to life. "Look, there's almost a full tank of gas! It's like it was left here for us. Like a miracle or some shit."

"Shouldn't that raise an alarm in your little head?" I hear his boots on the pavement as he walks around to the passenger side.

"Just think of all those feathers you could have in just a few hours," I tease. He pulls open the passenger door and gets in. "You don't want to drive?"

"I don't drive. I don't know how." He looks out the window into the forest. "Better get moving."

I unclip my backpack and set it in the back seat before buckling my seatbelt. "It's night, we don't have to worry about the dead right now."

"It's not the dead that worries me." He clips his seatbelt. He tips his head to the side. "Someone is coming. You had better drive, fast."

"What do–"

"Go!"

As I flick the headlights on and shift the Jeep into gear as a deep voice shouts from the woods. "Hey! Get out of my car!" I push down on the accelerator and drive off just as a gunshot rings through the night air.

"I think I just stole that guy's car," I tell Sparrow as I focus on the road in the night, accelerating the Jeep toward seventy miles per hour.

"It's probably better this way." Sparrow stares straight ahead.

"That I stole a car?"

"That we got away from that man in the woods. Sometimes the living should be feared more than the dead."

"What do you think he was doing?" I slow down to swerve between two parked cars in the middle of the highway.

"Hunting."

"Like deer or something?"

"Like two people walking down the highway in the middle of the night." A wrinkle of concern crosses his forehead.

"That's messed up." I accelerate the Jeep, speeding further away from the man in the forest.

Sparrow turns and looks out the back of the vehicle. "Just go. As fast as you can," he urges.

"What? Why?"

"Because it's following us."

"Wha–"

I lean to look behind us and sure as shit the man is running down the middle of the road at us, except it's not really a man. I can see what looks like horns protruding from his head. I blink, trying to focus my eyes in the dim moonlight.

"I have to touch you now," Sparrow warns me as I feel the pressure of his hand on my thigh as he pushes down, causing me to accelerate the Jeep.

"What was that?" I ask, hoping it was nothing more than shadows playing across that man's figure.

"Something worse than the dead which walk in the daylight."

...

I FOLLOW the highway signs to Syracuse. Sparrow is quiet. Each time I glance at him his face is covered in an awkward expression as though he's fighting something inside of himself or trying to remember something.

Driving to a zoo in the middle of a heavily populated city in the middle of the night definitely isn't a good idea. But now, I fear the day more than I fear the deep ghetto of the city.

"Look," I point out the passenger side window. "There's a huge mall. We could get new clothes or something." I glance at Sparrow's ripped coat. "You could get a new coat."

"Stay away from that mall," he warns. "Don't go there."

"Why?"

"Take a closer look."

I slow the Jeep and squint at the large building made of glass and cement. I can see movement and torches behind the plate glass windows.

"That's nothing more than a huge prison. Just like the one you left in Canada. Except this one is filled with people from the middle of a city with a booming crime rate. Who do you think is running that place? There's plenty of corruption in there and it's only a matter of time before their sins catch up with them."

"Okay." I pull away and continue driving, following the signs to the zoo.

...

"The parking lot is empty. That's a good sign. Right?" I ask, parking the Jeep near the front door of the zoo.

"Yeah, there's no one here."

We get out and head toward the front door, which I can see is already broken in. I follow Sparrow through the broken entrance and pull back as the stench of rot surrounds us.

"Holy crap." I pull my shirt over my mouth and nose.

"Cage up a bunch of animals, make them completely dependent on the humans caring for them, and then this happens." Sparrow shakes his head as he walks up an incline, past a gift shop and stops in front of the zoo map. "Aviary is over here."

I follow him as he pushes his hand against a door labeled *Birds of Paradise*.

"Jesus." I step out from behind Sparrow, watching where I put my feet. The floor is littered with dead birds.

Sparrow bends and lifts one in his hand, a small pink parrot-like bird. "This is too bad," he says as he grips the bird's flight feathers and yanks them off.

"That's gross."

"Yeah. Easier than chasing after live ones though."

"I thought you wanted flamingo feathers?"

"Those are outside." He points at a door. "You can wait out there for me if you want."

I walk past him, avoiding the dead birds that litter the ground and push open the door. Fresh air pours over me and I take a deep breath. I prop the door open with a garbage can so Sparrow can have some fresh air while he pillages the dead birds for their feathers.

There are dark forms on the ground in the gated enclosures, animals rotting into the soil. The sign directly in front of me says: *Lions*. I stand and walk to the thick observation glass, pressing my hands to it and seeing three lions on the ground, hipbones jutting out, and sides sunken in, dead.

I move on only to find a murky pool with a sign for penguins. The smell is so strong here that I step back and search the area for the walking dead. By the time I make it a few hundred yards, Sparrow catches up with me, his pockets full.

I read the sign in front of me. "Are you interested in Emu feathers?" Sparrow leans over the hip-height fencing and searches the cage. "Emu feathers are big."

"No they're not," he corrects me.

We stop in front of a fence with the label for a vulture. He grips the fence and launches himself into the cage and disappears into the shadows.

After a few moments he returns with a handful of large gray feathers clutched in his hand. "Good idea," he says as he reaches for the fencing and climbs out of the cage.

"I didn't suggest those ones," I point out.

He shrugs and moves on. A wooden sign points to the flamingo area. Sparrow walks so fast I can barely keep up with his fast pace. He grips the wooden fence of the flamingo enclosure, ready to launch himself over the side. He pauses when I catch up to him.

"Want to come with me?" he asks.

I get the general feeling that I might be ruining his fun if I went in there with him.

"No, I'll wait here for you."

"You're not going to run away on me again, are you?" he asks with a glimmer of humor in his eye.

"Go pillage the pretty pink birds, Sparrow. Before they come back to life and peck our eyes out."

He grips the wooden fence. "Animals don't walk like the dead, Meg. Their souls are pure." He jumps over the fence. I watch as he stops at each pink mound, stretching the wings of the dead birds and pulling out all of their feathers, stuffing his pockets until he looks like a child bundled for the winter snow.

...

WE HIT the zoos in Rochester and Buffalo. Sparrow took a bag from one of the gift shops to hold all the feathers we took.

With his craving for feathers sated, we stop in a little lakefront town on Lake Erie, just off the highway, Dunkirk. It's quaint, just a bit larger than Gouverneur. There's a breakwall with a little lighthouse out in the middle of the water.

I park the Jeep near the pier. As we make our way across the crumbling breakwall we can hear the sounds of the dead collecting on the shoreline. And when we are secure in the little lighthouse for the day, we watch the dead as the wobble across the peaks and valleys of the breakwall. We bet on which ones will fall into the lake next and which one will lose its footing and smack off the rocks on its way down.

Sparrow catches fish in the wee hours of the morning and we spend our night collecting gull feathers from the shoreline. There are so many that Sparrow doesn't even need to capture any of the birds, we simply pluck the good ones off the ground.

On our second day Sparrow stands up straight after

tucking a few feathers into his pockets and faces the small town.

"What's wrong?" I ask him.

"I need to go to the store." He begins walking across the breakwall toward town, now wearing a backpack that I know is stuffed full of feathers.

"What do you need from the store?"

"I'll know when I get there."

We drove through the town when we got here. There's one of everything; a doctor's office, a dentist, a Wal-Mart, a pharmacy... the list goes on. The only problem is they are a mile or more from where we've been staying.

"I'll drive," I suggest, skipping a few steps to get in front of Sparrow and lead him to the Jeep.

He shrugs and follows me.

We drive to the drug store.

...

"What do you need all of this glue for?" I ask Sparrow.

"Something," is all he tells me as he intently packs the glue into my backpack.

I leave his side and wander through the store. It's been mostly picked through. Probably from whoever lived here before, the survivors stocking up before they turned. I stop in front of the shaving supplies. I grab a men's razor and shaving cream. As I walk away, I reach for a women's razor. It's been a while since I shaved my legs.

When I find Sparrow again, my bag is bursting at the seams with glue. "Why didn't you use your bag?"

"My feathers are in there," he scoffs as though I should know better than to ask.

We retreat to the Jeep, but not before I search the store for something to eat. When I find a candy bar, I don't even ask Sparrow if he wants some of it, I know what his answer will be. I shove it in my mouth.

Something strange has come over us after the shopping spree. A lightness or something. Maybe it's the chocolate.

"Why don't you sing a song?" Sparrow suggests.

"Be careful what you wish for," I laugh. "What do you think we all listened to in the trailer park? Nothing more than seventies and eighties music blaring out of the boombox."

"So, what will you sing?"

"Do you know any Meatloaf?"

"Meatloaf," he says it as though he bit a lemon.

"Come on!" I tease. "I've been listening to you sing Bon Jovi for weeks."

"Yeah, but Bon Jovi is the man!" He reaches forward and slaps the dashboard.

"Well you need to stretch your wings bird-boy. On the playlist, right now, it's *Paradise by the Dashboard Light* by Meatloaf. The other man."

I sing loud, with my best shower voice. Sparrow chirps in, singing the chorus and at times the lead with me. It's not long before our voices break apart, Sparrow singing for Meatloaf and me singing for that strange looking lady in the white jumpsuit that I remember from the video. I accelerate and Sparrow stands in the passenger seat as he sings, extending through the open roof, his arms spread wide. I laugh out loud, throwing my head back with a full smile. Sparrow looks down at me, smiling wide himself. The sleeves of his coat billow in the wind.

"It's like you're flying," I tell him.

He freezes, the night suddenly empty of his voice, his smile gone as he slides down into the passenger seat.

"Oh, jeez." I pull over. "What's wrong? Are you okay? I... I didn't mean anything I was just..."

He turns to me and I see something pass over his face.

"What?" I ask.

"I just remembered something that I think is very important."

"What? Gosh. I'm sorry. I didn't mean to upset you." My hand hovers in the air as though I might touch him to comfort him. I don't though, because I know how both of us are. I've only touched him once and it was awkward, yet comforting. And I'm still not sure how I feel about it.

Sparrow tips his head as though he's studying me. "You're very pretty when you smile, Meg."

I sit back in my seat, dumbfounded. I wasn't expecting him to say that.

...

I WAKE to find Sparrow looking at me. No, he's lying on his side, propped up on his elbow, thoughtfully gazing at me. I scramble to sit up and move away from him, feeling my face for drool or something different, like death.

"What?" I ask.

He smiles that smile that I secretly love and I move further away from him, afraid that maybe he woke up changed just as Noah did that day—or maybe I have.

I stand, running my hands all over myself, feeling for something, anything to explain the look on Sparrow's face right now. "What's wrong? Why are you looking at me like that? Did I change? Am I waking up like one of them?" I run my hands through my hair, smell myself, touch my teeth. It's all still there, the same.

Sparrow stands and I notice his movements are different, slower, less like he usually is. His eyes don't flick from side-to-side, he doesn't check the buttons on his coat. He smiles as he speaks and tells me slowly, "I remembered something while you were sleeping."

"What's that?" I step further away from him.

"I'll tell you later," he promises.

I keep a close eye on Sparrow as we get ready to leave, and yup, Sparrow has definitely changed. He seems to no longer possess those odd quirks and movements and ways of speaking that made me truly believe he was cracked a bit in the head. While everyone around us has woken up a walking corpse, and I fear for the day when I do, it seems Sparrow has woken up completely normal.

...

THE LIGHTHOUSE HAS BEEN good to us, but we've cleaned the shoreline of feathers.

"Where do we go now?" I ask Sparrow, my head still full of unease at the way he's acting.

"We could hit some more zoos," he suggests.

"The next closest one is in Ohio. We'd have to get more gas."

"Let's go find some gas then."

We leave the lighthouse to walk across the breakwall for the last time. I drive down Washington Ave headed out of town. Suddenly, I see Sparrow's head turn quick as though he's noticed something in the shadows.

"What's wrong?"

"Stop the car." He reaches out, his hand hovering over mine.

Before I can shift the Jeep into park Sparrow has his door open and he's running to the sidewalk. He stops in front of a huge Gothic Church.

I get out and walk up next to him.

"What are we doing here, Sparrow?"

He turns to me, his green eyes ablaze. "You confessed your sins. Now, I must confess mine."

"What are you talking about?"

He looks at me, lucid and together, the crazy gone for this moment. Whatever he's saying, he's telling me the truth. "I had to collect the confessions of a sinner." He tips his head to the side, studying me. "You were that sinner."

"Sparrow," I step back from him, "I think you've gone and lost your nut."

He looks down the length of himself. "My nuts are fine." He blinks at me.

I choke out a laugh.

"Wait here." He runs up the steps and pulls the door to the church open. It closes behind him with a heavy thud.

I sit on the front steps, ready to retreat in case the bags of meat start moaning and gimping down the street. And I think about the last time I was in church, breathing in the dust motes and holy water spray during a school field trip. There was something comforting about the insides of a church, not one of those new Born-Again pole barn buildings, but a true brick and mortar Gothic creation with rows of candles and statues and the echoes of ritual. There was comfort, peace, a feeling of belonging. It was odd, feeling like that, especially since Daddy always said I'd burn to a cinder if I ever stepped foot in a church. Nothing ever happened during that school trip, I wonder if it would now?

Instead of finding out, I sit and when my butt goes numb, I stand and begin pacing the sidewalk in front of the church, wondering what the hell Sparrow is doing in there for so long. A few times I climb the stone steps and press my ear to the door. I can hear the murmuring of his deep voice in there speaking to someone, even though no one ever answers him.

Recognizing the pink-gray glow in the sky as the sunrise, I stop pacing and stare at the carved church door. If Sparrow takes much longer I'm going to have to interrupt the personal service he's having right now.

Throwing myself down on the cement steps to sit, I pull a feather out of my pocket, a bright green one from one of the dead parakeets at the zoo. I run it through my fingers and then stop, realizing it's a little too similar to one of Sparrow's odd quirks. I toss the feather into the night air, pull my knees to my chest and watch as it flutters down the street. Just as the feather travels further into the last shadows of the nearly ended night, until I can barely see it anymore, the ground shakes, and I mean it shakes *hard*, tipping me over. I roll down the steps, stopping myself at the bottom on my hands and knees

"Holy shit." I push myself off the ground. "Sparrow!" I yell, running to the door and tugging on the handle. The door doesn't budge, it doesn't even move. I can hear his voice through the thick wood; Sparrow Man talking, lucid and clear, just as when he told me he had to collect my sins. A deep shiver runs up my back. "Sparrow!" I yell, pounding on the wood with my fists. The sun rises higher in the sky and behind me I hear a deep moaning sound. Shit. Meat sacks. "Sparrow!" I scream, pounding so hard my entire arm throbs.

Finally, the doors push open and a long arm reaches out, pulling me into the safety of the church.

"Sparrow?" I ask as my eyes adjust to the dim light. I can only see the outline of his tall form in front of me. "The dead are awake. I heard them. They're headed this way."

"It's safe here. Hallowed ground. They can't get in," he replies.

"But we need to get out. We can't be trapped in here." The faces of strange statues stare down at us from the cathedral ceiling, watching, judging. "I can't be trapped in here." I look at my hands, at least I didn't burst into flames, seems Daddy was wrong about that.

"No." He turns from me. "We can't."

"What are you talking about?"

He paces the stone floor between the pews, a serpentine walk toward the altar.

"What do you mean we can't?" I ask. "Answer me, Sparrow! Did you remember something? Do you remember who you are?"

Stopping when he reaches the aisle, he runs his hands through his hair and his green eyes are wild as he turns to me. "Not quite. I need your help."

"What can I do?" I walk down the center aisle to him, my footsteps making muted sounds on the aged stone. "What can I do to help you?"

"Feathers." He starts moving to his backpack that's on the floor near the altar.

"You have all of your feathers, Sparrow. We just traipsed across the state collecting them. And then you were suddenly sane and now it's like you're regressing. What is happening to you?"

"Largest to smallest."

"What?"

"You... you have to arrange them, largest to smallest."

"I have no fucking clue what you are talking about, Sparrow!"

He turns after stepping up to the altar and I watch as he unbuttons his coat. He's wearing a loose ragged shirt and as he unbuttons it, his eyes are clear and focused as he stares at me. He pauses, his fingers smoothing over the last button. "Don't freak out, okay?"

"What?"

He presses his lips together and turns around.

I step back, blinking, taking in what I see.

His body is pale and well muscled, but... but his back... Jutting out of the skin at sharp angles is the skeletal form of a pair of wings.

Wings without feathers.

MEMORIES AND
THE DEAD

Sparrow turns around to face me, his eyes wide. "Help me with the wings?" he asks. No, he pleads.

Sparrow pushes his hands into the pockets of his pants and coat and starts pulling out handfuls of feathers. All the ones we've collected from owls and robins and finches and doves and chickadees. Hundreds of colors and sizes.

"What the…"

"Don't swear. We're in a church," he nips. "Help me, Meg. Please, will you help me?" His green eyes are wide and rimmed with red like he's been crying. "I need you," he begs. "I need you. Help me. You're the only one who can do it." He steps down off the altar and in a few long strides he's in front of me, reaching forward, taking my hand in his. "It has to be you. Please." He drops to the floor at my feet. "Please, please, please, Meg. Help me."

Standing still, barely able to move at the sight of Sparrow like this, on his knees in front of me, half-naked and begging. This is worse than when he lost his feathers near the dam.

I drop to my knees, into the thickness of feathers at my

feet, facing Sparrow and pick up a bright blue feather from a Blue Jay. I know this because I held my hand out, seed piled in my palm, so Sparrow could catch the bird and pull out two of its flight feathers. Pressing the soft tip of the feather to his bare chest, "What are you?" I ask.

Sparrow shakes his head. "I can't explain. I just know that I need your help."

"This is..." Sparrow's eyes flick to mine, a warning. "Messed up."

Sparrow reaches to the floor, grasping handfuls of feathers. "Will you help me?"

At this moment, staring at his wild, handsome face and his fistfuls of feathers, I realize I can't tell him no, not after all he's done for me since I've met him. "Okay," I whisper. "Okay."

Reaching down with a shaky hand, spreading the feathers out before me, and searching for the ones that I know are large: the vulture and eagle and flamingo feathers. I start sorting, biggest to smallest.

...

AFTER WHAT SEEMS like a very long time, long enough for my legs to fall asleep under me and for the feathers to blur into a dripping rainbow in front of my eyes, I look up.

Sparrow stands in front of me, clean shaven, his unruly hair combed. He's still without a shirt and he's taken off his boots and socks. A clean pair of jeans sits low on his hips. I gasp audibly. He looks amazing, like he walked off the pages of a magazine, like he walked out of that horny dream I had in the Safe House.

Suddenly self-conscious in front of him, I run my hand

over my face, feeling the tired skin and the awry hair sticking to my cheeks and neck. Shit. I never did pride myself on my looks much, but I'm sure disheveled doesn't even compare to what I look like right now.

Looking up at him again, my breath catches in my throat and I feel my face flame red from embarrassment. "When did you suddenly become not crazy?" I ask him, trying to smooth the wrinkles out of my shirt.

The corner of his mouth twitches. "Maybe I still am."

"No." I shake my head. "We've switched places. I'm sure of it."

Sparrow smiles that handsome smile that I love. Straight white teeth and dimples.

"Don't smile at me like that."

"Like what?" His left eye squints into an almost-wink.

"Like you know a secret and you're not going to tell me."

"Perhaps I do."

"I'm sure you do."

I bend my torso, resting an elbow on my leg and continue with my sorting. Eight bluish-black feathers of a dead crow, sixteen bright blue feathers from a dead parrot at the zoo, one sparkling white feather of a snowy owl, I grip that in my hand remembering the night he got them and the day he lost one.

"Those are my favorite," Sparrow says as he sits across from me, leaning back on his hands and crossing his legs that are stretched out in front of him at the ankle.

"I know. You spoke to that owl like she was a woman you wanted to take home to bed."

"Did that make you uncomfortable? Hearing me speak like that? Is that why you ran away?" he asks, his voice low and sultry.

I sit up, back suddenly straight, embarrassed that he

could read me so easily. "I liked you better when I knew you were crazy."

"Do I frighten you now?"

My eyes drift over him. Hell no, he makes me think about that dirty dream I had in that jail cell when he peeled my clothes off. "I knew what to expect from you then." I bend down again, setting the owl feather above the line of sorted feathers. Without its match, I'm not sure where to put it.

Time passes as I sort the feathers and when I look up again, Sparrow is gazing at me with a strange look in his eyes that I don't quite understand.

...

"WHAT HAPPENED TO YOU, SPARROW?" I ask as he stands still in front of me. I know he's watching me, silently.

"I will tell you when you tell me what happened to you."

I look up at him. He crouches down on his haunches and I think it's so strange to see him like he is now, without a coat or a shirt and the bony appendages visible behind his shoulders.

"What happened to you, Meg? The entire story." He tips his head to the side, waiting.

"There were men..." I start, running a large black feather through my fingers.

"How many?"

"Seven."

"Seven," he repeats quietly, tipping his head to the other side.

"Seven," I breathe out.

"Meg." He leans forward with his hands on the floor now. "Remember what happened."

I close my eyes. "I told them to go away. I told them to come back when Jim got home. But they wouldn't leave. They threatened to break down the door, said they had a paper from the Governor. That they had the right by law to search for guns. I opened the door." I pause, swallowing hard. "There are seven and I remember one looking at my stomach. I could tell by their faces, they looked bad, they felt bad. As they stormed the house, I ran for the stairs."

"What happened next, Meg?

"I'm... I'm not sure."

"Yes you are. Tell me."

I swallow hard. "I ran for the stairs. And then... then I noticed another man walk in the door."

"Who was it?" Sparrow asks.

"Oh..." I squeeze my eyes shut.

"Who?"

My heart contracts painfully. "It's Jim," I whisper. "Jim was there."

"Jim was there," Sparrow repeats.

"He saw... he didn't stop them... he pointed at me and said, *that's her.*"

"Meg?"

My eyes sting and my nose runs. I shake my head, wipe my sleeve across my face. I focus on the feathers. Choosing pink ones, the flamingo feathers, I lay them next to the large vulture feathers. I spread them apart down the center aisle of the church. Largest to smallest.

"Meg?" Sparrow asks.

"I'm done talking." My voice cracks. I clear my throat, swallow hard and focus on the feathers.

...

Sparrow sits in front of me, watching as I sort like a pet would, a devoted puppy waiting to play. He doesn't offer to help; instead he crosses his legs and starts humming. I recognize the tune immediately as *I'll be There for You*. He's hummed it before, at least every third day.

"Do you want to start at the beginning this time?" Sparrow asks when he is done with his song.

"This is the only way for you to tell me what you are?"

He gives a silent nod.

"Well, there was that time when I was born and killed my mother."

"You didn't kill her." Sparrow drops his hands from his knees and presses them to the stone floor.

"That's right." I pick up a pale gray feather and search the pile for its match. "You said that was unpossible." Finding the matching feather I place them in the line. "So there was that and the bad childhood–"

"Your father, tell me about him."

"Nothing to say. He hated me. I was a burden to him. Blamed me for everything and I never tried to be any different."

"What did he do to you?"

"Never laid a finger on me until I turned twelve." I look away from him. "This is embarrassing. I don't want to tell you how much my father disliked me and how he threw a butter knife at me one day because I didn't clear the dinner table fast enough and it lodged in the back of my leg." I run my hand over the scar behind my thigh. I can still feel it, even through my jeans. "You know what kind of hate can cause a blunt object to lodge in skin? A steak knife would have been too easy, he wouldn't have had to throw it as hard."

"You can tell me."

"I don't want to. I try not to think about all that crap. I left him as soon as I could and never spoke another word to that asshole."

"Then tell me something else," Sparrow suggests.

"When I inherited that money, I packed up all the clothes I had and went downstate to college. Just far enough away that I didn't feel out of place. Things were going good. I had escaped my crappy town for a few years, almost put all that behind me. And then I went to a party one weekend, ran into Jim." A soft laugh escapes as I speak, now recognizing the absurdity of the whole situation. "I didn't realize how much I missed that town, even though I hated it and almost everyone there." I pick up a new feather, this one a sharp black.

"What happened with Jim?" Sparrow presses.

I stare at the floor as I talk, focusing on the feathers, the embarrassment of my sour life burning my cheeks. "We had drinks at the party, more than a few, until I couldn't feel whatever it is that makes me... me. I drank until I couldn't remember all that pain, until I felt free and all I could focus on was the handsome guy across the room who was staring at me." I drop the feather and pick up a new one, bright red, from the parrots at the zoo.

"Focus, Meg," Sparrow urges.

"I drank until I couldn't feel myself anymore. Until I couldn't feel whatever it is inside me that makes me act this way. You know, bad, and all. That guy I saw sat down next to me; put his arm behind my neck... We had sex and I got pregnant." I squeeze the quill of the feather between my nails. I can't bear to look up at Sparrow. It's too hard with the shame of it all and the way he makes me feel. I keep remembering that damn dream now that he's gone and changed on me, looking so amazing and asking me all these personal questions.

"So he brought you home?"

"Yeah, said he wanted to keep the baby, proposed and all."

Strangely, Sparrow asks, "Did you love him?"

I drop the red feather and rest my hands on my jean-clad legs. "I thought I did, but... I'm not really sure what love feels like. It might have been close."

"Did he love you?"

"I don't know. He said he did. He asked me to marry him. Isn't that enough?"

I reach forward and pick up the red feather again. Twirling it between my fingers, I search for others like it.

"Did you ever get the feeling you were meant for something more? Something better?" Sparrow asks.

Finding another red feather I pick it up and say, "Nope. I believed what everyone told me, every day of my life: Nothin' but trash. That's what I am and that's how I've acted. I know nothing different."

"Maybe you're wrong."

Not bothering to face him, knowing my face is flaming red, I say to the floor, "Maybe you're wrong, Sparrow."

...

"YOU'RE DONE," Sparrow whispers from behind me.

I jump, startled. I didn't know he was so close. Standing to stretch my numb legs, I get a good look at the long line of feathers stretching down the middle aisle of the church.

"Are you ready for the next step?" He walks away and lifts my backpack from the pew it was set on.

"What's the next step?"

He dumps the glue out of the bag. "I need you to glue them on."

"On what?"

He turns and points to the bony appendages on his back.

"Oh," I mouth.

"Will you–"

I don't give him time to finish, mostly because I'm afraid he'll drop to his knees and beg me, and I don't think I can bear to see him in that position again. "Sure."

I bend and pick up one of the bottles of glue.

Sparrow lies across the stone floor on his stomach, his cheek resting on his folded hands. I look between his wing scaffold and the long string of feathers stretched down the church aisle.

Dropping to my knees at his side, I reach for a feather.

He tips his head up. "Remember, biggest to smallest."

"I got it!" I snap at him.

Pinching a dark feather between my fingers and moving to him, I place my free hand on his back as I bend down, steadying myself. Using the glue, I dab a bit of it on the quill of the feather before pressing it into the empty shaft of his skeletal wings. I hold it in place, breathing shallow, waiting for the glue to dry. It's during those seconds of waiting that I remember my hand on his back. My fingers twitch over his skin, it's taut and silky. I have a sudden flash of that filthy dream I had about him naked and pressing against me in my cell. I lift my hand from his back and I swear to God I see the corner of his mouth quirk up.

Sparrow starts humming *It's my Life*.

"Sparrow."

"Huh?"

"Shut up."

I reach for another feather, the matching one for the other side of his wings.

…

"WHAT HAPPENED WITH THOSE MEN?" Sparrow presses on as I glue his feathers.

"I don't want to talk about it." I lean away from him and have to try very hard to control the urge to get closer.

"You have to, Meg. You have to talk about it."

"They broke down the door, chased me across the house, upstairs to the bedroom." I open a new bottle of glue, watching as the cap falls and bounces across the stone floor. "The bedroom was the only door with a lock on it. I tried to lock the door. But they just kicked it in."

Sparrow's focus on me is intense.

"I don't want to tell you this," my voice drops.

"I know," he replies.

"No, you don't understand, Sparrow. I really, really don't want to tell you this."

"I won't judge you."

"I don't care if you judge me. People have been judging me my whole life. I just don't want the way you look at me to change," I tell him in a fleeting moment of truth.

"Unpossible."

"Sparrow…" I feel the burn of tears behind my eyes and with a sniff, I swallow them down. Big girls don't cry. And trailer trash don't cry, we get a beer and drown it.

"It's okay. You have to get it out."

"Maybe later," I suggest.

"We don't have forever, Meg."

I shake my head. Reaching for a bright green parrot feather and dabbing glue onto it, I press the quill into place.

...

"IT SEEMS WE'VE CHANGED PLACES," I tell Sparrow, holding another pink flamingo feather in place as the glue dries.

"What do you mean, Meg?"

"Now I'm thinking I'm the one that's crazy."

"You're not crazy."

"I'm in a church, gluing feathers to your back, and you have wings or... or something. You used to be cracked in the head and now you're perfectly lucid and here I am doing all this. This is fucked up, Sparrow."

"You're not crazy. But you still shouldn't swear in church."

"What are you?" I ask, my hands shaking as I reach for the other pink flamingo feather.

"I'll tell you later."

"How much later? We've been here for days, maybe even a week I think." I sit up and try to remember how long we've been inside this musty church. When I look to the stained glass windows I see it's dark outside. Only, I don't remember ever sleeping. I can smell dust, musky bricks; feel the weight of years of confessions cluttering the air in this space. Sparrow lit candles around me, what must have been hours ago. A perfect circle of votives and tall wax candles give his skin a soft glowing appearance.

"I told you, when you tell me what happened to you, I will tell you what happened to me."

I take a deep breath, and when I exhale, the feathers that

I've already glued to his wing bones flutter. Sparrow makes a strange noise in the back of his throat and closes his eyes.

"Does that hurt?" I ask.

"I'm not sure."

"How can you not be sure?" And just to test him I purse my lips and blow a stream of air across his feathers. I watch as they flutter and notice the bottom ones brushing up against the smooth skin of his ribcage.

"Dear God, Meg, stop it," he says with a half-groan as he shifts his hips against the stone floor.

I do it for just a second longer, knowing that I'm teasing him, just like I have before. I stop when I realize he may never look at me the same again if I tell him everything that happened.

Talk about a mood-buster.

...

A STRANGE SENSATION causes me to press my hand to my stomach. It feels perfectly flat, taut from weeks of walking and running. The sensation gets stronger and when I raise my head and look around.

"What's wrong?" Sparrow asks from the floor next to me.

"When was the last time I ate?"

His eyes seem to darken a bit. I can see that he's biting his cheeks, trying not to tell me something.

"Sparrow?" I run my hands over my face. "Am... am I dead? Did I wake up like this?" I stand, frantically running my hands over my body, under my shirt, over my pants.

"You're fine."

"No, no. I can't be. To be alive I have to eat. I have to

sleep. I haven't eaten, how long has it been?" I stand, turning myself in a tight circle, my hair whipping across my face.

Sparrow stands and grips my wrists, his thumbs circling over the sensitive skin laced with blue veins. It has a calming effect. "You're fine," he tells me in a soothing voice. "You ate already. Look." He points at the floor next to me where I see an empty plate and my bottle of water.

I certainly don't feel like I ate anything. Of course, lately I never feel absolutely full, no matter how many crackers or candy bars or roast deer I eat. I'm never full, the hunger is never gone.

"I... I don't remember," I say.

"Because you're focusing too hard. Look, you're almost done." He points at the small pile of feathers next to us.

I close my eyes, feeling his thumbs and index fingers continue to circle around my wrists. Even though he's just trying to help me, his touch, it feels... different.

"You're fine," he tells me.

I kneel in front of the small pile of feathers and run my hand through it before picking one up.

"What else happened, Meg?"

I can feel his gaze on me, waiting for an answer, waiting for me to tell him everything.

"Jim was there," I whisper, staring at the tiny yellow feather in my hand. It's not a bright yellow but a soft pale yellow, just like the nursery.

"Jim was there," Sparrow repeats. "And then?"

I shake my head. "Let me finish this first."

Sparrow lies on his stomach, still as a stone as I secure the last few downy feathers onto his wings. When I am done, I sit up on my knees.

"There's just this one tiny shaft left that's empty." I

touch the spot in the middle of his back with my fingertip. "I'm out of feathers."

"Oh," Sparrow moves his arm from under his head and reaches into his pocket. "I almost forgot about this one."

He holds his hand out to me and in his palm I see the small white feather from the snowy owl that I gave him that night I apologized for trying to sneak a peek under his coat.

"You still have this?"

"Of course. No one has ever given me a feather before." He rests his head on his hands and waits.

I dab the glue onto the quill and place the feather into the last empty space. The muscles in his back twitch, he flexes his shoulders.

"Okay," I scan his back. "I think I'm done now." I stand and move away from him.

Sparrow rolls and sits up so he's facing me, his face expectant. "Jim was there," Sparrow repeats. "And then?" he asks, folding his hands in his lap, waiting.

"Jim was there," I whisper, flashing back to that day, to that moment when I asked the men to come back when Jim was there. "They didn't wait outside. They laughed, kicked in the door, chased me all the way upstairs where I tried to lock myself in the bedroom. They kicked down that door too, did things that no men should do to a pregnant woman."

"That's why you don't like to be touched?" Sparrow leans closer to me.

"I've always been like that." I shrug. "Jim was there." I look up at the stone statues secured to the vaulted ceiling; seven giant gargoyles watch us with stony eyes. "He watched, said terrible things to me."

Sparrow sits still as a stone in front of me. His face calm as he listens.

"They pushed me down the stairs after." My hands

flutter to my stomach. It is flat now. My stomach has been back to being flat for a long time. "Hauled me up by my arms and dropped me over the stairwell. That killed the baby. I felt it when I landed. The baby stopped moving inside me." Pausing, shaking my head, trying to hold that in, I continue after a beat. "In the stairwell there was a step with a hidden compartment."

"What was in there?" Sparrow asks. "What was in the compartment?"

"A gun. It was loaded. Jim always kept that one loaded."

"What did you do?"

"I shot them. I... shot those men."

"And Jim, what happened to him?"

I look up at Sparrow, feeling the burn in my eyes, the tightness in my throat. "Oh my God, I shot him. I... I killed him. I killed Jim!"

"He tried to kill you."

"Oh my God." My arms drop to my sides. "He... he killed the baby. He tried to kill me. He did this to us!" A sob that I can't even think of containing racks my body.

"It's okay," I hear Sparrow's soft voice in my ear. He's so close to me. "Can I touch you?" he asks.

I nod my head, sobbing too hard to form words.

"Shhh." He wraps his arms around me. "It is okay, Meg." I feel his lips on my cheek, my temple, where the hot tears leak from my eyes. "It's okay. I can help you."

"You knew didn't you? You've known this entire time!" I pound my fists on his chest. "Sparrow, you've lied to me this entire time!"

"Shhh. No, I didn't. I promise. I swear to you. I'll help the pain go away. I can help you feel better." His hand moves so his palm is resting in the center of my chest, over the spot where my heart beats at such a rapid pace. "I can't make it go away forever, what you're feeling right now, but for a little while I can make it stop. Do you want that?"

I nod my head, feel his lips on mine, lips that I've stared at and dreamt of. It's so strange, this feeling inside of my chest. It's something strong, stronger than grief and pain. But as his lips move over mine it starts to dissipate, it starts to leave, and I can almost think clearly again.

"You helped me," Sparrow whispers on my lips. "Now I will help you, but only if you say yes."

I nod my head. "Okay."

He grips my chin between his fingers. "Only if you say yes, Meg. You have to say yes. You have to give me permission."

"Yes," I tell him in a desperate whisper.

...

MY WORLD SHIFTS as I feel him sweep my legs off the ground and carry me away. There is no cot here as there was in my dream, just a thick Persian rug in an empty space to the right of the altar.

He murmurs sweet words into my ear just like he did to that snowy owl, like no one has ever spoken to me, the tip of his nose rubbing against the sensitive skin of my ear sending a deep tremble down the back of my neck. I turn, wrapping my arms around his shoulders, pushing my fingers into that unruly hair of his. Once his lips are back on mine his murmurings stop. He sets me on my feet, one strong arm wrapped around my back, holding me to him. He pulls his lips away with a regretful groan. His free hand moves to the buttons on my shirt as he speaks in a hurried mumble, "So, so beautiful."

His feather light touch moves my arm from his neck as he pushes the shirt off my shoulders and kisses me thoroughly until I forget what else I planned to ask. I feel his fingers trail across my abdomen, sending my blood aflame.

"Ah, Meg," he whispers on my lips as his fingers dip lower, unbuttoning my jeans and pushing them down my hips to the floor. "I've dreamed of you like this." My hands move to his chest and around his neck, gripping onto him. "Dear God," Sparrow breathes, his mouth moving to my neck and down my chest.

"Jesus," I pant as his mouth moves lower, nipping at the thin bra covering my breasts.

"I thought you didn't believe?" Sparrow stops, looking at me with a wicked grin.

"I don't. You're just going too fucking slow." I unclasp my hands from his neck, run them down his chest and abdomen, relishing the feel of his smooth skin over tight muscle. I reach for his jeans, flick the button and begin to push at them. Sparrow's eyes open, heavy and dark with desire. Now he moves at a faster pace, sweeping his fingers across my bra and unhooks it before crushing our bodies together and dragging me to the floor with him.

"You're so perfect," he whispers between searing kisses, his hand moving from my face to my neck, lower.

"Sparrow..." I whisper between breaths, running my hands over his body in frantic movement. "I want to feel you."

"You will," he promises.

My back arches, my hips tilt, wanting more. He inhales through his teeth as my hands graze his unbuttoned groin. I try to press my hand into his jeans so I can feel him but he shifts his body so he's covering me, his elbows positioned on each side of my head, my arms trapped at my sides. He dips his head, kissing me, his tongue spreading the seam of my lips, dipping into my mouth. Sweet Jesus, he even tastes like all those things; Christmas and cake batter and I can't even remember what else I thought in that dream. I press myself to him, trying to feel him on me. Sparrow lowers his body onto mine and I wiggle to move my arms.

"Sparrow, I want to touch you."

"Slow down," he whispers as he nips at my ear and grabs both of my hands, holding them up by my head. "I've waited so long for this." He nips my shoulder. "For you." He nips my collarbone, then moves lower, kissing and nipping his way across my body. I tilt my head back and try to move, pressing myself closer to him.

"Patience, Meg," he whispers as he trails down my abdomen, stopping to lick a circle around my belly button before moving lower, pressing his mouth to the skin in the hollow of my hip. Pulling my hands down, he grasps them across my stomach with one hand, securing them in place. Using his free hand, he runs it up my leg, stopping just before I want him to. "Open your legs," he instructs me and I do it, trying to press my hips up at the same time, but he holds me down with his hand on my abdomen.

His mouth is on me and my blood feels like it's boiling, like fire in my veins, like I've never felt before with anyone. Stars and lights burst behind my closed eyes and I grit my teeth trying not to scream. When I open my eyes and look down Sparrow is watching me with a satisfied grin.

"Sparrow," I breathe his name.

"Tell me what you need."

"You," I breathe out, panting. "I just want you. Now. Like I've never wanted anyone ever in my entire life."

His green eyes brighten as he pulls away. I lay there boneless. I hear him taking off his pants and then his hands are on me, searing my skin everywhere he touches me. "This is how you should be loved. You should be pleased over and over and over again."

He presses his lips to mine before I can say anything; before I can tell him that all my one-night stands and middle of the night trysts were never like this. Sparrow's eyes graze over my body before locking with mine. He gives a little grin before he covers my body with his. It's not long before we are both coated in a thin sheen of sweat. He whispers things in my ear, sweet words and compliments, so much like what he said to that snowy owl, things that have never been spoken to me before.

My head swims, my body aches for more of him and just before I don't think I can take another second of this, Sparrow twists his hips, targeting in on some sensitive area inside my body I never knew I had. The effect is explosive. I arch my back, tighten my legs around him, throw my head back and call his name.

Sparrow collapses onto me, his face buried in my neck. I can feel him panting like he ran five miles and he can't catch his breath. And I know I'm breathing the same way as the vibrations continue to run through my body. He rolls, pulling me with him into an embrace, pressing his lips to my forehead. I lay there, my head on his shoulder, one of his arms wrapped tight around me, and for the first time in my life I am without words.

Sparrow turns, shifting me in his arms. "I didn't hurt you, did I?" he asks, his eyes heavy with concern as he brushes a thumb across my cheek.

My throat tightens and something beats heavy in my chest. "No, not even close," I manage to get out, not telling him that sex was never like that, not with anyone, not at any time, ever.

He looks down at me, his eyes focus on my tattoos. I suddenly feel self-conscious again.

"You don't like them?" I ask.

His eyes move to mine and he leans closer to me, pressing his lips to mine. "They're perfect. Just like you." He bends, pressing his lips to the feather across my collarbone. "This one." He rolls me to the side, pressing his lips to the stars on my shoulder. "These." He bends, pressing his lips to the heart on my hip and the anchor on my ribcage. I notice his eyes move lower. "And this one, I didn't notice before." His fingers graze the inside of my thigh, up high, almost to where my leg meets my hip, but low enough for it to show when wearing a pair of short shorts.

I look down to see his eyes focused on the mark on my upper thigh. "That's not a tattoo," I tell him, my voice sounding thick and abnormal.

"It's not?" He sounds distracted, kissing and touching, his fingertips running across my legs, sending a sharp tingle to my lower stomach.

"No. It's a birthmark. Daddy always said it was my mark of the devil."

"Are you sure that's a birthmark?" he dips his head to inspect the patch of skin that looks like nothing more than an uneven-edged circle.

"Yes. Why?"

"Because... I think that changes everything." He presses his left thumb to the mark on my thigh, hard, mumbling words in a language I've never heard.

A bright white light erupts behind my eyes and a noise that sounds like an air horn fills my ears.

......

I wake, no longer feeling the hard stone of the church floor under me or Sparrow's body wrapped around mine. I sit up straight.

"Sparrow?"

My eyes focus on the pastel colors and white sheets of a hospital room. Dread fills me. He's gone.

"Sparrow!" I scream at the top of my lungs.

This brings a flurry of activity.

First it is a nurse, a middle-aged woman with dark hair and glasses. "Oh my," are her words as she walks into the room and sees me sitting up straight, screaming for Sparrow. She rushes to me, her arm extended, ready to give comfort.

I flinch away. "Don't touch me!"

She stops in her tracks and eases herself onto the edge of my bed.

"You're awake," she says, eyes wide as though she didn't expect it.

"No shit, lady." The alarms behind my bed scream and blink as I reach for the leads attached to my chest, ready to pull them off. "Where's Sparrow?"

"There's no one here by that name." She frowns and looks me over "Do you know where you are?"

"No." I look around. "Where the hell am I?"

"Gouverneur County Hospital." She stands and pulls a chart from the foot of my bed.

"What the fu–" I run my hands over my face and hair, feeling its length as it covers the back of my neck as though I never cut it. I pull the plaid hospital gown away from my body and I am relieved to see the tattoos that I remember are supposed to be there. It seems that this is my body, and I am very much alive.

"Let me go get the doctor." She pauses at the door. "You woke at a bad time. The docs are doing their rounds. Your room is about to become very full," she warns me.

The nurse leaves the room, carrying the chart with her. I hear footsteps in the hall and the chatter of voices, both young and old. The room seems to shrink as they all walk inside. Fresh faces stare down at me, twelve of them as they write on their notepads. A plain looking man in a wheelchair rolls in behind them and up to the side of my bed. I look at the tag hanging off his white coat and see in bold print that it says *Doctor*.

"So, what we have here is a twenty-four year old female who has just woken from a–" He pauses as he reads my chart, then turns it, his finger on the paper for everyone else to see.

I'm sure I know what it says in there: rape, stillborn, hysterectomy. I'm sure there's more too; strange medical terms I don't understand that mean nothing good. The looks start, faces drawn, eyebrows tilted, concerned furrows appear as they look between me and my papers.

I hate being looked at like this, like a pitiful case study for these people. Their stares and looks of pity inflame an anger inside of me. I would rather have them look at me like I was nothing but trash than submit to this.

"Get the fuck out of my room," I tell them, glaring at the doctor in the wheelchair.

The doctor swallows hard, the students all look up from their notepads. "Please miss, these walls aren't soundproof."

"No shit. And I see you don't need legs to be a genius or a doctor. Get the hell out of here, all of you!"

Wheels glares at me as he ushers everyone out of my room. The nurse steps in just after they're all gone.

"It will be okay," she assures me as she holds out a thermometer to take my temperature.

"I'm not apologizing for that," I warn her.

"Don't need to." She writes something down on a piece of paper. "It's about time someone brought them down from their pedestals, even if it's only for five minutes."

"I'm looking for a friend. His name is Sparrow. Has he been here?"

The nurse shakes her head. "No one has been here to see you but your father."

I tense at the use of that word.

"Let me just listen to you quick and then I'll see if the docs will let you eat something."

...

My first real visitor is a trooper, I can tell by the way he walks down the hallway, the way the people out there stop talking, and I recognize the jingle of the handcuffs that are attached to his belt. I recognize him as soon as he walks in the door.

"Noah," I whisper as I see him walk around the curtain. When his head lifts, I sink back into the bed.

"Haven't heard his name in quite a while," the trooper smiles. No, this isn't Noah, it is his older brother, Jack. "Hey, Meg." He flashes me his lady-killer smile, something this family seems to have in common. White teeth, handsome face, just like Noah.

"Shit, Jack." I stare at him with wide eyes, feeling my fingers tremble as I grip the quilt that covers my bed. "I thought you were him."

He sighs. "I'm sure no one told you but he passed, not too long ago after this happened." He swoops a finger in the air across the hospital bed.

"I thought he was supposed to be in the state pen?"

"Wrong again." He pulls a chair across the room and sits

next to me. "There was an accident on the drive to Auburn. Noah didn't make it."

"Oh, Jesus..."

Jack gives a sad smile. "I just need to get your statement." Jack pulls a notebook out of his back pocket.

"I already gave one."

"Meg," his eyes sweep over me. "You've been in a coma for weeks, you didn't tell anyone nothin'."

"I don't understand." I had a bedside hearing. I went to County lockup already. I don't get how I'm back in a hospital bed.

He smiles and looks so much like Noah that I almost forget to breathe.

"You've been in a coma," he repeats as he flips the pages on his notebook. "After what happened to you, this will be hard, so just start at the beginning."

I blink hard and stare at his notebook, remembering how difficult it was to say those words to Sparrow. "No. I can't. Not right now. I'm sorry." My heart seems to sink a little in my chest. I know it's not for the shame of being unable to repeat all of that crap, it's because he's gone. Sparrow's gone.

Jack folds his notebook and tucks the pen into his pocket. He reaches out with his hand as though he's going to say something but the motion is interrupted by the sound of footsteps in the hall. These ones are swift, angry, and I recognize them right away: they are the footsteps of my father.

He bursts into the room. Muddy work boots, worn pants, grease stained tank top. If he isn't the epitome of trailer, I'm not sure what is.

Jack stands. "I'll give you two some privacy. Just push that red button there if you need anything." I look to Jack's hand and see the call button next to my fingers. When I look up at his face, he winks before turning and walking out of the room.

My father doesn't say anything. He just paces the floor at the foot of my bed, rubs his scruffy beard. I guess he's searching for the right words. I just never expect him to say what he finally does. Maybe I was hoping for something nicer, something that led me to believe he actually loved me as a father does a daughter.

"You used to have quite the mouth on ya. Guess Jim boy finally beat that outta you, 'bout time." He stops at the foot of my bed and places his hands on the plastic footboard.

"Go away," I tell him.

He laughs that same wicked laugh he did when I was a kid, when I knew a beating was coming. Moving away, he picks up a spare pillow from the windowsill and squishes it between his hands as though he's testing its fluffiness.

"The state took that pretty little house you bought. Confiscated it to pay for your medical bills since you had no insurance. They were about to use your trust money too."

"I already got the trust money," I remind him, whispering. "I spent it on the house."

He laughs and squeezes the pillow tighter. "You are a little trashy idiot. If you had kept your mouth shut, I could have finished what I was about to say."

My mouth snaps shut.

"Your mother was a very rich woman. Don't know why she was slumming in around this redneck town. Actually, I do. She was nothing but trash deep down, just like her daughter. There was more money, a lot more money and no man wants a baby around when there's that much money involved. When I found out how much she was worth..." He pauses and looks down at the pillow gripped in his hands. Then walks to the door and closes it gently.

Unease fills me and I hold the call button down with my finger.

"Let's just say, falling down the stairs isn't the best way to get rid of a baby during the end of a pregnancy."

"What did you do to her?" I ask.

"Found her papers from the lawyer. Found out how much she was worth. Found out that she signed it all over to her unborn child." He takes a step closer to me. "You know the clause she put in there? Of course you don't, cause you're dumb. Full payment on the child's twenty-fifth birthday. All we had was two more weeks."

"We?"

"Oh, forgot, Jimmy boy's dead now. Thanks to you. Fine with me. More for myself. He was going to waste it on a bunker in the woods, near that stupid cabin you bought in Canada. What a waste of money. Don't know where you found that boy, but he was paranoid as shit, kept talking about putting a bunker in the ground to prepare for the apocalypse. Looks like he didn't want no stupid woman or a baby to drag around with him." He looks at the pillow again. "Thought about doin' this all those times you were knocked out in that coma, with a tube down your throat. Woulda' been easier then. They said you weren't going to make it anyways. The money was going to be mine. It was always mine. I put up with the bullshit from your trashy mother, jumping from bed to bed in this town, and I'll go to hell before your scrawny ass gets any of it. Guess now is as good a time as any."

My father moves faster than I've ever seen him move before, crossing the room and pressing the pillow down onto my face. I try to scream, but the sound is only muffled. I let go of the call button and try to push him away. I try to grasp at the pillow but he crushes my chest with a knee and presses harder.

I hear the door slam against the wall and the sound of footsteps running, bodies struggling. Pressing the call button must have worked. The pressure is released from my face; the pillow falls just as I see Jack kick my father to the ground. With one knee pressed to his back, Jack handcuffs him.

My father spits at me as Jack lifts him by his elbows to his feet, "You shoulda died a long time ago!"

...

THEY KEEP me for a week with a trooper outside the door, some overweight man on the edge of retirement. He chats with the nursing staff yet says no words to me. At night, his relief plays on his smartphone, the beeps and clicks not as soothing as listening to Sparrow's voice each night singing Bon Jovi tunes.

On my twenty-fifth birthday, my nurse brings a gift, a set of sea-green scrubs. A new outfit to walk out of this place in since they had to cut the clothes off my back the day they brought me in and the state sold everything at my house. There's nothing like starting over, with nothing to call your own.

I call the bank and check my account. Just like Daddy said, there is enough money to last the rest of my life. Now this is a strange feeling, never having nothin' and now my bank account is bursting at the seams. Still, I feel emptier than ever. I blame it on the memories; the coma dreams that I'm having a hard time convincing myself weren't real.

On my day of discharge, Jack shows up to walk me out. And as I sit in the front seat of his cruiser I realize how this must look, me leaving the hospital in scrubs with a trooper.

I probably look crazy. We drive around town, over the bridges, past his grandmother's house. I can't stop the image of Sparrow cutting off Noah's head in the basement from running through my head.

"Do you want to see your old house?" Jack asks. "I mean, I know they sold it, but..." He turns to glance at me and stops talking. "Sorry, that's a pretty bad idea."

While his hands are gripping the steering wheel that I notice the gold band across his left ring-finger.

"You're married?" I ask.

"Yeah." He stretches his fingers. "Almost a year now."

"Congratulations," I tell him, turning away to look out the window. "I need a car."

"There's the dealership on Route Eleven," he suggests.

"Can you take me there?"

Jack drives me and waits as I decide on one of those hybrid vehicles that use less gas. I call the bank and have them transfer the entire amount. While we sit in the car as the salesman goes inside to finish the paperwork, Jack turns to me. "Where will you go, Meg?" he asks.

"I don't know. I had a dream I went to jail for what I did." I turn to face Jack, my stomach dropping with the change of his expressions.

"The state buried it. You won't go to jail. The Governor's waiting for you to sue over what those men did. Now that you're wealthy and can afford a lawyer." Jack adjusts the badge on his chest pocket. "They should've never hired those goons. Or passed those gun laws." He exhales a long breath and my focus turns to the pistol on his hip. I consider asking for it, remembering Sparrow's words, *guns can't help you now*. I guess they can't, and an officer won't give me his weapon, but I can go down to the hunting store and buy a shit load of weapons now. Maybe another day.

"So, where will you go?" Jack asks again.

"Not sure. I just can't stay here."

I feel his arm grip me around the shoulders and I lean into him, resting my head on his shoulder. I think this is the first person I haven't flinched away from.

"I'm sorry Noah got you into so much trouble as a kid. I didn't know that was how your father treated you. Noah never said a thing."

"Doesn't matter," I tell him. "Can't change it."

The salesman interrupts us. "Well, you're good to go, miss."

I take the keys, I hug Jack, and then I sit for a long time at the edge of the dealership parking lot trying to decide which way to go and what to do with my life, feeling emptier than I ever have before.

Looking down at the scrubs I'm wearing, I decide that my first stop is to find a store for some new clothes. I drive away from Gouverneur, toward Watertown, where I have less of a chance of running into someone who recognizes me.

Sitting in the J. C. Penney parking lot I find myself filled with apprehension. Before I knew what I wanted; I'd run into Wal-Mart and grab the shortest jean skirt and tightest tank-top I could find.

After what seems like forever, I unlatch my seatbelt and get out of the car. Standing next to the new car, key-fob in hand, I can't seem to remember how to lock the darn thing. Staring at the buttons for too long, I give up and head into the store.

Opening the glass doors, I look over the sea of clothing racks, suddenly insecure about what to do next.

"Can I help you, miss?" a lady with curled gray hair and a nametag asks me.

"Women's dresses?"

"Sure. Follow me," she says with a pleasant smile. Her

heels click on the floor as she walks. "What type of dress are you looking for?" she turns her head to ask me.

"Just something... nice," I reply with a shrug.

She stops in front of a rack of dresses. "Day, evening and night." Her wrists jangle with bracelets as she points at the racks of clothing.

"Thanks." I smile at her.

I search the racks, finding a few dresses that I think might fit. In the fitting room, I settle on a gauzy teal one that hits at the knee. Next I search for the shoes, choosing a pair of sandals, real sandals with leather straps, not plastic flip-flops like we wore in the trailer park. I pass a salon. Backing up, I walk in and see if they have any appointments available.

As the hairdresser works to cut my long, dark hair, every clip of her scissors brings back the memory of Sparrow slicing his blade across my ponytail and throwing my hair into the trees. I close my eyes and fight with the memories, the emptiness in my chest. I tell myself it wasn't real. Those were just dreams from the coma, my brain trying to figure things out.

"You work the night shift, hon?" the hairdresser asks.

"What?"

"You a nurse or something?" I look down at the scrubs I'm still wearing. "You work nights? Is that why your eyes are closed or are you too afraid to see all this pretty hair gone?"

"Uh..." I search for some answer. "I'm just tired."

"Almost done here," she replies between chewing on her gum.

She clips a few more times before the comb and scissors are replaced by a hairdryer. I feel her spin the chair.

"All done, hon. What do you think?"

My eyes open and I look at my reflection in the mirror.

I'm sure the cropped haircut is better than the one Sparrow gave me. My eyes look bigger, my cheeks flushed. "It looks great." I smile. "Thanks."

The hairdresser whips the hair covered apron off me and I watch all the dark pieces of hair fall to the floor. Running my hand across my now bare neck, I follow the lady to the cash register.

...

AFTER CHANGING my clothes in the store bathroom, I sit in my new car with my new outfit and new haircut, feeling empty, still.

Where will you go? Jack's words echo in my ears.

Away, is all I can think, far away from here.

Getting on 81 south, I find myself on the same route as I took with Sparrow in my dream. I drive, stopping at a highway rest stop by mid-afternoon. I just sit for a while and stare off into the forest until my bladder spasms.

When I come back from using the bathroom, I find a white feather on my windshield. I look around the parking lot before reaching for the feather, noting that I am the only one here. As I hold the feather in my hand and twirl it in my fingers I notice the light brown spots on the edge of it. It's a snowy owl feather.

"Sparrow?" I whisper, looking around the empty parking lot.

No one answers. I set the feather in my purse and drive away.

...

I find myself following the signs for Syracuse and the zoo.

As I walk to the entrance, I realize this must look odd, me being here alone, without a family or a child. The ticket man says nothing as he takes my money and stamps my hand. I head for the exhibit labeled *Birds of Paradise*.

Sitting in the aviary, I can't help but think that the last time I was here this place was littered with dead birds. No. Wait. That wasn't real. A green conure flies over my head, dropping a feather, which flutters down to the bench beside me. I reach over to pick it up, stopping when I realize what I'm going to do with it: shove it in my purse. Fuck, now I'm turning into a crazy sparrow woman.

A small parrot lands on the bench next to me. I can't help but recognize it as one that Sparrow held in his hand and pulled the feathers from. The parrot chirps a light trill at me be before flapping off into the trees.

This is where I sit for hours, trying to figure out what this empty feeling is inside of me and trying to push the memories of Jim, of my lost baby, of my hurtful father, and of Sparrow, to the back of my brain where I might forget them.

At the end of the day, when the children and families have filtered out and the lights outside come on, I hear the soft brush of leaves against something, a whistle, someone talking softly. No, they're not talking, they're singing or humming.

I stand and turn to find a man in jeans and a blue shirt standing not too far from me. He's singing to a large parrot that's perched on a branch in front of him. He turns to face me as I take a deep breath in, and smiles. I recognize him instantly. It's Sparrow, in the flesh; wingless and standing before me.

"Hello," he says with a smile. The smile I've missed so much.

How can this be, the man from my coma dreams, here, alive, real? I take a hesitant step to him. "Do they call you Sparrow Man?" I ask.

"Yeah," he laughs, moving one arm to rub the back of his neck.

I reach into my purse and pull out the snowy owl feather that I found on my car. I hold it out to him, my fingers shaking. His sparkling green eyes focus on the feather and then back to me.

"No one has ever given me a feather before," he says, reaching for the feather.

"I know," I reply, trying to contain the urge to touch him and make sure he's real. I give up. "I... I know this is weird, coming from a stranger and all, but... can I touch you?"

He nods.

I step closer, reach my arms around his neck, run my hands over his shoulders and down his shoulder blades where I feel nothing but taut smooth skin underneath. Something inside of me sinks when I don't feel wings. Maybe this is not the Sparrow I'm looking for and miss so much.

"This would be strange, Meg," he whispers in my ear. "But we are not strangers."

I remember that I haven't even told him my name, just felt him up a little. "How do you know my name?" I ask, pulling myself away from him, dropping my arms to my sides.

He looks me up and down from my head to my toes. "You look nice, Meg." He tips his head to the side, just like he did so many times in my head, in my coma dreams, studying me.

"I bought a dress, like a lady." Before I would have added 'and shit'. But I refrain. "I don't understand how you're here?"

"This is new for me too." He does that smile, the one that leads me to believe he knows some secret.

I watch him closely as he takes a pink feather out of his pocket and tucks it behind my ear. This barely makes sense, any of it. A glimmer of something deeper begins to ripple through my chest, and for a moment I wonder if maybe I'm starting to believe in something greater than all of this.

Sparrow smiles and my heart stops for a second. "Meg?" he asks, leaning into me.

"Yes, Sparrow?"

"I'm going to kiss you," he tells me. His eyelashes brush against his cheeks as he looks down at me.

I stare up at him at that moment, in awe at how much he'd changed from an odd crazed person into this handsome man standing in front of me.

"Okay," I tell him.

Sparrow leans closer to me; his soft lips hover just over mine. I feel his hand trace down my side, to my leg, pushing my skirt up.

"Sparrow!" I scold, trying to push the skirt down; after all, I'm trying to become a lady.

"It's okay." He smiles and then presses his thumb to the birthmark on my thigh and his lips to mine. And just like before there is a blinding white light and the sound of a thousand sirens blaring, which makes my eardrums rattle.

·····

As my eyes flutter open I see the dusky church and Sparrow standing over me.

"What the shit was that?" I yell, pushing and slapping at him to get away from me. He stands still, watching me as I pace, naked as the day I was born. "What was that, Sparrow?" I yell at him, running my hands through my hair. "I was back... things were back to normal. I was free. I had money and a car and I was free of that town and I found you at the zoo. What was that?"

"I think... I think that was a life you were never meant to live, Meg."

"But what was that, how was I there and now back here?"

"You just closed that door. Shed that skin." He takes a step to me.

I take two back.

"What if I didn't want to?" I yell at him. "What if I wanted that life, not this... whatever this is now?" I point at the door. "At least I had a life, not this... this... whatever the hell this is."

"I just saw a glimpse of that life. Was it really all that great? You looked very sad."

"What the fuck do you know, Sparrow? You can't remember shit. For all you know I was a fucking princess!"

"I have remembered a few things."

"Not enough!" I point at the wings behind his back. "You can't even explain to me what you are or who you are!"

"I've remembered a few things," he repeats walking closer.

"Like what?"

"Like that I really, really like you."

"Well I sure hope so, Sparrow. For Christ's sake we just had sex in a church." I point to the carpet a few feet away from us. "I sure as hell hope you like me if we just did that!"

He takes another step in my direction. I take two more back. His tall nakedness is slightly intimidating.

"How do you know I was never meant to live that life?" I ask, nervous at what just happened. It all seemed so real. And I do feel a bit different now. Although I'm not sure how to describe the difference I feel.

"Let's just say I have a feeling about it."

"What the hell is going on, Sparrow? Who are you?" I focus on the feathers behind his back. "What are you?"

"I'm still not one-hundred percent, but I think I have an idea." The corner of his mouth tips up. "You want to see?"

I give him a hesitant nod.

Sparrow backs away from me and stands facing the altar. All I can see are his legs, his broad shoulders, the back of his head, and the wings I just glued back together, the colorful feathers all arranged just like he asked. Sparrow begins extending the wings. I circle around him to see that sweat beads his brow and he lets out a groan of pain, as though he's using a muscle that hasn't been stretched in a long time.

I step back, mouth agape. I don't want to say it out loud. I know that would just make this whole situation seem even crazier. What he is, a man with wings who seems to know strange stuff. That can only mean he is one thing. "Oh my God, you're–"

"I think so," Sparrow says with a strained voice.

"This is so fucked up," I mutter on a breath.

He exhales loudly and the wings retract. "Would you stop swearing?" Sparrow glances at the altar.

"Why?"

He points at the altar.

"I don't care."

"Well maybe you should. Have some respect."

"I don't care where we are and I won't show respect for something I don't believe in. I don't believe in God, not one that let me live a life like I did. Not one that would let my father and Jim treat me like they did."

As soon as the words are out of my mouth, the ground shakes, just as hard as it did when I was outside alone waiting for Sparrow. The entire church shudders, cracking the plaster walls and coating us in a layer of white dust.

I take in a deep breath and scrunch up my nose.

"What?" Sparrow asks.

"What's that smell?"

"It seems," he looks to the door at the end of the isle that runs down the middle of the church, "that is the smell of failure and death."

"What–"

Before I can finish Sparrow focuses on the front door of the church and the large oak door heaves as something pushes on it from the outside.

"Meg, get your clothes on," Sparrow offers, calmly.

We scramble to get dressed.

"I thought you said they couldn't come onto hallowed ground?"

"This must not be hallowed enough," he replies.

Sparrow slips on his pants and buttons them just as I'm tying my boots. "Is there any chance you could believe right now?" he asks. "Someone might send us some help."

"I don't think that kind of thing can happen in five minutes."

The door bulges again with a collective thud, the sound of hundreds of bodies surging. Just as I clip my backpack across my shoulder, the sound of splitting wood echoes through the church.

Sparrow grabs my sleeve, pulling me through the back hallways of the church, and through a door marked exit. We run down the street in the broad daylight, although the light doesn't seem as bright as it should be, nor as bright as I remember it.

"What the hell good are those things if you can't use them?" I point to the sky. "Can't you fly?"

He pauses and stretches the wings, disappointment cloaks his face. "It seems I've forgotten how."

"Do I need to push you off a cliff or something? Like your momma bird?"

"Don't have time for that right now." He looks behind us to see the shuffling dead trickle out of the back door of the church. "Let's get going."

We run.

When we are far enough away, we both slow to a fast paced walk. Sparrow is still shirtless with his machete fastened to his belt loops, hanging down his leg. Now I see him in the daylight and it's better than what he looked like in that dusky church. He's broad shouldered, muscular but not too bulky, his jeans hang from his narrow hips. The sight of him, like this, now, is very distracting.

"I think we need to find you a shirt."

His lip tips upwards. "Why? Does my near-nakedness make you nervous?"

"No. It makes me think dirty thoughts and I can't focus on where we're going right now."

"I remember a time when you had no problem stripping down to your skin in front of me and I don't think you gave a damn whether I could focus or not."

"Whatever," I mutter to him, keeping my focus on the road in front of us, trying to sort out what I was just given a glimpse of and what's real.

"Let's loop around to the Jeep. I bet it's clear there by now," Sparrow suggests.

We jog around the block, making way for the Jeep that I left on the side of the road. The dead trail behind, too slow to reach us. I open the driver's side door and climb in, just as Sparrow launches himself over the passenger door. The engine hums to life as I turn the ignition and speed away.

As I follow the signs for 81, Sparrow gazes at me, twirling a piece of my hair around his finger.

"Stop." I shrug my shoulder and pull away from him. "I don't like to be touched."

"You didn't mind me touching you earlier."

I give him a look. "Where are we headed?" I ask.

"I think we need to figure out what's going on with you." He adjusts himself in the seat. "Who was your father?"

"Besides a bastard?"

"Meg?" He gives me a look now.

"His name was John Lewis."

"But that isn't your last name, Meg Clark."

"No. He didn't give me his last name. He told me because they weren't married that the state put my mother's last name on the birth certificate. He never attempted to change it. That's probably a good thing."

"I think we need to go back to his house. We need to figure out who you are."

"I don't want to go back there."

"Don't you want answers, Meg?"

"What are answers going to get us, Sparrow? You might get some of your memory back. But what about me? I left my father and never looked back, you know why? Because he was an asshole and I hated him. Never once in my life did he show that he ever cared about me. Those are memories I don't want to live a second time."

"Did you ever get the feeling that you were something more? Better than all of that?"

"No, Sparrow, I believed every word my father and the rest of that hick town told me. I don't know why you think

I'm something special, because I'm not." I notice a feather fluttering behind him. "I'm not the one with wings," I add.

"I think you're wrong." He settles one elbow on the door and the other hand in his lap.

"Well, since you're still half-crazy, I'll take you to where my father lives. If he's even still alive."

"I think I'm significantly less crazy than I was before."

I glance at him from the corner of my eye as I drive. He's right. He's way less crazy than he was before. The quirks are gone and the odd motions as well. He's not shoving his hands in his pockets every five minutes to stroke off to a bunch of feathers. I guess I could say, besides his memory loss, Sparrow is pretty much a normal guy now. Well, besides those wings. Those are definitely fucked up.

...

A DILAPIDATED, single-wide trailer sits in front of us, looking darker and crappier than it did when I was a kid.

"This is where you grew up?" Sparrow asks.

"I know, you're jealous. Don't be."

Sparrow gives a quick smirk before stepping ahead of me, one hand on his machete and the other reaching for the door handle, turning it and pushing it open.

"Well, it's about fuckin' time!" A familiar voice hollers as we step into the living room. "Look what we have here, the hero stripped of his wings and the little slut."

I step around Sparrow to find my father sitting in his worn pleather easy chair, just where I remember him sitting almost every day of my life.

He stands and I can see that something has changed about him, he's taller, his skin darker, tinted a red hue almost, and it seems as though the top of his head and backs of his hands are covered in rough scales.

"Daddy?" I ask, unable to control the quiver in my voice.

His eyes narrow on me, darker than ever. "No, sweetheart, you were never my daughter. A true daughter of mine would never be as weak as you are." His gaze flicks to Sparrow.

"Is this about the money?" I ask, remembering how he tried to smother me in the hospital, when I... well, I guess I'm not sure what really happened when I went back to when everything was normal again.

He laughs. "It's not about the money *here*, dear Meg. Your mother left you something very important, but it wasn't money. Didn't figure it all out 'till I made it down here." He takes a step toward us. "The Heavens thought that you were going to be their secret weapon." He throws his head back and laughs. "But you're weak, and still nothin' but a piece of garbage." He takes another step closer us, his laughter burning me deep. I remember the look on his face when he tried to smother me with a pillow. It's worse now—there is no love there, and I can't understand how this person raised me and can have no feelings toward me whatsoever. "Nothin' but a stupid–"

"Hey!" Sparrow starts, taking a step in front of me.

At the interruption my father takes two quick steps, his hand reaching out, moving faster than I've ever seen him move before, faster than when he tried to smother me, grabbing Sparrow by the throat.

"It's amazing that you're the one who's here with her," my father sneers. "One of the Legion. Aren't you the one who lost her in the first place?" He reaches for Sparrow's wings, plucking a feather out and crushing it in his hand. "Looks like she put Humpty Dumpty back together again.

Seems a fitting punishment, take the only thing from you that matters." My father's gaze flicks to mine. "All these assholes do is sit around and preen their feathers like a fuckin' prized goose." He focuses back on Sparrow. "Did you tell her why your wings were stripped? Or did they wipe your memories too? I hear those flying monkeys up in the heavens save that punishment for the worst offenders."

Even though my father's hand is gripping Sparrow's throat, Sparrow's head tips to the side, his eyes widen as though he's trying to piece something together in his head.

"Have you remembered yet? This is your punishment for losing her." He looks back to me. "If you want someone to blame for your life, Meg, blame him, the one who lost you in the first place." He turns back to Sparrow. "And now you're nothing but a crazy man, trying to piece yourself back together. This little slut isn't going to help you at all. It doesn't matter what you and your winged tribe think. She is nothing."

I hear a gurgle escape Sparrow's throat and his hands fly to my father's arms. I run at them, throw myself onto my father's arms, trying to get him to let go. "Leave him alone! You're hurting him!" I yell as I try to pry him away.

In one quick movement my father backhands me, just like he's done hundreds of times since I passed the age of twelve. Only this time, it's harder, hard enough to send me flying across the living room. I hit the wall and roll, pushing myself to my knees just in time to see Sparrow reach for the machete at his side. It seems to glow in the dark trailer, illuminating the room in a golden shine as he twists his wrist and slices across my father's arms.

I push myself to my feet, hearing my father roar in pain, staring at the stumps for arms that end just below his elbows. Sparrow brushes the lifeless hands off his neck and assumes a fighter's stance, feet apart, knees bent, ready for action. I can tell by the hard look on his face, that he's remembered something.

A dark chuckle escapes my father's chest as he holds his arm nubs up. "Nice try," he laughs as his arms begin to grow and reform new hands.

Sparrow raises his machete and in one swift move he slices my father's head clean off. It hits the floor of the trailer with a resounding thud, and I swear I see the face flinch. Sparrow moves to stand over the wobbling head.

"Killing just me can't help you, bird man. More will be coming for you." The eyes from my father's decapitated head flick to me. "They'll be coming for you too, slut!" The head gives a deep, horrific laugh just before Sparrow kicks it down the hallway, holsters his machete to his hip, and starts toward me.

"Meg..." His hands reach out for me, but I step back, trying to process what just happened. "Are you okay?" he asks. I blink hard, but it doesn't clear my vision. All I can see is my father's lifeless body on the floor and hear his head still making noise from down the hallway. "Meg?" Sparrow asks again.

I step back, move my eyes to his face and see that he's changed, again. All that uncertainty Sparrow has always had is now replaced with a true knowledge. I can see it in the hard lines of his face, the angles of his jaw clenching.

"Is what he said true? You remember now?" I shake my head and clutch my hands to my chest.

"A few more things," Sparrow replies with a low voice. "That's all. Not everything."

"I don't understand what just happened. What he said..."

"What didn't you understand?"

"What makes me so special?"

"I can't remember."

"But you remembered something! And you need me for something. That's... that's what he said."

Sparrow presses his lips together and nods.

"And the reason why I grew up here, why I experience all of those years of... all that shit was because you *lost* me? What the hell does that mean?"

"I–" Sparrow starts, but something feels like it's going to explode inside me. All the grief and pain of realizing my entire life has been a lie, wells up so strong I can barely contain it.

"I need air," I gasp, pushing Sparrow away from me and running out the door.

"Meg, wait!"

I push open the screen door and leap off the small porch, just as I did when I was a kid. My feet hit the gravel driveway with a satisfying crunch and I have the memory of watching the dust swirl around my feet when I did this as a kid. The only difference is it is night now and I'm an adult.

There are lights on in the other trailers, casting an eerie glow over the pebbled gravel road. Just as I hear the sound of Sparrow's footsteps run up behind me, the sound of screen doors squeaking open fill the night. As I look around the trailer park at all of the neighbors, I realize they are not the neighbors I remember and they are not truly human any longer. They are something else.

"Meg!" Sparrow grips my shoulder and pulls me behind him as he draws out his weapon, ready to defend us.

"What are they?" I ask.

"Demons."

"Demons?"

He nods, bending his knees and gripping his weapon in front of him. I peer around the edge of his left wing and step aside from him.

"How do I know you're any different?" I ask.

"This is not the time for this conversation," he informs me with a stern tone that I've never heard from him before. "Get behind me," he orders.

Seeing my neighbors, the demons, descend their porches and walk to us. I move behind Sparrow wishing I had some type of a weapon to help defend us. I curse those bastards who took my guns.

"What are you going to do?" I ask.

"Cut their heads off."

Before I can ask him how or what the hell or run screaming into the forest because all of this is so fucking crazy, all six of the neighbors run for us, their skin changed to a leathery red hue, some have horns, protruding teeth, scales, and odd patches of hair on their bodies. My heart gives a few hundred rapid panicked beats in my chest.

Sparrow steps forward, his machete in hand, swinging it and lopping off the heads of the first two. He moves fast, with a skill I never knew he possessed, and as the second two run for him, their teeth bared, he repeats the same action. Two more heads fall to the ground. The last two look at each other, then back at us, before they run off into the woods behind the trailer park.

Sparrow turns and takes my arm. "You're coming with me. Let's go."

"Screw you." I rip my arm away from him. "I'm not going anywhere with you."

"Then where will you go, Meg? Are you going to run off and scamper up into a tree like the last time you ran away from me?"

"Fuck off! I am so sick of people bossing me around and treating me like crap. I don't need it from you too."

"No. You don't." He takes one long step toward me, stopping when our chests are almost touching. "Two more of those things are still alive. You think they'll stay away? As soon as they sense you are alone, they'll come back for you. Now come on. You're coming with me."

Sparrow reaches for my arm again but I step back. "The hell I am. I don't understand this. Any of it. What happened to my father? How are there demons running around in this place with the walking dead? This doesn't make sense." I point a finger at him. "And you're different. I liked you better when you were crazy."

"There's still time for me to go back to crazy." He tips his head, a motion that reminds me of the man he was just a few days ago. "We need to get out of here."

"Tell me what the shit is going on first."

Sparrow's eyes flick to the forest where the last two demons ran. "I think... I think we are in Hell." He looks around us. "Or something like that."

"So I'm dead!"

"No." Sparrow shakes his head. "Not dead. Before you were–"

"I was dead before?" I almost scream at him, freaking out.

"Before you were in a coma, your soul teetering on the edge. And then in the church... your birthmark..." He presses his fingers to his forehead. "There's something special about you. I just can't put together all the pieces right now." His eyes flick to the bodies on the ground. "Come on, we need to go."

"No! I'm not going anywhere with you."

"Why?"

"Because, you are nothing but a liar!" I raise my hand to shove him away from me, but Sparrow moves lightning-fast and grabs my arm.

"Not being able to remember doesn't make me a liar."

"Then what were you doing at Noah's? Huh? Just waiting for me to show up?"

His grip on my arm loosens. "I just had a feeling and then everything happened."

"Yeah, and now you remember."

"Only a few things."

"Like what?"

"Like I'm supposed to protect you and bring you somewhere."

"I'm not going anywhere with you."

"Yes, you are." Sparrow reaches down, grasping my hips and tossing me over his shoulder.

Spewing a stream of very unladylike words, I pound on his back with my fists and twist my hips. "Let go of me, you royal dickweed."

I feel him chuckling as he walks. "You know, you shouldn't talk like that. I'm pretty sure I've told you this before."

"Oh yeah, how would you rather I talk? You want me to whisper sweet nothings in your ear?"

"Can't hurt. I kinda liked the things you whispered to me back in that church."

"I don't think so." I cross my arms and press my elbows into the firm muscle of his back, just underneath where his wings connect.

"Could you move your arms? That's very uncomfortable."

"Screw you and I'm never talking to you like that again, ever."

Sparrow stops, drops me to my feet, and bends down so his face is just in front of mine. Nose to nose. I can see nothing but his clear green eyes boring into mine. "Tell me you didn't like it."

I lean away from him, pressing my lips together, refusing to talk. I don't need him to explain what he wants me to tell him. I know exactly what he means; the sex, the best sex I've ever had in my entire life. Just the memory of it makes my lady parts tingle.

"Tell me it was bad, Meg." He presses on. "Tell me it was the worst time of your life. Because from what I saw, it looked like you were enjoying yourself and everything I was doing to you. Every second of it."

I narrow my eyes.

"Yeah, you can't even pretend." Some cocky smile appears on his face as his eyes trail down my body.

"Fuck. You." I mouth to him.

"Hm." Sparrow turns with a satisfied grin and starts walking.

"Where are you going?" I ask.

He keeps walking.

I turn in a circle and take a look at the four bodies lying in the narrow road that runs through the trailer park and a tiny part of me is thankful we didn't live in one of those fancy parks with their own zip code. A shudder runs through me as I realize he's right, I have nowhere else to go and no one else to go to. I run up next to Sparrow and catch a glimpse of the smile that starts across his face.

"Shut up."

"Told you so," he responds triumphantly.

"Fu–"

Sparrow turns so fast I barely see him move, I just feel his finger on my lips, silencing me. "Don't you even say that to me. I swear to God, Meg, if you use that word one more time in front of me that's exactly what I'm going to do. To you."

Now, even though I'm pretty mad at him right now and confused and pissed at this whole situation, I put a pin in that shit to remember later.

He stands up straight and looks down the road. I see

that we are almost to the Jeep I parked on the side of the road. Sparrow starts for the driver's side door.

"What are you doing?" I ask him as I skip a few steps to follow him.

"Driving."

"I thought you didn't drive?"

"I just remembered how." He slams the driver's side door. "Get in," he tells me over his shoulder.

"I think I liked you better when you were balls-to-the-walls crazy," I grumble on my way to the passenger side. Sparrow turns and stares at me as I buckle my seat belt. "What?" I ask.

"I was just thinking I like you better naked."

I want to tell him to fuck-off, but I remember the warning he gave me just a few minutes ago. So instead, I let my cheeks turn a nice shade of red as I cross my arms over my chest and stare straight ahead. And just as though Sparrow has been driving this entire trip, he turns the Jeep on, shifts it into gear, and accelerates down the road.

...

"Why did those men target you?" Sparrow asks me as he speeds out of town.

"Why would you care?"

"Because I need to know. I think it might help figure out where we need to go."

"I don't know why."

"Think."

"You know, that is the same question the people in Kingston asked me. Why is it that everyone wants to know the things I have no knowledge of?"

"Think, Meg. There has to be something."

"How about, instead, you tell me something. Like how you said that what happened to me should have killed me, but it didn't, and now you think we're in Hell with all the demons and shit. So that must mean I'm dead. That must mean I did die. Those men and Jim did kill me. So I don't really care anymore. If I'm dead right now then it doesn't matter. The only question I have is how are there people here? Noah and his group, the old guy at the Country Store, everyone we met in Canada. That doesn't make sense that they're all here if this is Hell."

"Maybe this is their Hell too? They must be dead." He rubs the stubble on his chin. "We need to go back to your house."

"We just left it."

"No, not your father's house. Your house, the one you lived in with Jim."

"I don't want to go back there." I shudder at the memories.

"We have to." The tires of the Jeep squeal as he turns sharp in the middle of the road.

Why is it that I keep coming back here? All I have ever wanted was to get the hell out of this town, and all this bull-shit keeps pulling me back. I look to the sky and see the first hints of sunrise. "Shouldn't we rest somewhere and wait until night?"

"This will be quick. We'll be fine," Sparrow assures me with the confidence he has always had when it comes to safety and the dead.

I give him the directions to my house.

...

Sparrow parks the Jeep across the street. The house looks just the same as it did a few weeks ago when I came here for clothes and supplies. I follow Sparrow through the open door. The downstairs is still overrun with cats, they scamper away as we walk through the living room.

"I hate cats," Sparrow whispers.

I kick at an old pair of sneakers by the door, thinking about replacing these hiking boots with them.

"Where would Jim have put important papers?" Sparrow asks.

"I don't know." I walk to the kitchen in search of food.

"Weren't you going to marry him? How can you not know where he kept things?"

"I didn't really pay attention."

I hear Sparrow's footsteps as he searches the house.

"Watch your step," I warn him.

"Why?" He stops at the threshold of the kitchen.

"Upstairs." I open a cupboard door only to find it empty. "They never cleaned up the blood."

The next thing I hear is Sparrow's footsteps as he walks upstairs. Giving up on finding any food, I follow him. When I reach the second floor landing I notice the door to the nursery is open.

"Sparrow, did you go in the nursery?" I ask.

There's no answer. I head to the open door, drawn to it by some unknown force. Walking into the room, I immediately wish I hadn't. A pressure hits my chest. I clutch at my shirt, pulling it away from my body, trying to stop the choking feeling.

The walls are still painted the light yellow and green hues, the crib decorated in soft linens and stuffed animals. It's the only room in the house that doesn't look dank and dirty.

My hand smoothes over my stomach, missing the feeling

of having the baby in there, and I realize that I'm never going to have that chance again. Babies grow in a uterus and mine has left the building. I swipe at a tear, blink hard. *Grow the fuck up.* I tell myself. I should have never walked through the goddamned door. Somehow, I'm on my knees, my fingers pressing into the beige shag carpet. I stand, walk out of the room, and slam the door.

"Noise!" I hear Sparrow's harsh whisper from down the hall.

"Shit," I mumble to myself, hoping that the dead didn't hear the door slamming.

"Sparrow?" I call down the hallway. I search the spare room and bathroom on my way to the master bedroom. On my way, I give up trying to step around the dark stains in the carpet. There's too many of them. "Sparrow?" He looks up, staring at me with some odd look, like he's crazy again or I'm a bird whose feathers he's getting ready to pluck. "What's wrong with you?" I demand. "I've been calling your name."

"I... I was going to say something, but it seems... It seems I've lost my words." He runs his hand through his hair and looks around confused.

Walking to him, I find a picture of my mother in his hand. "Where did you find this? I thought I lost it in the move."

He points to the floor where I find an open lockbox. Bending, I inspect the other papers. There is a yellowed folded piece of paper. I open it to find my birth certificate. There's more, a letter from a lawyer in Syracuse stating the large sum of money I was about to inherit, and a letter from my bank.

My hands sift through the papers as my brain works overtime, piecing it all together. Jim knew, he knew about the money and he knew about my mother. Part of me now wonders if he knew all of this before he drove downstate and got me pregnant, if the baby and killing us was always his plan.

My eyes focus on the picture of my mother. The mother I never met, the mother I killed the day I was born. There's nothing to signify who she was in this picture, just a pretty woman standing near a tree in a park. The image is blurry like someone tried to get her to stand still but the only part that came out clearly was the smile on her face.

"There's so much blood spilled here." I look up from the papers to find Sparrow has moved across the room. He now stares at the stains on the carpet.

"I know." I close the top of the lockbox and stand up, leaving the papers and the picture. "It's mine."

Sparrow turns and the look on his face is one that can only be described as deep sympathy.

"Don't look at me like that," I tell him, walking around the side of the bed to him. "I hate it when people look at me like that."

"Something terrible happened to you here."

"I fucking know that, Sparrow. Remember? I told you all about it." I head for the door.

"No." He steps forward, blocking my exit from the room. "Something terrible." He steps in front of me and places his hand over my heart. "Right here."

"Stop it." I brush his hand away. "I don't need your little pity party." I start walking away from him.

"No, Meg." He grabs my arm and pulls me back to him. "It's not pity. It's regret. I can't help but feel like this..." He waves at the bloodstains on the carpet. "This is my fault."

"How could it be your fault, Sparrow? You didn't know me when this happened."

"I–"

His words are interrupted by the sound of footsteps on

the first level of the house. I wish all I were hearing is the sound of a single person's footsteps, but it's not, it's the sound of dozens of footsteps, dragging and scraping across the floor beneath us.

"I knew we should have waited until night to come here," I say.

Sparrow looks around the room before stepping into the hallway and looking down the stairwell. "They'll make it up these stairs," he whispers.

"I thought they couldn't climb?"

"They can't climb ladders. But stairs, stairs are angled just enough that they can fall and drag their rotting bodies up them. We have to block them." He moves to the bedroom and lifts a nightstand. "Come on. Help me throw some stuff down the stairs to block them."

"Uh, shouldn't you choose something bigger, like a dresser?" I suggest.

"Layers, you have to block them with layers. We start with the nightstands then the dressers."

I move, lifting and tossing, the commotion only seeming to draw the walking dead to the bottom of the stairs. The sound of heavy wood being pushed across the floor makes me turn to see Sparrow pushing my dresser across the floor.

I move back and watch as he shoves it down the stairwell. We follow that with Jim's dresser, a chair, the mattress and box springs from the bed.

"If we take the bed apart, the headboard and footboard should be enough to block them until night. Then we can climb over everything and get out."

I pace the floor, look at the bloodstains on the carpets, the broken mirror in the bathroom. I feel a sharp pain in my side, remembering how it got broken. And just as though Sparrow were remembering right along with me, I hear him inhale sharply from across the room.

I turn to him. "I can't."

"It's just until night, Meg." Sparrow walks closer to me and I back away from him.

"No. I can't stay in this house with all these memories for twelve hours or more."

A sad understanding crosses his face. His eyes sweep across the stains on the floor. "You want to talk–" he starts.

"No. I've talked about it enough with you. You're already giving me these looks of pity. I'm done talking about it. I never want to talk about it again."

"Okay." He rubs his jaw and looks around the room. "That leaves only one option." He walks to the large window that faces a neighbor's yard and opens it. "Come on." He beckons me to his side.

I cross the room to him. "What are you doing?"

"Getting you out of here." I follow Sparrow through the window and to the small roof that covers the side entry into the house. Sparrow holds his finger up in the air. He turns to the left, then the right, before he turns to me. "We need to get higher. Climb up onto the roof."

I feel his hand on my shoulder as he turns me and points to the low pitched area of the roof. I climb, Sparrow pushing at my backside to get me higher, my boots gripping the rough shingles. I straighten as Sparrow stands next to me.

"I need you to put your arms around my neck." He tells me as he reaches for my hands and draws them up his bare chest.

"You need a shirt."

He winks. "Hold tight."

"What are you doing?"

"Getting you out of here. Just like you asked." He pulls me by my waist, jerking me against him. "Don't let go," he whispers into my ear. His wings spread wide and when I look up to his face, I can see the beads of sweat starting on his brow. I think to pull back, to stop him. I know he can't fly and this, this isn't going to get us anything but some broken bones and then we'll definitely be meat sack surprise for dinner.

"Spa–," I start, finishing with a gasp as he leans forward and drops us off the roof. My arms tighten around his neck to the point where I'm sure I'm choking him. His feathers flutter in the sunlight as we descend the roof. Landing on the ground, Sparrow stumbles, dropping down to one knee while holding me tight against his chest.

"I thought you couldn't fly?" I finally breathe out.

"Well," he starts as he stands. "I didn't really. Just glided down." He smiles at me. "But if you want, you can keep looking at me like I flew."

"It was kind of amaz–" Sparrow bends and presses his lips to mine before I can finish. A burning fire warms my chest and spreads throughout my veins as I feel his lips move over mine. I push my fingers into his hair and press my body closer to him. Too soon he pulls away.

"I'd like to finish this." He looks down at me in his arms. "But we have to go."

He pulls me to my feet and I fight to catch my breath as his arm leaves my back.

"Let's get back to the Jeep," he says with a gruff voice. "We need to get moving before more show up."

He takes my hand and we run through the neighbor's yard, around the side of the house, down the street and just as we make a left to reach the Jeep where I left it parked in the road, we skid to a stop.

"Shit," Sparrow spits.

"Motherfucker," I mumble.

There are dozens of them, the dead, pouring into my

little house. And as we stop in the street, they all turn and look at us.

…

"Get in the Jeep, Meg!" Sparrow shouts as he moves for the driver's side door.

For some reason, I can't seem to move my feet.

"Meg!" Sparrow shouts.

I feel my lower jaw drop and every ounce of energy I once possessed drains from me.

"What's wrong with you?" He moves away from the vehicle, steps toward me, scowling. "Let's go."

"I shouldn't have come here. Back to this place. I tried so hard to forget it all." I hear the words come from my lips but it doesn't feel like I said them. "I can't do this anymore. You shouldn't have made me come back here."

"Meg, now, we have to go." Urgency entwines with his voice.

I look past him, watching as the horde of the dead leave my little house and amble in our direction. "I'm dead anyways so it doesn't matter."

Sparrow grips my shoulders, trying to direct me toward the Jeep. I don't move. I can't even find the strength or the want to move. A calmness washes over me with the thought that I could just stand here and end all of this right now, let the memories go, be done with dragging them around in my soul.

"Goddammit, Meg." Sparrow turns, removes his machete from his hip and readies himself.

"You should just go, Sparrow."

"I'm not leaving you."

"I think you should. Dragging me around isn't helping you. I just want to end this. There's more I will remember. I can feel it. And I don't want to remember any of it."

"Don't be stupid." I notice him cringe after he says it. "I didn't mean that..."

"No, that's what I am. Stupid trash. And there's no way out. I don't want to do this anymore. I thought you were the one with lost memories, but it seems this problem is afflicting both of us. This is wrong, Sparrow."

The horde and their moaning get closer. "Don't say that."

"They're coming," I warn him. "You should leave. I'm just dragging you down."

"Not happening."

"You should go. You should move on. You'll be better off without me. My father was right."

"Unpossible."

I close my eyes, waiting for the end, waiting to hear Sparrow's footsteps as he runs away, for the rumble of the engine of the jeep starting. I never hear them. Instead, my ears are filled with the sound of Sparrow's machete blade slicing and the wet thwacking of body parts hitting the ground.

"Are you over this yet?" My eyes open with Sparrow's voice.

He turns to face me, blood and sweat and things I don't care to mention dripping off him, looking like nothing but a hulking warrior and so different from the Sparrow that I've grown to love. He's no longer my sweet, slightly confused Sparrow who dragged me all over the state searching for feathers.

"Let's go. In the Jeep!" he orders.

I stand still in the road, surrounded by the newly decapitated dead. "I can't do this anymore," I tell him, feeling a heavy weight in my chest and I'm not sure why.

"We still have to find Jim. We have to get answers from him."

"Jim's gone, Sparrow. He wasn't in Kingston. The Safe House there couldn't find him. I'm sure he's here somewhere. God knows he should be in Hell for what he did. But he doesn't want to be found. And frankly, I don't think I can face him. Not after what he let those men do to me."

"Meg, we have–"

"No!" I feel my bottom lip and chin trembling. "I should have never walked back into that house. I should have never looked at that empty nursery or that picture of my mother." I draw a shuddering breath. I used to know exactly who I was, what was expected of me. But now, with all of this, Sparrow pushing me for answers and these memories springing up from wherever I pushed them, I suddenly have no idea who I am anymore.

"Meg." He shakes my shoulder.

"Damn you, Sparrow." I brush his hand away. "I don't want to!"

He blows out a breath of frustration and runs his dirty hands through his hair, looking around us as though there might be a solution out here. "I can give you just a glimpse of that normal life. Like last time. But just for a few minutes. Will that help you?"

I nod, brushing the hot tears from the corners of my eyes.

He grips my thigh, pressing his thumb to the birthmark on my leg and whispers the same strange words he said in the church. A bright light erupts from behind my eyes and I hear that blasted horn sound.

PERSPECTIVES
AND PAIN

When my eyes flutter open, I find that I am standing in the zoo. The same place I left off in the aviary, with Sparrow standing in front of me, fully clothed, his wings gone but his strong green gaze just the same.

I can feel my hair brushing against my neck as I move my head from side to side, taking in the normalness of the bustling zoo. It seems when we do this, the time is the same as it is in Hell. Daytime, now. The dress I'm wearing suddenly feels tight even though there is a slight breeze brushing it by my legs. I step away from Sparrow, putting an arm's length between us.

Sparrow frowns at me and his beautiful green eyes widen with the knowledge of what I'm about to do. "What's wrong?" he asks.

Shaking my head at him, knowing without a doubt that this is my chance to escape, to get away, run from all of those memories and all the bullshit. Because I know he's going to make me go back there, to that Hell where all my nightmares live. I can't do it, not for one more second. I can't go back there and continue on with this. I don't even give him the chance to say two more words before I turn and run away from him as fast as I can, with the burn of looming tears behind my eyes, making my vision blurry.

The zoo visitors step aside and watch as I run past them, choking down a feeling of pain that's aching deep in my heart like I have never known.

......

Sparrow

Watching as Meg runs away from me, I remember this is not like the last time. This is not like how I lost her so long ago when she was nothing but a baby and I couldn't bear to be demoralized as a babysitter. I was a warrior, after all. Born, bred and trained to fight. Not babysit. It didn't help that every time I looked at her all I could see was a future, of us, together. One that is forbidden. So I never looked at her again, and I lost her.

Remembering all of this now, I guess my punishment was sufficient. When I think of all that I put her through, there is a deep pang in my gut.

Hearing a loud cracking sound I look to my left and find a huge man glaring down at me. His hair is black and long to his shoulders, but it's the bright blue hue of his eyes that tell me who he really is.

I know this man. I remember him. Meg's real father.

Shit.

"You really fucked up good this time, Sparrow." He steps closer to me.

I hold my ground as he advances. He's so tall that this is

one of the few times when I ever have to look up to some-one. It's strange that he's in the human realm. I glance around to make sure no one is watching us.

"You really, really fucked this one up," he continues, his voice low and threatening. "This was your chance to redeem yourself, get her on board, and now there she goes, running away from you." He palms a fist and cracks his knuckles.

Double shit.

"I tried–"

"You've almost failed. Again. The rules are simple." He reaches out and flicks something off my shirt. It's an intimi-dating move but I stand straight and still, like the warrior I'm supposed to be. "I ought to banish you back to Hell for not keeping your pants on, boy. Of all the females available to you, you choose my daughter."

"You have hundreds of daughters," I remind him. I remember that much.

He laughs. "Not like this one. There was a reason why you were ordered to watch over her in the first place." He palms his opposite fist and resumes cracking his knuckles. "You better fix this, Sparrow. She has a place and I need her in it. She's the youngest. There will be no more from my bloodline."

"I–"

"Fix it!" He takes a long blink and sighs. "And if she is the one you've chosen, perhaps you should ask for my blessing."

I clear my throat. "You mean, we can... I thought... It's always been forbidden with humans."

"She's not like the others. That was the reason for you guarding her in the first place, dumb-dumb."

Triple shit.

"Why is she different from the others?"

"You already found out who her mother is. That should explain it all."

"It doesn't explain how she got here."

Meg's father blinks at me. "She got here because her mother was a very stubborn woman, just like Meg. She wanted a different life for her daughter, one without monarchies and rules and rituals. That is why you were supposed to be guarding her in the first place. But you obviously got a little distracted. And now I see why."

I remember the photo of her mother. "But she doesn't have wings?"

"Neither do I. Unless I need them"

"But... that would make her pure–"

"Seriously, Sparrow, I know you were supposed to be one of our best, but I think taking your memories damaged your brain." He moves his index finger in front of my face. "Let me help you a bit. Listening to your blubbering is extremely annoying." He flicks the top of my forehead, hard. "You can thank me later."

I press my hands to the sides of my head, feeling it ache as memories rush me. "Okay."

"Sparrow, you forgot to ask."

"Ask wha... Oh. May I have your blessing?" One dark eyebrow rises on his face. "Sir?" I add.

He leans down, the tip of his nose almost touching mine. "You fuck up again, the only thing you'll get is a lifetime in Hell and I won't let her get you out of there again. Now, get her back on course, stop letting her flash back here, and get her ass to Jim so she can remember who she really is."

"She's given up already, Sir. Was ready to drop in the road and let the dead have her."

"She can do this. She's strong. She just needs to see it in her heart." He lays his open palm on his chest. "She has to see that all those people were wrong about her and feel it, right here. If she doesn't see the good, we can't release either of you." He points in the direction Meg ran. "Go fix this, yesterday."

"Yes, Sir." I stand there awkwardly for a moment.

"Get the hell out of here and go after her already!"

I run in the direction that Meg ran, hearing the voice behind me say, "You have my blessing."

....

Meg

Chest burning, I stop running, pace a few steps, try to sort everything out in my head, but all I can hear are the people talking, children laughing, noise from the animals, and the smells. My stomach feels like it's going to crawl out of my abdomen. I'm so hungry and all I smell is candy apples and popcorn and pretzels. I stop in front of a stand selling fried dough.

"Can I help you, Miss?" a middle-aged man in an apron asks me.

I lick my lips, remembering the lonely nights feasting on rats, the meals Sparrow and I have pieced together. None of it filling the void and none of it smelling as good as this fried dough does right now.

"Would you like an order?" the man asks.

I nod my head. "Yes..." I look around me. Feel my pockets. Shit, I don't have pockets in this skirt and no cash in this purse. "It seems I don't have any cash on me." I turn seeing

Sparrow headed my way. "But my husband is on his way," I lie, pointing behind me. "That handsome devil with the green eyes who needs a haircut. He'll pay for it. Promise." I give the sweetest smile I can muster.

"You want sugar or cinnamon?" the man asks.

I decide to be greedy. Who am I kidding, I'm always greedy. "Both," I tell him. I grab a few napkins and watch as he pulls a large piece of dough from the fryer and sprinkles the sugar and cinnamon on it. He sets the dough on a plate and hands it across the counter to me.

"Thanks." I take it and walk as fast as I can to a bench that's hidden behind a cart selling toys. That was easier than stealing candy and condoms from the Country Store back home.

Peeking out from behind the cart, I watch as the man at the dough-stand points in the direction I went. He's talking to a younger version of himself who's also wearing an apron. I take a giant bite of the dough and watch while they argue. Sparrow walks right by them and they don't even notice him. I wonder if the man is blind? I eat the dough. All of it. When I am done, my stomach grumbles, wanting more.

Sparrow walks to me, a look of disbelief on his face. "What the heck was that?" he asks.

"I was hungry."

"Have I ever let you starve? You could have said something to me." He crosses his arms over his chest. "Well, was it worth it? Lying and stealing."

"It was fucking delicious." I lick the sugar off my fingers as his gaze darkens on me. "I've decided." I pause to clean another finger. "I like you, Sparrow. Even with all the bullshit that has happened. I'm willing to finish this with you." I circle a clean finger in the air. "Whatever the hell this is that we are doing. Because, well, frankly, I have nothing better to do right now. And your price to pay was the fried dough. I don't know what went through me in the road back there. Maybe my blood sugar was low, but it's good now. So whatever it is we need to do, we can finish it, here, where it's normal. I'm not going back there to Hell."

Sparrow sighs. "We have to go back there."

"No. I can't. I won't."

"There's still unfinished business, Meg."

"But why can't we stay here? It's nice here. Everything is normal. The sun is brighter. No one's dead. And there's delicious food."

"We have to finish what we started. We have to finish searching for answers. That's what we were doing. It's important, Meg. Very important."

"I can't." Sparrow kneels in front of me. "What are you doing?" I ask. "People are watching. They're going to think you're weird." Looking around I notice I'm wrong, no one's watching. It's like we're invisible, or Sparrow is.

"I don't care what they think." Sparrow moves the empty plate coated with grease and sugar off my lap.

A huge man walks by us, his eyes as blue as the sky. He clears his throat loudly. Sparrow's back straightens as though someone kicked him. The man winks at me and waltzes off.

"Who the hell was that?" I focus behind Sparrow and watch the tall man walk away.

"Your real father."

I try to stand, wanting to run after him and grab onto him and ask him what all this is about. But Sparrow grips my hands and presses them to my legs so I can't stand. The man disappears into the crowd.

"Not yet," he tells me.

"Who is he?" I ask.

"I can't tell you. Not yet. That is what he said. You have to find who you are." Sparrow presses his hand to my chest. "Here."

I look down at Sparrow. There's a red mark on his forehead like someone hit him there and absolutely no confusion left in his eyes. "You remember, don't you?"

"Yes. I remember now. All of it. Your father, your real father, he gave me back my memories."

"And?"

"This is my fault."

"How can it be your fault?"

His eyes bore into mine. "Trust me. It is. I'm so sorry that I lost you, that I–"

"But... I've never met you before. You haven't lost me."

"This was before. When you were a baby."

"How?"

"I was entrusted with guarding your mother and her child. Let's just say I failed. I failed miserably."

Ever since I met Sparrow, and all we've been through these past few weeks together, he's been there for me, always. Each time I have needed him, he's been there to help me, to rescue me, to guide me through all the memories of everything that happened to me. We've been there for each other. And a tiny part of me thinks that I should be mad at him, but I can't find the anger because I've never felt like this with another person at my side. I've never felt so... so complete. Something clicks inside me.

Sparrow sits back on his heels, his shoulders slump. "I'm so–"

I press a finger to his lips, silencing him. "I don't care. I don't care about any of that. I spent my whole life listening to people call me names and treat me like crap, and when I really think about it, you're the only person who's ever treated me differently. You were there for me when I needed you. I don't care that you failed in the past. I only care that you are by my side. I think I can do this, whatever it is I need to do. I can do this forever with you here, just like this. I just don't want to go back to Hell."

He tips his head, leans forward and presses his forehead to mine. "I'll never leave you alone again. I promise."

"How am I supposed to know if this is real?" I whisper, feeling his solid body pressing against my thighs.

"It's all real."

"Is this still about believing in God?"

"No. Not right now." He shakes his head. "It's about you and me. We're almost done. We have to go back, Meg. This one last time. We have to get answers from Jim. And then... then we'll be free. We won't have to go back there anymore." He rests his palms on both sides of my face.

"Jim was a dick. I don't want to see him again."

"I know. But I'll be there, by your side. I'll never leave you, ever again."

"Okay," I whisper.

Sparrow leans, pressing his lips to mine in a soft kiss, and another, and another, until I barely hear him when he whispers the words and runs his thumb over the mark on my leg.

......

This time, when my eyes open, I am greeted by the feeling of a large hand wrapped around my throat. Trying to speak, I can only get out a gurgle.

"Dumb shits," I hear the familiar voice of my father, or ex-father, the demon-thing, John Lewis.

I tip my head to see he holds Sparrow the same way. Hand around his throat, arms in the air. My feet dangle as I try to kick them. I try to kick him. Sparrow struggles. It seems with my father's reincarnation he has developed some super strength and size. He's huge.

I try to kick harder, but he just laughs and jerks us by our necks, cracking the backs of our skulls together as though we were a set of cymbals. I hear Sparrow groan as everything goes black behind my eyes.

...

"HEY, MEG," someone whispers in my ear while trailing a finger down the side of my cheek. "Wake up, my sweet little angel."

That voice, it's so familiar. It's the same voice that greeted me at that party when I was in college, the same voice that whispered in my ear as he stripped my clothes off me that night. The same voice that told me we were going back home to be a family. The same voice that told those seven men that I was the target. It's not a nice voice, not a snowy owl voice. It's a voice that only ever says bad things to me.

It's fucking Jim.

My eyes flick open to find him standing in front of me. Smirk on his face, eyes as gray as a storm, he swipes at the thick strands of blonde hair across his forehead.

"Get the hell away from me." I try to move but find that I can't. My arms ache like never before. Looking up I find that they are secured above me, my wrists wrapped in metal, chains dangling from the ceiling. A quick glance around tells me that I am in some kind of a cave, with torches lighting the large room.

"Now, this is how I've dreamed of seeing you, Meg," Jim continues. "Chained up just like you belong, shouting dirty words at me. You always had quite the mouth on you." He reaches out, snaking his fingers down my throat, between my breasts, settling on the waist of my jeans before leaning forward and kissing me hard, pressing my lips against my teeth so hard I can feel blood in my mouth. I might have welcomed the touch and the kiss, if I hadn't already remembered what he did to me.

I pull my head back and thrust it forward in one hard jerk, bouncing my skull off his. "Asshole!" Jim staggers back a few feet.

"You bitch," Jim spits. The back of his hand slaps me hard across the side of my face and I swear I hear my teeth rattle.

The realization comes to me right then, this isn't the first time Jim's hit me. There have been others, plenty of others. I must've tucked those memories away, way in the back of my mind. Now they come flooding forward. I let my head hang down as I remember every single backhand he gave me: after burning dinner, forgetting to give him my gas receipt, folding his laundry wrong, when the hanging flower baskets wilted because I forgot to water them one day. It didn't matter that I was pregnant, he still hit me.

As I hang there, I hate myself for not getting away from him, for telling myself it's what I deserved. After all, that's what my father had told me my entire life and I had already spent all my money on the house and the cabin in Canada. I couldn't raise a baby on my own. I remember telling myself that.

"That's better." He straightens his back, rolls his shoulders, and adjusts his shirt. "'Bout time you learned your place."

I look across the room to find Sparrow lying on the floor, unconscious. Jim laughs. I look away from Sparrow, trying to keep the focus on me. "I searched for you. The Safe

House couldn't find you. Trekked all over the state. That was before I remembered what you did to me."

"Those places are only for the lost souls who want to repent, for another chance to fly up to Heaven. I know better than to step foot in one of those places. I'd burn in one of those prisons." Jim tells me.

"Why did you do this? I thought..." I shake my head. "You asked me to marry you. I was pregnant with your child."

"Was it really mine, Meg? I mean, you are quite the slut."

I close my eyes, tilt my head, focus on the feeling of the metal cutting into the skin of my wrists, the fact that my feet are barely touching the floor right now. "The baby was yours." I open my eyes to find him grinning in front of me.

"I don't believe you."

"Whatever." I give up that argument. It seems like there's no point now that the baby is dead.

"Did he tell you what you can do?"

"He doesn't know anything and he can't do anything, besides sing Bon Jovi."

"Nice try. But word down here is that you can travel back and forth between realms, without the portal. You should really keep those tricks in your pocket and say, not practice them in the middle of the street. Word travels fast down here. Wicked fast." He chuckles. "You know why you keep flitting back and forth between Hell and the earthen plane?"

"If I knew, then I get the feeling I wouldn't be strung up in your little cave right now."

Jim raises his hand but this time I don't flinch, I simply glare at him.

"Hmm." Jim wanders over to where John Lewis has Sparrow pinned to the floor with a foot to his throat, his hands tied with rope. "Bird-man knows why you can flit back and forth." Jim reaches out with his index finger, stroking the pink flamingo feather attached to Sparrow's wings. "I bet he's not allowed to tell you though." Jim glances at me, his lip curled, his eye in a half-wink. He closes his finger over the feather and rips it out before standing and walking back to where I hang. "You'll find out. Soon enough."

"Leave him alone," I whisper to Jim. "He doesn't know anything." For a split-second I wish Sparrow were still crazy, then I might be able to protect him.

"Or what?" Jim holds the tip of the feather to the base of my neck. "What will you do, Meg? You have no idea who you really are. You have no idea *what* you really are." He trails the feather across my neck, from side-to-side, as though he were slicing it open. "Did he at least tell you about this Hell? Your Hell?"

"He said he can't."

"Oh, that's right. He can't because it's his fault you two are here. But I can. What has he told you?"

"He told me he lost me."

"Oh yeah, he lost you. Turned his back on his one duty." I focus behind Jim and see Sparrow's eyes watching us. His chest rising and falling rapidly. "Sounds like a pretty stupid idea to me anyways. Send one warrior to watch over the future of the monarchy." Jim leans into my face, his eyes focused on my lips. I lean back. "Did he tell you why he lost you?"

I shake my head.

"Doesn't surprise me much." Jim wanders in a circle. "Of course, how do you tell your superiors that you've abandoned your post because you're in love with an infant?"

Looking back to Sparrow I see his eyes close and his breathing slow. "What?" I ask.

"I know." Jim chuckles. "It's kinda sick. Falling in love with a baby. I'd run away too. He didn't know who you really were, but I'm sure when he saw how trashy you are, he knew he had to get away."

"Meg–" Sparrow starts but the boot to his throat ends whatever words he was going to say.

"Don't worry about it, bird-man. I'll fill her in on everything. Did you know his kind live a very long time? Your kind, Meg, you're one of them." He waves a hand at Sparrow.

"No, I'm not. I don't have wings," I reply, shaking my head.

"Wings." Jim sneers and walks to Sparrow. "You mean these?" He reaches down and pulls on the tip of Sparrows wings. "Wings... haha!" I watch in horror as he stomps down with his booted foot, crushing the bone.

Sparrow flinches and groans.

"Leave him alone!" I twist my arms in the chains, wishing I could break free from them.

"You see, Meg. You don't have wings because none of the monarchy does. Only their warriors have wings, even the feeble ones." He stops and drops his chin. "Is it clicking in your little brain yet? Meg? You're a fucking princess."

"Shit," I mumble. I look to Sparrow who tips his head in agreement. "You're wrong. I'm not."

"You're wrong." He points at me. "Wish I had known that before I tried to kill you the first time. I could have been a prince. Lived in luxury." Jim sighs and walks toward me. "You killed us that night, Meg. Me and the guys. Shot us dead. Wasn't expecting that." He grinds the feather he's been holding in his hand and drops it to the floor. "We were after you for the money back then. But now, now it's for the blood."

"You took enough of my blood. I needed three transfusions."

"Oh, suck it up. You would have survived without the transfusions. Didn't he tell you?" Jim twists on his heels and points at Sparrow on the floor. "Guess not." Jim shrugs, waltzes over to Sparrow and rips another feather out of his wings. "Let's see, where did I leave off? Oh yeah, you killed us that night. And we bad, bad men descended to the bowels of Hell for what we did."

"It's where you belong."

Jim's eyebrow quirks up. "But is it where you belong?"

"I don't give a fuck."

"You might." Jim holds the most recent feather he's plucked from Sparrow. A bright red one. He taps me on the nose with it. "Did you know that Hell is filled with gossip and murmurings and tales of the lost child of the heavens who would one day show up down here, along with her banished Legion commander?" I swallow hard. This doesn't go unnoticed by Jim. He smiles and tips his head to Sparrow. "Your father here, John, he showed up not long after that little punk Jack smacked him upside his head with his Billy-club, on his way to county lock-up. Guess you woke up from that coma, Meg."

My father stands over Sparrow. He smiles, palms his fist and cracks the knuckles. "Wait 'till that little bastard shows up down here. He's going to get what's coming to him."

"Yes, well, remember, we hope to be out of here by the time Jack meets his maker," Jim adds.

"I hate you both," I breathe out.

"You never really loved either of us anyways, so what does it matter now? Hmm. Where was I? Oh yes, did you know that if the blood of that lost child is spilled, those who drink it can release themselves from the bowels of Hell? We can crawl out of this cesspool as though we never died in the first place."

"So where's your lost child?" I ask Jim with a flatness in my voice like never before.

"Haha! Oh my dear, sweet, trashy, stupid Meg."

"Hey!" I hear Sparrow's voice from behind Jim. He groans as the boot across his neck presses harder. Jim walks to Sparrow, kicks him hard in the side, reaches down and pulls out an entire handful of feathers and tosses them in the air. They flutter to the floor, covering Sparrow.

Jim leans down. "Shut up, dumbass. You got yourself into this mess." He reaches down again, pulling out one of the large gray eagle feathers. "You!" Jim points the tip of the feather at me as he turns and walks swiftly to me with renewed focus. "I didn't just chain your scrawny ass up because I like to see you like this." He brushes the feather over my left cheek. "Although, I admit it's a damn good look for you. I should have tried this when we were living together. Might have made those cold winter nights a little more enjoyable than watching you paint that fuckin' nursery for a baby that was never going to see the light of day." Darkness cloaks Jim's eyes. He drops the feather, reaches forward with both hands and starts unbuttoning my shirt.

"Don't touch me, you bastard!" I jerk my body. The chains jangle but don't loosen.

"I will do with you whatever I please," Jim replies with a swift backhand that makes my vision blurry. "That includes a little fun before spilling your blood." He pulls on my shirt, popping all of the buttons off. He brushes his hand across my abdomen.

A whimper escapes my throat.

"Don't touch her!" Sparrow yells from the ground, struggling against my father's boot.

Jim whips around. "What's wrong, bird-man? Don't want me to lick your candy? Did she tell you how used up she was already? I mean, before me there was, what?" He twists toward me with his finger on his chin. "How many were there before me, slut? At least ten. And then there were the seven just before I died. Did she tell you that already?" Jim turns back to Sparrow, walking swiftly to his side and bending down. "Did she tell you how she enjoyed those seven men as I watched? And she was pregnant at the time! Just like a true strumpet, spreading her legs for anyone."

This time he kicks Sparrow in the side of the skull and I see Sparrow blink rapidly before his head flops to the side.

"Leave him alone!" I scream at Jim.

"Well, now, why would I do that?" A scraping sound in the corner of the cave causes Jim to turn toward the shadows. "Settle down."

I focus on the shadows, my eyes adjusting to the dim light. There are forms standing in a line, watching. "Who are they?"

Jim laughs. "You know them already. Quite well, actually."

He waves a hand. Boots scrape across the rock floor as a group of men step forward. Seven men.

"Fuck," I whisper.

"Yeah. I'd say that too if I were you."

I glance around the room, the severity of our current situation strikes me. We are shit out of luck here.

"Just kill me already. That's what you want."

"Wait." Jim scratches his head. "I was tellin' a fuckin' story but everyone keeps interrupting me." He hollers. "Now, where was I?"

"You were talking bullshit about some lost child you have yet to find," I remind him.

"Oh yes! Thank you so much for reminding me, Meg."

He takes a step closer to me, shakes his index finger in my direction. "You should have died that day. You should have been dead and then we were going to split all that money. It's absurd really, letting your woman live in a strange place, give her lots of money to survive on but only send one stupid Legion Commander to watch over them."

"You don't know anything about my mother."

"I know plenty. Your daddy here filled me in, along with the rumor mill down here. I'm pretty certain I have this little story all figured out. Your pregnant little momma left her home in the heavens to escape a life of royalty, rules, and council meetings so her daughter could have a different life. A free life. One where men didn't rule over her every move. Her lover packed her up with pockets full of money and a baby in her belly, sent her down to play with the humans. But your momma was just as stupid as you are. Found the tiniest town in the North Country, flapped her lips about all the money, shacked up with your demon-daddy over there and wasn't strong enough to get away from him. She was weak. Just like you."

"I'm nothing special. You and him told me that my whole life." I twist my wrists against the chains.

"Of course he told you that. If you knew you carried royal blood from the heavens, I get the feeling you wouldn't have stuck around. But this time, this time you're going to die." Jim reaches behind his back and draws out a dagger. He holds the sharp tip of it to the base of my neck. "You're going to die, just as soon as I get done with that menace over there on the ground."

Jim turns and begins a swift, purposeful walk to where Sparrow lies unconscious on the ground. His shoes make hollow noise as he walks and I know without a doubt that Jim is going to kill Sparrow, right now, in front of me.

"No!" I scream. "No! No! No! Stop!" I scream so loud

that Jim jerks upright and turns back to me, a sick half-smile on his lips.

I look at Sparrow on the ground across from me. The old Meg would have run off and left him there as a distraction. I've been called nothing but trash my entire life and all I've ever done was back up the names with my actions. Never had a reason to act any different, I never had anyone to impress... now I do. I'm not going to listen to them. I'm not going to give them any reasons to think of me like this anymore. Maybe I could do this one good thing. Maybe that could make a difference. With this one act, for once in my life I can stop trying to prove them right. With this death, I can prove them all wrong.

"Stop, please." I beg Jim. "Just leave him alone. Take me. Kill me first. I'm who you want anyway."

"Spilling the blood of royalty will bring us great power, more than enough to deal with big-bird afterwards." John Lewis suggests. I think it's the only good thing he's ever done, agreeing with me, even if he didn't mean it.

I can do this. I tell myself. I can save his life. "Take me first. Just, let him go," I plead.

"Hmm. Bartering on your death bed?" Jim asks.

"You don't need him. You said yourself you only need my blood. So take it. Just promise me you'll let him go."

Jim turns to Sparrow on the ground, and flicks his finger at my father, who then removes his boot from Sparrow's neck and lifts him to stand.

"As you wish, *princess*," Jim says with a sneer as he turns to face me.

This isn't the first time someone has tried to kill me. My blood has been spilled more than once and I get the feeling that maybe Sparrow was right; this is a life I was never meant to live, here or in the earthen realm.

Jim walks toward me, blade in hand. He presses the

point to the base of my neck. "There are no guns for you to find this time." He glances at my bound hands, strung above my head.

"I know," I whisper.

"I'm only doing this because I feel just the tiniest bit awful about you not dying the first time."

The old Meg, she would have told him to fuck off. Maybe even spit in his face, tried to kick him in the balls. I'm pretty sure I did it fifteen minutes ago, but now, now I give him a soft smile. "I will forgive you," I whisper just loud enough for him to hear. And for the first time in my life, I think I might actually mean it. "Thank you."

The last thing I see is Sparrow's face as he opens his eyes to look at me. His handsome features morphing into that of understanding and dread. I try not to remember what he told me about this being his punishment. He can live on. He can find someone else to spend his time with, someone better.

I close my eyes, feel a few hot tears drip down my face, and wait to feel something, the slice of a blade, the puncturing of my heart. Whatever it's going to be, I'm sure it will feel nothing like what I've endured my entire life. At least all that I've been through has prepared me for the pain of death, just not the pain of leaving Sparrow behind.

A white-hot throbbing starts in the middle of my chest, spreads throughout my body. I'm sure what I'm feeling is Jim's blade. It has to be, because no emotion could hurt this bad. A bright light bursts from behind my eyes and I hear my own voice in my ears, screaming. Then there is nothing.

Except... the sound of someone struggling!

I open my eyes to find myself still dangling, a knife sticking out of the center of my chest, and Sparrow wrestling with my ex-father.

Jim slinks toward them, Sparrow's machete in his hand.

He raises his arm, the blade gleaming in the dim firelight. As he brings it down to Sparrow's back, I hear myself yell and then my voice collapses with exhaustion as the blade only hits Sparrow with a blunt force, just like the time I tried to use it against the dead.

Sparrow turns, one hand twisting my ex-father's face, the other grasping the shaft of the machete and twisting it out of Jim's hand. Sparrow moves swiftly, swiping the blade across my father's neck.

Jim steps back. I hear his voice, the voices of those seven men in the shadows as he calls on them to go after Sparrow. I recognize their laughter; it's the same as when they came after me.

Jim looks to me, seeing my eyes open he walks closer. "Good. You're awake. This is about to get interesting."

"You're a bastard."

"Possibly." He shrugs.

"I don't understand how you've become so evil." Noticing the sharp pain of the knife in my chest, I wince, try to slow my breathing.

"I'm surprised you didn't notice before, Meg. Our little podunk town holds more secrets than you have come to realize. I'm more than just the son of a small town sheriff." He gives a satisfied grin. "You think it was a coincidence I showed up downstate at your college campus? It wasn't. And there's a reason why my father wanted you to get an abortion and not taint our bloodlines. Maybe John was right. Maybe you really are just incredibly stupid."

Jim stops talking at the sounds of bodies colliding. Sparrow kicks one of the men in the chest hard enough to knock him down. Turning, he slices the blade across another's throat, sending a spray of blood across his own chest, staining the feathers that peek from behind his shoulders. He swivels and ducks, nearly missing the set of arms coming from behind him. He kicks at another chest, swipes his blade at another throat. Three down, four to go.

Knowing what those men are capable of, watching Sparrow is kind of mesmerizing. I have never seen his body move so fluidly, his focus so intent. He swings the machete, another head drops. Three to go. The floor sticky with the fluids of death, Sparrow's footing slips and he goes down, rolling to his side, away from the last three. Like a vulture to a carcass they descend on him, but Sparrow slices at their legs, bringing two more down. The last man gives Sparrow a hard blow to the chest with his elbow. It doesn't seem to faze Sparrow; he's on his feet and swinging, bringing the last man down before turning to the two injured ones on the ground and finishing them.

I turn. Jim is no longer at my side pestering me with tiny clues. Sparrow takes in his surroundings, breathing heavy, before making eye contact with me.

"Meg!" Sparrow runs to me. He glances at the knife in my chest. "Don't look at that." I don't, I only look at him. He's sweating, tense, covered in blood–his own and others. "I have to pull this out." He reaches for the knife.

"No! Wait. I don't think you're supposed to do that."

He grips the blade. "I can't leave it in."

"Sparrow!" I gasp, fearing the pain.

"Hold your breath. I'll count to three."

I nod, taking a deep breath. Waiting to hear his words.

"Ready?"

I nod again.

"Three." He pulls the blade and drops it to the floor.

"Sparrow!"

"What?"

"You ass, you didn't even count!"

"I know." The corner of his mouth tips up in a quick

grin. "Oh crap." His voice turns gruff as I feel his hands on my chest, covering the knife wound.

I've seen my blood before, as I lay on the floor of my house. For some reason this time it seems to exit my body faster, maybe it's because I'm strung up like a turkey. "It's bad?" I ask.

"You'll live."

"Jim..." I look around to see if he has re-appeared. "He said I'd live forever?"

Sparrow tilts his head. "Unless you suffer a mortal wound."

"Like what?"

"Like... let's talk about that later." I look down to see thick streams of blood dripping around his fingers.

"A wound like this?" I start to panic.

Sparrow's brow furrows. "Let's hope not. I have to get you down from there." His hands leave my chest as he reaches for the metal clasps around my wrists. My blood drips down his arms and the chains he touches.

"Where's Jim?" I ask.

"Ran off."

"Are you serious?"

"Said he'd catch up with us later."

"What a loser."

"No f-bombs?" Sparrow asks as I feel the metal loosen from around my wrists.

"I'm not feeling very feisty right now," I mumble, fighting the heavy feeling in my eyelids. "I think I've felt like this before. I think I've lost too much blood."

There's a sharp clang, my arms drop. Sparrow catches me and lowers me to the ground. "You'll be fine. You just need to rest and heal." I feel his hands move to the wound on my chest and resume pressure.

"Sparrow?"

"What?" His eyes search the room as I speak.

"I'm sorry I gave up."

"You didn't give up." His eyes are back on mine.

"Yes I did. Twice now. Back on the road and here, just now. I'm sorry. It was selfish."

"It's okay. You gave your life for me even though you barely know me. That is admirable." I feel him lessen the pressure on my wound.

It hurts, not the wound, but having spent all these weeks with the crazy Sparrow and to have him change on me. "You're some kind of a warrior?" I ask.

He nods. "I haven't been for about twenty-five years. That was part of my punishment for losing you. I was expelled from the Legion, the collection of warriors from the heavens."

"You knew you loved me when I was a baby?"

Sparrow's face drops and he leans away from me. I know this look: shame.

"I know it was wrong. That's why I left. That's why this is my fault. All of it."

I move my hand over his. "No, it's fine. It's… sweet. In a fucked up kind of way. No one has ever really cared about me enough to say they love me. I remember that from my life. Those words never came out of my father's mouth or Jim's."

Sparrow looks at me, his eyes sad even though he smiles slightly. "I should be the one apologizing."

"Why?"

"Because I gave up on you just like everyone else. I didn't know who you were. I judged you, hated the position I was put in, and look where that led."

"But you're here now."

"I'm not sure if that's enough."

"I hope it is." I stare at the rocky ceiling, swallow hard.

"So if I survive this, what comes next?"

"You'll survive. You know who you are now."

"I think so, if what Jim said was the truth. It's still kinda blowing my mind though."

"Good. Can you walk? We have to get out of here before they regenerate."

"Who?"

He tips his head toward the decapitated corpses. "Come on." Sparrow stretches an arm under my shoulders and helps me stand. What little blood is left in my body seems to trickle to my feet, leaving me light-headed and wobbly. Sparrow holds me tight to his side as we walk to a shadowed corner of the cave. In the dim torchlight I can see a dark hallway.

"How do we get out?"

"This way. If I remember correctly."

"Did you see how they got us in here?"

"Yeah."

"Can't you do that thing to make us poof back to the real world?" I ask, almost out of breath.

"Poof?" He chuckles a little. "I guess that's a good name for it. I don't do that, you do. And you're too weak right now."

"Me?"

"Yeah, you. Normally, we can't do that."

"Oh." His grip tightens across my shoulders, my head spins. "Sparrow?"

"Yeah." I hear a few stones roll under his feet and echo in the granite hallway Sparrow has walked us to.

"I think I'm going to faint."

"Just hang in there."

My head feels dizzy, my skin like it's on fire, and my vision blurs just as my knees give out.

"Told you," I whisper as everything goes to black.

SHIT JUST GOT REAL...
FUCKED UP

"WILL SHE BE OKAY?" I hear Sparrow's concerned voice.

This is followed by a much more feminine voice. "She's fine. She's coming around now."

When my eyes flutter open it seems we are still in the cave. I try to sit up, only to be stopped with a firm hand pressing on my shoulder. "No. You stay down," the female voice tells me.

Turning to face the sound, I find a woman at my side. She has a strong nose, large hazel eyes, and short cropped blonde hair. The downy white feathers visible from behind her shoulders don't go unnoticed. She's striking.

"Who are you?" I ask.

She leans back and presses her perfectly pouty lips into a thin line before standing and walking away from my side.

Sparrow takes her place. The blood and gore have been cleaned off him, his bare chest replaced with a black shirt stretched tight across his shoulders.

"Who is that?"

"That's Teari." He leans back. "And this is Marcus." He

gestures to a dark skinned man of similar build near where Teari went to stand.

"What are they doing here?"

"Reinforcements. It seems Jim has been up to no good down here. The Legion got word of what he's been doing." He glances at my chest. "And you needed healing."

"How did they get here?"

"Seems your real father is a bit impatient. Sent them to help."

"No, I mean, how?" I wince at the sharp pain in my chest.

"Oh, there's a portal, a long ways from here. On true hallowed ground."

"How long until we get there?" I ask, hopeful for this to end.

Sparrow starts to shake his head.

"We're not done?" I ask.

"No."

My head falls back in disappointment, *thunking* on the hard rock underneath me. "Ow."

"Meg." Sparrow's voice drops just above a whisper. "Can you do something for me?"

"What?"

He leans close, the smell of him igniting those tingles deep in my stomach. "Don't tell them how crazy I was. Don't let them know what I was like before I remembered everything. The feathers, the... all of it. Just forget it all."

Tingles gone.

"Why?"

He glances back at Teari and Marcus, who I see are tall, lean and winged, just like him. But their wings aren't broken. "I don't want them to know me like that."

"Like what, Sparrow?"

"Weak."

"You weren't weak," I remind him. "You kept me alive."

"I wasn't strong enough. I almost dove into a river of the dead to go after those feathers. I remember."

"And us?"

"What about us?" he asks as he stands, his tone completely nonchalant.

I get a sinking feeling in my chest. Now that Sparrow is surrounded by his peers, everything is going to change, including how he acts toward me. I shouldn't be surprised, no matter who I am now, it's the same way everyone has acted toward me.

"Whatever," I mutter. As I move to stand Sparrow reaches down to help me. I push his hand away. "No. Don't touch me."

"What's wrong?" Sparrow steps closer.

Teari and Marcus turn to watch us.

I would like to punch him in the throat and I'm sure it wouldn't look so bad, now that he's not crazy anymore. "I don't need your pity."

"I don't pity you."

"And I don't need you telling them what happened to me." The faces of those doctors flash through my memory, the looks they gave me as I sat in that hospital bed.

"I'm not going to tell them anything."

"Then why do they keep looking at me like that?"

"Like what?" Sparrow turns to the other two.

"Like they don't trust me."

"They don't. But they will, Meg. Just give them time. The only thing they know is that I was banished because of you. They know nothing more about you."

"And now they've been sent down here to clean up the mess?"

"No. They've been sent down here to help us. This is what the Legion does, keeps the demons of Hell in check.

Your Father, your real father, wants Jim dead for all he's done to you. And Teari has already started healing you. What more do you want?"

I want to scream at him. That's what I want. I want to scream in his face and point out the fact that I just gave my life for him. I just took a knife to the chest to save him, and in return he wants me to keep the weeks we spent together a secret. He wants me to forget collecting all those feathers, gluing him back together, watching him smile at me as though he didn't have a care in the world. Those moments with him are some of the best I've ever had in my pathetic life.

I stand, feeling the rush of lightheadedness and a sharp pain in my chest. Looking down I see that my shirt is torn, stained with blood, hanging open. I grip it closed as I try to steady myself, my fingers rubbing against the bandage taped to my chest.

"You need to sit," Sparrow warns me.

"I don't need to do shit. Get away from me."

"Meg," he warns, as I take a few shaky steps and fall flat on my face.

...

"You need to get your human under control," Teari warns Sparrow.

I turn my head and see them standing outside an open door. It seems we've moved from the cavern to a house, or a... trailer. Perfect. I look around the dim room; find my backpack on the floor and a bed under me.

Sparrow's eyes lock on Teari in a completely pissed way.

"She's not human. You know that. That wound would have killed a normal human."

The bedsprings squeak under me as I move. Marcus reaches out with one long, dark arm and slaps the door closed. They start talking again, muffled, but still clear enough for me to make out.

"She's slowing us down. We could've been done with this by now. Killed Jim and flown to the portal in no time, instead of waiting in this shitty trailer for her to heal."

"Did you forget I can't fly, Teari?" Sparrow's voice sounds agitated. "And you need her. She was engaged to Jim. She can draw him out. He wants her."

"That sack-a-shit Jim only wants her so he can escape from here. What makes you think she won't help him?" I hear the deep voice of Marcus.

"She would never help him," Sparrow replies.

"How can you be so sure?" Marcus asks.

"He stuck a knife in her chest, among other things."

"The King will be pissed if you screw this up, Sparrow. I'm pretty sure this is your last chance at redemption," Teari warns.

"Yeah, I know!"

"Then why don't we forget about her and get moving?" Marcus urges.

"Because I left her once and it wasn't good."

"What are you talking about?" asks Teari's unconcerned voice.

"Twenty-five years ago one of our own left to live amongst the humans. She was pregnant with the King's child."

"He has hundreds of children."

"Not like her."

The mocking voice of Marcus sounds next. "What makes her so special? We saw her tattoos, her scars. We know her kind. She teach you how to play beer pong or something else that shows more skin?"

The sound of a hard thud against the wall shocks my eyes open. Boots shuffle, all three voices are shouting at each other, followed by the unmistakable sound of someone getting punched.

"You have no idea what we've been through. What she has been through." Sparrow's voice is angry. He's pissed, worse than when I tried to peek under his coat that one day. "If neither of you want to help then go back."

"We can't go back," Marcus' strained voice replies. "We are under strict orders to kill Jim Sullivan and John Lewis and bring you both back."

The conversation seems to end with the sound of footsteps that stop outside the door. Sparrow steps in and closes the door behind him. He glances at me before dropping to one knee and searching my backpack.

"What are you doing?" I ask.

"Looking for a change of clothes. That shirt has seen better days."

I look down at myself and see the same ripped, stained shirt I had on before I fell flat on my face. Moving my hand to my chin, I wince, feeling a few rough scabs and a raised welt. I run my tongue across my teeth to make sure they're all still here.

"Don't mind them," Sparrow continues as he pulls out a clean shirt.

"Why don't they know about me?" I ask. "Everyone down here does."

"We are a very stubborn breed. You don't win the wars of good and evil by trusting everyone. They'll come around."

I lay back on the bed. "It's fine. It's not like I haven't

been treated like that my entire life. I'm just wondering what comes next, the trailer park jokes or the idiot jokes."

Sparrow stands over me, gripping my blue shirt in his hands. "No jokes allowed from them." He sits on the edge of the bed. "Sit up. I'll help you get that off." He motions to my torn shirt. "Your father wants Jim dead," he tells me as I move.

"I heard. So why am I here?" I pull the torn shirt from my shoulders and toss it on the floor.

"You're too weak to *poof* yourself out of here. We kill Jim, John, and then travel back to the portal which will transport us home."

"Two birds with one stone, huh?"

"Yeah." Sparrow glances down at the shirt in his hands.

"Are you going to give me that so I can put it on?" His eyes settle on the bandage in the middle of my chest. "Sparrow?" His eyes drop lower.

"No one has ever given their life for me," he says softly.

"Me either. And no one has ever asked me to forget all of the things that made me love them."

Sparrow tips his head. "I don't want you to forget them." His eyes are on mine as he leans closer to me. "It seems I am always losing you or watching someone try to kill you."

"That seems to be a repeating theme in my life."

"I'm not letting you out of my sight, ever again."

"Well, in that case, can I have my shirt?" I shiver, not from the cold, but from the closeness of Sparrow sitting next to me, the heat radiating off him, heat that my body is currently craving.

His eyes graze down my body. He tosses the shirt across the room. "Nope."

"Sparrow–" he muffles my protests with a kiss. Warm lips, wet tongue, it's enough to make me forget what those other two said about me. As his mouth moves to my neck I ask, "I thought we needed to find Jim?"

"Not until you're better and not in the daylight."

"Who is Jim, really?"

Sparrow sits back, his hands kneading my shoulders. "The son of a very bad demon."

"But, his father was the Sheriff."

Sparrow shakes his head. "Nope, that was his Watcher, like a babysitter. Sometimes demons can get out of here, just like we can get out of Heaven, and live amongst the humans."

I press my fingers to my head. "But, I don't understand how those corpses walk down here. And Noah... he was normal-ish, until he turned."

Sparrow pulls my hands away from my face and tucks the loose strands of hair behind my ears in a sweet movement that tears at my heart. "When you are new down here, freshly dead, your soul remains as it was when you were alive, looking normal and human. It's so they can find a Safe House and repent. Get one last chance at Heaven."

"And if they don't go to a Safe House?"

"Then they wake up a walking corpse and this is their Hell."

"But it looks so normal down here, just... darker."

"It is."

I shiver again. "How did I get down here? Did I die? Was I not really in a coma?"

Sparrow rubs my bare arms. "You were in a coma, your soul teetering until we found each other and you woke. Now, you are very much alive. You can *poof* yourself, your whole body, between realms. If you are here, you are not on the earthen plane, and when you are on the earthen plane you are not in Hell. Understand?"

"This is so fu–" I press my fingers to my lips, stopping myself from finishing that sentence.

"Hm. Seems you remember my warning." I catch a glimpse of humor in his eyes.

"Oh, I remember," I smile. "I'm not allowed to say fuck around you."

He leans closer. "You know what's going to happen now."

"Won't they hear us?" I look to the closed door as my head hits the pillow.

"No. I'll be quiet and slow."

"You were slow last time," I remind him. Painfully slow and sinfully good.

"Then this might take forever." Sparrow shifts on the bed, toeing his boots off in the process, pressing me down on the mattress.

I run my hands over his shoulders. "I see you've finally found a shirt." I pinch the thin cotton between my fingers, wanting to feel his skin instead of the soft fabric.

"You like it?" he grins, running his hand through my hair, pressing his lips to the corner of my mouth.

"I'd like it better off." I reach for the hem of his shirt.

He shifts again, sitting up on his hip, raising his arms to pull the shirt over his head. "As you wish."

Sunlight filters in from the small window near the bed, a few faint scars are visible across Sparrow's arms and chest. I run my fingers over a long mark on his bicep. "What's this from?"

"Battle, long ago." He reaches for my bra, eyes fixed on mine as he flicks his finger across the clasp.

I forget about the marks on his skin and focus on the warmth, the strength, the intensity radiating off him.

...

Sparrow leans over me, propped up on one elbow. "I'm sorry I didn't warn you before touching you."

I smile. "It's okay. I like it when you touch me."

He runs a finger across my collarbone. "Me too."

"How will you kill Jim if they can regenerate?" I ask.

"Burn the body."

"Why didn't we do that before?"

"Never had matches or enough time while we were running."

"Oh." I look around the room, my head thrumming with questions.

"Ask," Sparrow urges.

"So, Teari and Marcus, they eat sunlight and never sleep like you?"

Sparrow chuckles. "They eat food and sleep. Just do less of both than you do."

"Oh. And you?"

Sparrow frowns and looks away for a moment before shifting, moving so we are eye to eye. Noticing the piece of broken wing jutting out from behind his back, I reach out and touch it. "Did it hurt?"

"Not as much as watching Jim stab that knife into your chest." He tips his shoulder away from me while drawing my hand down with his, holding it to his bare chest.

I shiver at the memory of Jim stomping on Sparrow's wing.

"Let's get you dressed." Sparrow sits, pulling me up with him. "Then you can sleep."

I stand, steadying myself with my hand on the wall. I manage my underwear, jeans, socks and bra by myself. Sparrow collects the shirt he got out for me and walks to me with it in his hand.

"You look pale," Sparrow says.

I tip my head, not quite able to find my words. My head turns foggy, vision blurs.

"Shit." Sparrow takes my shoulders in his hands, leads me to the bed and sits me down. "I think standing was a bad idea." He stretches the shirt over my head. I glance down to see blood staining the bandage on my chest.

"Maybe it wasn't the standing," I mumble, feeling awfully lightheaded.

"Lay down."

He doesn't have to tell me twice. I drop onto my side on the bed. Feeling the mattress give as Sparrow settles next to me, I roll slightly. He tucks his chin into my neck, wraps an arm around my stomach. "Sleep, Meg," he whispers in my ear. "I won't leave you." He presses a kiss to my shoulder.

"Promise?" I ask.

"A promise is a promise." He gives me a slight squeeze as I feel myself drift off to sleep.

"Can you sing to me?" It's been days since I last heard him hum Bon Jovi before bed. "Is that still allowed?"

"Sure, they won't think anything of that. Always been a Bon Jovi fan."

"Sing something for me?" I ask, wanting so badly to have a glimpse back at that sweet and crazy Sparrow, even if it's just for a few minutes.

"Sure, Meg." He starts to hum *Always*.

...

TEARI STANDS POSSESSIVELY at my side, giving Sparrow dirty looks. Even in the moonlight, with the way she twists her face at Sparrow, she looks stunning. It's strange watching her act like this. I've never had a woman act protective of me. I heard her giving Sparrow flack about the time he spent alone with me. She said she knows we weren't just sleeping and she couldn't heal me if he wasn't going to keep his pants on.

Now, with her standing next to me as we decide which route to take, I am hit with a sudden feeling of inadequateness; it's like setting caviar next to a slug. She's tall. Almost as tall as Sparrow. Which would put her over six feet. And with Marcus being just as tall as Sparrow, I suddenly feel very short with my completely average height of five-foot-six.

I get a good look at Marcus; his dark features, olive skin and even darker hair. He's wearing black cargo pants, boots and a gray shirt. Just like Teari. But Marcus has added straps across his thigh, biceps and chest that hold a variety of weapons. I try to contain a shudder. He's intimidating, even when he's not looking at you.

Sparrow wears his coat once again. The only difference is this time it's not buttoned up to his neck. It's hanging open, the fitted shirt visible. I wonder if they've asked him where the colorful feathers came from, since theirs are a downy white and his are... not.

I stand there and listen as they prepare a plan to find Jim, cut his head off, and burn the corpse.

I look around, not recognizing the area. "Where are we?"

"Southern New York," Marcus replies quickly, his voice curt. I get the feeling he still would rather me not be here.

I turn to look at him and notice a raised bruise across his left cheekbone. No doubt Sparrow gave it to him yesterday when he was talking about me. It looks like it hurts.

That was the first time anyone has ever stuck up for me. Never once did anyone stand up to the way my father or Jim treated me. The entire town simply turned a blind eye.

"We need to keep going south." Marcus points down the road we stand in.

Sparrow nods. "To the burning caves? I was hoping we wouldn't have to take her there." He nods in my direction.

"What are the burning caves?" I ask.

"You might know the area as Centralia, Pennsylvania." Teari turns to me. "In the human realm, the earthen planes, it's a place of ever-burning underground mines. Here, there are still fires but it's the demons' home. We have our castle, they have their cave."

"You live in a castle?" I ask.

She nods. "Some are nicer than others, but yes."

The thought of living in a castle pretty much blows my mind. Especially with the images of that shitty trailer I grew up with so fresh in my memories.

"That's over a hundred miles from here." Sparrow stands with his feet apart, hands on his hips, and his brow creased. "Since we've lost the Jeep, that trek is going to take us a while."

"We could fly," Marcus suggests.

"That would do nothing but warn them ahead of time. We've got to stay hidden," Teari tells them as she eyes me apprehensively. "She's injured and I'm not carrying Sparrow on my back."

"I can go by myself," Marcus suggests. "I'll keep low, scout the area, find a vehicle and shelter for when the sun rises."

Marcus and Teari both eye Sparrow's coat. Awkward wouldn't even describe the moments that pass. Sparrow's nostrils flare. Teari's eyes flick to the bandage on my chest. Marcus rubs his jaw.

"Night's not getting any darker," Sparrow finally breaks

the silence as he reaches for my hand. "Let's get walking. I'm sure we'll find a ride on the way there."

We walk, the road feeling crowded with four. Sparrow keeps a tight grip on my hand as I hear the other two murmuring behind us.

...

We stop at a crossroads. From the signs we've passed I know we're near the Pennsylvania border but for the last few miles the road signs have been too damaged to read or cut off their metal supports. I guess they don't have road crews in Hell.

Teari and Marcus are close behind us; we wait for them to catch up.

Feeling a sharp pain in my chest, I glance down, noticing the blood seeping through the white bandage taped there. I pull my shirt over it and move my free arm across my stomach. The last thing I need is them thinking I'm weak, more than they already do.

"What do you think, Meg?" Sparrow asks from my side, taking my free hand.

It's been so long since any of them asked me my opinion that it takes me a moment to answer. "I don't know these roads. I never made it any further south than Cortland."

Sparrow nods. "There are three directions we could go in."

"You lost?" Marcus asks as he gets closer.

"Crossroads." Teari shakes her head. "You need to get in the air," she tells Marcus. "See which route is the best."

I watch, in awe, as he spreads his wings and in one

powerful movement, thrusts himself into the night sky. Teari watches him before her eyes move to Sparrow.

"He's just being cautious," she says.

"He's just being a dick," Sparrow replies.

"You used to be the same way, Sparrow. I remember a time when Marcus was new to the Legion and you gave him flack at every turn. He's grown since you've been gone. Twenty-five years can change one of us. You of all people should know that. You were his mentor, he looked up to you and then when you were banished... it took a long time for him to come around."

"Then why did the King send him?"

"Maybe it's because you need each other, more than you think. You were like a father to him. Do you know what it's like going on for twenty-five years thinking someone you hold as close as family is as good as dead? That's what we were told, Sparrow. The King said you failed and you were banished. We all know the punishment you received. Being sent down here without your memories, not knowing who or what you really are. That's enough to drive one of us crazy. That's enough to get one of us killed."

Sparrow's entire body stiffens; his grip on my hand tightens. I grit my teeth; try to keep my face emotionless. I try my best not to give away Sparrow's secret: he was crazy, bat-shit crazy.

"Since you've been gone, leadership in the Legion has been... pitiable. Marcus was just about to take your place. The King was going to make an announcement, and then we got word that you were down here and needed help." There is a long pause. "You're hurting her." Teari tips her head toward our hands.

I look down and see that my fingertips are blanched white. Sparrow drops my hand and turns away from us, facing the open roads ahead. "Doesn't matter," Sparrow mutters. "I'm done with that. I doubt the King will reappoint me after all this."

"Like I said, it hasn't been the same without you."

Sparrow's only response is a grunt of dissatisfaction.

"How's your injury?" Teari asks, taking a step closer to me.

I tighten my grip on my shirt. "It's fine."

"You're not supposed to be able to lie." She narrows her eyes at me. It's a distrustful look, one that these two have been giving me as soon as they showed up.

I sigh and open my shirt for her to see. She frowns at the blood soaked bandage. "We need to get you someplace to rest."

Just as soon as the words are out of her mouth a harsh breeze brushes by us and Marcus lands behind Teari.

"What did you find?" she asks him.

"There's a few vehicles off the highway, maybe thirty miles down that road." He points to the road that veers off to the left.

"Is that the road to the burning caves?" Teari asks.

He shakes his head no and points to the empty road straight ahead of us. "That road leads directly to the burning caves."

"So why don't we take that road?" Sparrow asks, turning to face us.

"Because that road is littered with corpses that will rise with the sun and nothing but forest on either side. We need to go around. There's an old town not far from here. We can find shelter for the day, maybe get a car running." He looks directly at me. "We're moving too slow. Before long the rumor mill will get around to Jim that we're all here and looking for him."

"I'm sure he's looking for me too," I reply. "Jim wants

my blood and he's already shown that he plans on getting it."

Marcus glares at me. "Let's get moving. Daylight is coming and if we walk any slower those corpses might catch up with us."

...

THERE IS A SMALL TOWN. Small and deserted. As we near it, Teari stops in the middle of the road. "There's a Safe House here." She turns to Marcus. "Why didn't you tell us there's a Safe House here?"

Marcus shrugs. "We can't go in those. I didn't think it would matter."

"They can direct us to shelter and give us supplies, food."

"Why can't we go in them?" I ask. "I did."

"That's forbidden. Why didn't you stop her?" Marcus asks Sparrow, his voice escalating. "You know the reprimand for one of us going in those places."

"Her soul was on the edge. She was in a coma. And how was I supposed to remember? That's what happens when someone takes your memories; you don't remember things like that," Sparrow replies.

"Shit." Marcus brushes a hand over his close-cropped hair. "Did you go in? Where were you while she was in Quarantine?"

Sparrow shrugs. "I was outside."

"What did they say to you?" Marcus asks me.

"They just questioned me. I told them I was looking for Jim. But that was before I remembered that he tried to kill me."

"Fuck!" Marcus shakes his head and walks in a tight circle. "We are fucked if they recognize you." He jabs his finger in the air toward me. "Their Deacons are the biggest gossipers of any. They have their ear to the ground, searching for others to repent. That's all they care about; numbers–how many souls they can send to the heavens. They'll do anything and that includes selling gossip to the demons down here."

"Settle down, Marcus," Teari starts in a calming voice. "They obviously didn't recognize them. We have our own people in the Safe Houses, we would have heard something."

"I still don't trust them." He glares at me and I know what he's saying, he trusts me even less now. Marcus turns to Sparrow. "What did you do after? You two have been down here a long time. Where did you go?"

I wait to hear if Sparrow is going to confess that we trekked across the state searching for feathers, that we spent a week in an abandoned church while I glued them on his wings.

"It doesn't matter what we did." Sparrow takes a step closer to Marcus, his hands balled into tight fists.

"Calm down, boys." Teari steps between them, laying a hand on each of their shoulders. "We need to move. Morning's coming and Meg can't outrun the dead. Not in her condition."

We walk an uncomfortable, tense walk. The only sound is the echo of our shoes on the crumbling pavement.

We pass the Safe House on our way into town. A prison, surrounded by chain-link fence, topped with barbed-wire, just like in Kingston. The guards at the gate stare at us, an intense gaze. Teari walks over to them, leaving us in the middle of the street. One of the guards points down a narrow road and places something in Teari's hand.

"There's a secure house up here. They said we can stay there." Teari tells us when she returns. We follow in the direction the guard pointed, the morning getting brighter with each step we take. Finally we come upon a barricaded, empty house. Teari reaches for the gate lock, holding a key in her hand from the guard. Just as she turns the key there is movement in the streets, a moaning and stumbling I recognize as the dead waking and walking.

"Hurry up," Sparrow urges Teari as he steps closer to me, drawing his machete from where it's attached to his waistband. Marcus does the same, ready for action.

The chain link fence rattles. Teari swears as she twists the key and jerks on the lock.

"Let's go..." Marcus warns.

I back against the fence, unable to see over Sparrow's shoulders. He backs against me, so close it presses me harder into the fence. There is a loud clang, followed by the squeal of the fence gate opening.

"We're in!" Teari announces. She pulls on my arm, dragging me through the gate and into the secure yard. Sparrow and Marcus follow, slamming the gate and locking it.

The house is small, single-story. We enter through the garage door. There's a Jeep parked in it.

Marcus opens the driver's side door. "Gassed up and stocked, the key is in the ignition. Guess we'll be getting to the burning caves in no time."

"Why do we only seem to find Jeeps here?" I ask.

"Last American car company that hasn't sold production overseas," Teari responds.

"Oh," I respond, not understanding what the hell she's referring to.

Teari continues, "The only way the majority shareholders could keep the company American-made was to make a deal with the devil. As a result, the demons down here get a few freebies every year. Drive them through the portal between here and the human realm."

"So what happened to the other car companies?"

Teari shrugs. "Not sure. But I do know one company that made a good deal."

"Which one's that?"

"Let's just say we've got Cadillacs up there," she gestures at the sky.

Okay, that's got to be the weirdest shit I've ever heard. But it's a car, which means no more walking and less time for conversation. I hope.

...

JUST AS I'M raiding the cupboards, dipping a spoon into a jar of peanut butter while simultaneously reaching for a box of crackers, there's a knock on the door. Sparrow closes the fridge and stands up straight, two bottles of water in his hand. Marcus moves for the door.

The dead don't knock, they moan and barge in.

"Who is it?" I ask Sparrow.

He shrugs and walks closer to me. Twisting the cap on the bottle of water and handing it to me. "You need to drink something."

I decide to lick the peanut butter off the spoon first.

Marcus opens the door, steps aside. I recognize the figure on the front step. The clothing mostly. It's a Deacon.

Marcus lets him in. "What are you doing here?" Marcus asks.

"There's a bounty on your heads," the Deacon warns, hooking his finger into his collar and pulling on it. "The payment is a good one, one-hundred and fifty souls to repent. I've come to warn you."

"You've come to turn us in," Teari counters, walking toward the man dressed in black.

"Maybe I have." The Deacon swipes nervously at his brow. "A bounty like that is hard to come by. That's one-hundred and fifty souls to send to the heavens and secure my place there when my time is done here. And since you all just showed up here, so close to the burning caves, I could have them here in no time to collect you." His eyes flick to me. "Now. Tell me why I shouldn't."

"We'll tell King Gabriel what you have planned." Teari says. "You'll never secure your place in the heavens."

"The King is weak, withering, bored. That's the only reason why he sent help to find his lost daughter. He needs some excitement in his life before he dies. None of you will make it out of here alive." The Deacon's eyes move to Sparrow. "You're pretty much already dead."

"We're making it out of here. The King wants Jim dead. Tell us how to get to him and I'll put a personal word in for you. That's better than all those souls," Teari says.

The Deacon's eyes flick between us.

"What do we have to do to draw him out?" Teari asks.

"There's only one thing Jim wants and that's her blood." The Deacon points at me. "There's never been a bounty that high before. For anyone. Who are you?"

The Deacon steps closer to me, gets blocked by Teari moving between us. "She's no one. Just a lost soul passing through."

The Deacon's eyes narrow on Teari. "Lying is not one of your strong suits, cherub."

Marcus grabs the Deacon from behind, holding his machete to the Deacon's neck. "You're staying with us. Until we're ready to leave. Teari! Get me some rope."

Sparrow wraps an arm around my shoulders. I set my spoon on the counter, suddenly full. "Come on." Sparrow pulls me to his side. "Let's find a room for you to rest. Let them take care of the Deacon."

...

Something helped me sleep like the dead. I'm not sure if it was the clean sheets, the warmth of Sparrow's body next to me, or the thought that finally I have people on my side, people who might actually care for me. It's a feeling that I've never experienced before in my life.

When I wake up Sparrow is gone. I roll over, my feet dropping to the floor. There are clean clothes on the chair near the door. While putting them on I hear the sound of voices down the hall.

I turn the door handle slowly, trying to make as little noise as possible. As I reach the living room, Sparrow is there, with Teari and Marcus sitting on the simple furniture. The Deacon is gone.

"Nothing brings those fuckers running like a party. The Deacon already confirmed that. Give them food and a spectacle. That will draw him out." Marcus turns to me, gives me a knowing look.

"So who's the food and who's the spectacle?" I ask, crossing the living room, taking a seat next to Sparrow on the threadbare plaid couch.

"You're the food." Marcus says with a curt tone. "The spectacle will have to be a fight."

"That sounds wonderful. Tie me onto a spit and light a flame. So, who will fight?" I ask.

Marcus glares at Sparrow, and that's all the answer I

need. If they were once chummy, they no longer are. Whatever bond Teari mentioned is long gone.

"What about Teari?" I ask.

"She can stand by," Marcus answers. "Get to the portal and get help if we need it."

"We won't need it," Sparrow interrupts. "This plan is not happening."

I exhale a breath I didn't know I was holding and ignore Sparrow's warning. "So you want to string me up like a hooker under a streetlamp and wait for him to come and get me?"

"No. Not happening." Sparrow steps forward. "We aren't going to hang her like a fresh piece of meat for him and his kind. They'll tear her apart."

Teari and Marcus look at each other, then me. There's no other choice. This is the fastest way. "I'll do it," I say.

"Meg, you can't!" Sparrow stands and shouts at me.

"I can, Sparrow. There's nothing I want more than to see Jim gone forever." Sparrow shakes his head. Hating the feeling of him towering over me, I stand. "Besides, if it gets too dangerous I'll just *poof* myself out of there."

"You think you're strong enough for that?" he asks. "You think you're strong enough to go up against him, again. Twice now, he's almost killed you–"

"And everyone I've known stood by and watched," I remind him. As soon as the words exit my mouth, I see the pained expression on Sparrow's face. Knowing what I just did, I feel like shit. I just punched him in the ball-sack where he keeps all that guilt stored up.

He said he wouldn't be able to deal with losing me again. This plan is just pushing his limits. Sparrow's head tilts to the side and he studies me for just a moment before reaching behind him and plucking one of the feathers off his wings. He twirls it in front of his face, his focus narrowing on the damaged dark colored feather just before he turns and leaves the room.

A warning, that's what that action was. A fear sinks into me that maybe he's relapsing, maybe he's going back to crazy and his greatest fear, the others seeing him like this, may come true.

I close my eyes, take a deep breath, focus on the feeling deep in my gut. My fear of Sparrow regressing seems to be overshadowed by the gnawing need to ruin Jim for all he's put me through. To be free of Jim and that thing that raised me, there's nothing more that I want at this second.

Looking down at the bandage covering my chest, I start to peel it away. My wound hasn't bled in a while and I'm curious. Underneath there is a faint red line from where Jim stabbed me.

Teari moves closer to me and holds her hand over the wound. "It's not fully healed, but enough," she says as she moves her hand away and looks toward the door.

"Where's the Deacon?" I ask.

Teari frowns. "Sent him back."

"And he'll keep his mouth shut?"

She gives a quick nod.

"What's wrong with Sparrow?" I ask, sensing something.

"You should go to him," she says softly, concern flooding her voice.

I walk to the door, opening it and walking to the enclosed yard. Sparrow is bent over the narrow sidewalk. Something dark lies on the cement.

"Sparrow?" I ask, walking to him.

He reaches out, nudging the mass on the ground. As I walk closer in the early evening light, my eyes focus on the object. I see the gleam of its pointy beak, the twig-like legs lying lifeless. It's a dead bird, left here like a taunt.

"Sparrow!" I run to him, my hand landing on his shoulder as he reaches out and rips the feathers out of the wings. Oh God, Oh God, I thought he was done with this. I thought he was over this! "Sparrow! They'll see you," I warn him.

"Good."

"But... I thought you didn't want them to know how crazy you were?" I whisper.

"I am."

"What?"

"How crazy I am."

He stands to his full height of six and a half feet, towering over me, thrusting a handful of feathers into his pocket.

"You're not–" I start but he cuts me off.

"We need to leave." He weaves around me and walks toward the garage.

...

TEARI DRIVES the Jeep at breakneck speed as I sit in the backseat with Sparrow. He doesn't touch me. He doesn't look at me. He just stares out the window into the night. I hear his hand in his pocket. And I know what he's doing, touching the feathers in there.

Hours pass. The night blurs. Every now and then I catch the Jeep's headlights illuminating a road sign that points to some small Pennsylvania town.

Finally, Teari pulls off the side of the road and parks the Jeep in the shadows of the trees. "We can walk the rest of the way," she says as she shuts the Jeep off and sets the keys in the cup holder.

We walk down the road, fear seeping into my chest as I realize what I'm about to do. Offer myself up to Jim on a freakin' platter and hope to heaven that these people come and save me.

The road turns bumpy. The asphalt broken, shifted at odd angles. The cover of the trees is gone and in the early morning light I can see nothing but open space, dead grass and trees, and smoke rising from breaks in the ground. It smells like sulfur.

We stop at a withered tree with nothing but hard-packed dirt ground surrounding it for a few hundred yards.

Marcus stands with his hands on his hips. "This should be a good spot." He kicks at the ground.

Teari walks toward me, pulling a short knife out of the holster on her waist. "I need to cut open your wound, just a little."

I look to Sparrow, hoping to get some type of notion from him that it's okay. He still won't look at me. I unbutton the top of my shirt, pull the clean bandage off. Teari uses the knife to open the wound, just enough to make it bleed. I hear myself take a sharp intake of breath as she punctures my skin, slides the knife down the red scar where Jim stabbed me.

"They'll smell the blood." She wipes the knife on her black pants before securing it on her waist holster.

"Because I'm the food." I leave the shirt open, watch as the blood soaks into my bra.

"Right." Teari frowns.

Teari and Marcus walk away, speaking for a few moments before Teari opens her wings and lifts herself into the sky and disappears.

"Will you help me up?" I ask Sparrow as we stand next to the barren tree.

He bends, offering his hands for me to step on, lifting

me so I can reach the lower branches. I seat myself on the lowest branch, watch as a drop of blood drips onto the bark near my hand.

"Give me something, Sparrow." He gives me a look, since he's so tall that I'm barely a head above him, I catch every angle of his face. There's sadness, anger, and something else. "Give me a song to remember, one of your Bon Jovi songs, so I can do this."

He tilts his head to the side, studying me. A movement I haven't seen him make in days. "I don't want you to do this."

"I know."

He presses his hand against the rough bark near where my feet dangle. "If I refuse? Will you stop this and try something else?"

"No. I have to do this. I have to end him. This is the fastest way." I shake my head, try to clear my mind, change the subject. "Is this because you don't want to fight Marcus?"

Sparrow glances back to where Marcus stands on the dusty ground in the early morning light, arms crossed, looking pissed. "Definitely want to kick his ass."

"Please?" I ask him, hoping that he sings something before the urge to jump out of this tree and run away overcomes me.

Sparrow takes off his coat, throws it on the ground and reaches his arm across his shoulders, to his back, pulling two feathers from his broken wings. One gray, one white. The gray one, he tucks behind my ear. The white one, he swipes through the blood dripping down my chest, bringing the white feather to his mouth, his tongue flicks out and he tastes it.

My stomach churns. He's definitely gone back to being

crazy, even with his memories. "That's kinda gross, Sparrow."

His green, green eyes bore into mine. "I've lost you too many times. I can't live with losing you again."

"This is the last." I try to assure him, and myself.

"You promise?"

"I promise," I tell him, hoping to hell that I make it out of this alive.

"A promise is a promise, Meg." I nod my head, the image of him ready to leap into that river of the dead after all those feathers flashing through my mind.

He leans his shoulder against the tree, twirls the blood-stained feather in front of his face, and starts to sing *Captain Crash & The Beauty Queen from Mars*.

...

Shirt ripped, fresh blood dripping down my chest, I crawl higher into the tree. From this height I can see the smoking entrance to the burning caves.

"Just remember, Meg. You and me, we're invincible together." Sparrow pushes off the tree and walks to where Marcus is standing a few feet away. He leaves his coat on the ground at the base of the tree.

It's those words that make me wonder if this plan is nothing but one big stupid mistake.

Marcus and Sparrow begin the fight. At first Sparrow just stands there ignoring the advances from Marcus, the taunts, the quick jabbing punches. Sparrow glares. Marcus says something I can't hear; just as his mouth closes he turns to me and gives a snide glare. I might not be able to hear him, but I can read his lips. I've heard those words before: stupid, slut, dead.

Sparrow moves fast, punching Marcus in the face, every muscle in his body flexing and rippling. Now, it's a full blown brawl. The spectacle is on. Marcus falls on his back, only to kick Sparrow with both of his feet in the center of his chest. Sparrow staggers back, tries to catch his breath. Marcus leaps to his feet and barrels toward Sparrow, leaping on him, knocking him to the ground. They roll, dust clouding around them.

My teeth bite into my lip, my nails grip the tree. I hear the sounds I recognize as the dead waking.

"Oh, Sparrow," I whisper as the dead amble closer to the spectacle. Looking at the cave I see forms running at us. I count them, seven... no, eight. I guess the Deacon was right, food and spectacle will bring those fuckers running.

I look toward the fight. Now there is a tight circle of the dead around them, ready to grasp at Sparrow and Marcus. The dust clears. There's blood on both of their faces, scratches on their bodies. Marcus looks around, the dead move closer. He grips Sparrow under his arms, lifts Sparrow into the air, and flies off with him into the pink morning sky.

...

THIS TIME, the seven men and Jim, they haven't chased me across my house and up to my room. They've simply met me at a tree, where I sit, waiting for them.

I should have brought a weapon.

"Ah, Meg." Jim smiles up at me, same gray eyes, same blonde hair. "I see you've come back to me. I always knew you would. Where's your bird-man? He get bored and flutter off with the rest of his flock?"

"Yeah, that's exactly what happened." I grip the bark of the tree tighter, unable to shake the image of Marcus flying away with a fighting Sparrow dangling in his arms. Sparrow was pissed and I'm not sure if it was at me or his kin.

"Come down then, before I send these men up after you."

I start to move, the sweat dripping down my spine and pooling along the waistband of my jeans.

"Hurry now, Meg." Jim glances at his wrist. "I don't have time for your games. I'd like to drain you and make it to Denny's before the bars let out. I've been absolutely dying for a Moons Over My Hammy."

I stumble a few times, nearly falling out of the tree, unable to stop my arms from shaking. I drop to the ground, going straight to my knees. Jim pulls me to my feet with a tight grip around my upper arm.

"You stabbed me in the fucking chest," I finally say. I want nothing more than to spit in his face, but I hold it in.

"I'd like to do worse," Jim replies.

"You're such an asshole. I can't believe I ever agreed to marry you." I flinch, waiting to feel the backhand, but it never comes.

"Yeah, and I'd like nothing more than to teach you a lesson. But I need to conserve your blood so I can get the hell out of this place. Splattering your insides all over this dirt isn't going to help me with that."

My knees wobble and I start to fall. Sparrow was right, this is a bad idea. Jim hauls me over his shoulder, his hand creeping a little too high on my hamstring.

The seven men, no... demons, whatever the hell they are, they circle around Jim and keep the walking dead at bay. I can feel the blood from my wound dripping down my neck now, trailing into my hair as I flop over Jim's shoulder. My head feels foggy. I think Teari cut the wound open a little more than she needed to.

Jim walks fast. The morning sunlight disappears as he steps into the cave. The rock hallway is lit with bare bulbs and while I was expecting to smell brimstone or fire, all I notice is the slight scent of woodsmoke and pine.

Jim takes a few turns. The seven follow. The dead never enter the burning cave, which I find strange but don't bother to ask about.

The floor turns from damp rock to dark throw-rugs to aged tile. Jim stops, lowers me to the floor, holds me tight to his side so I don't drop. He reaches for a heavy wooden door and pushes it open.

We walk through.

Jesus Christ, I've been brought to the most magnificent bachelor pad ever. There's overstuffed leather furniture, a flat-screen TV, weapons hang on one wall, a bar is built into another. And there are rows and rows of liquor.

"Get her a drink," Jim orders one of the men as he directs me to sit on one of the couches.

I watch as one of the seven walks to the bar, grabs a glass from the shelf attached to the rock wall, and pours a dark liquid in it. He pauses, flicking the button on an old-school boombox that sits on the counter. *The House of the Rising Sun* starts playing.

"Fucking fantastic," I mutter to myself. I hate this creepy ass song.

Jim chuckles. He knows this. He played it every Friday night as I made his dinner. Steak and fries and broccoli. And if I didn't make it just right, he gave me a punishment I wouldn't forget. I shudder. I haven't forgotten.

The man with the glass walks closer to me.

"What are they?" I ask Jim, tipping my head to the others. "I mean, besides rapists and murderers."

"My own personal guard. The King has his Legion of bird-men. I have my own band of elite warriors: the Hellions."

I am handed a glass and make the mistake of looking up at the Hellion. Leaning away, sucking in a breath, I remember this one, the scars on his face as he came at me in my house. This was the one that tossed me down the stairs. The ice cube in the glass chinks against the side as my hand shakes. The Hellion gives me an evil smile before turning and joining the others.

"Drink it. It's your favorite, bourbon," Jim urges.

I look at the dark liquid in the glass. "I hate bourbon."

"I know." He smiles, turns, walks to the wall that holds all the weapons. He removes a short dagger and walks back to where I'm sitting. "This is kinda how we met. Bought you a drink, you drank it, and then the only thing that separated us was something hard and pointy."

I down the bourbon. Cough. "You were never that hard."

"Well, it's difficult to get it up for a slut who opens her legs for anyone." He points the dagger at my throat.

I try to ignore the seven sets of eyes that are on me and stop myself from looking at the door they brought me through. I hope to hell Sparrow and the others come running in. Settling into the couch, the open space of the room feels cavernous. I need another plan, but my only option is to kick him in the balls and run. Jim steps closer. My heart starts thumping faster than it ever has.

Oh, wait, I can *poof* myself out of here! My thumb rubs over the birthmark on my leg. I close my eyes, trying to remember the strange words Sparrow mumbled.

"Jim?" One of the seven Hellions speaks. My eyes open.

"She's more valuable alive. You can drain her little by little, get what you need to escape and leave her here for us."

"What would you want with her?"

"Maybe you didn't want to taint your bloodlines, but ours... we could use the ability to flash between realms. Keep us off the radar of those fucking bird-men," the Hellion replies.

Jim ponders the thought, the same as I do. And I wonder if that is why I am suddenly so valuable to my father, if he is old and dying and needs heirs to the throne. What better than to have heirs with special powers? Except... my baby-making parts are gone. Cut out of my body after these assholes nearly killed me.

I let them depict a plan to bleed me almost dry, let me heal, and then use me as their own personal demon breeder, my skin crawling the entire time and I can't stop thinking, Where the fuck are Sparrow, Teari, and Marcus?

......

SPARROW

"Take me to the portal!" I shout at Marcus between the flapping of his wings.

"I don't take orders from dead men." He stares straight ahead and continues flying.

I reach for the machete at my hip, twist, press the tip of it to his groin. "Take me to the portal."

"What the fuck do you think you're doing? You can't go through that portal."

"You're going to get her killed, sending her into that den of demons. She doesn't stand a chance against those Hellions. They nearly killed her once already."

"I don't give a shit about her. This fuck-up will be your fault. You're done. Forever. Second chance done and gone. It's time the heavens moved on and quit wishing you'd come back."

"You think the King will let you take my place? You don't think he will suspect something?" He has to suspect something, or he wouldn't have given me back my memories, he wouldn't have given me his blessing.

"I don't care what he thi–"

I press the tip of the machete harder against his balls, tearing the fabric of his pants. "Take me to the portal or I swear to God in Heaven I will disembowel you. Starting with your nutsack."

"You can't go through it." His fingers dig into my shoulders where he's holding me. "You're dead."

"I know." I figured that out the moment that guy Meg stole the fried dough from looked right through me. It seems she can flash a soul out of Hell, nice trick. I just hope this plan works or we're screwed.

"Fly faster, fuckhead. I might be dead, but down here this weapon still slices through everything like it's made of butter." I press the machete harder between his legs.

"This isn't going to work." Marcus picks up speed. "You're fucking crazed. Been down here too long."

I notice the clearing ahead of us, true sacred ground. Marcus drops me in front of the portal. Nothing but a stone arch in the middle of the clearing.

Marcus inspects the hole in his crotch. "Damn it. I just got these!"

Looking at the stone arch, praying that this works, I pull the white feather stained with her blood from my pocket. Marcus' eyes widen as I suck Meg's blood off the feather.

"That's disgusting." Marcus curls his lip in repulsion.

"It's not as bad as what the King's going to do to you." I turn to the portal and run through it.

...

EVEN THOUGH TWENTY-FIVE years have passed, the feeling of passing through realms is familiar. There's the tingling, the lightness, feeling like I'm flying even though I haven't been able to since I've been banished.

Exiting the other side, I am met with a sharp gasp. I recognize Teari's voice, and the light–a brightness I haven't seen in a quarter of a century. I forgot how bright it is here, home.

"You can't be here." Teari places a hand on my shoulder.

"Have to be." I push myself to stand, shield my eyes from the light. It doesn't come from the sun in the sky, but from everything. It sparkles and shimmers and I want nothing more than for Meg to see this for herself. "I have to speak to the King."

Teari stares at me, her mouth agape.

"Gather a team, we're going back to save her," I tell her.

"You don't give orders. You aren't our leader anymore, Sparrow."

"I don't give a shit, Teari! Marcus planned on leaving Meg behind. Did you know?"

She shakes her head.

"Gather a team. Now! I'll be back." I run for the castle.

...

I RUN, ready myself for a fight. The guards at the front door do nothing but stare as I push the doors open, run down the marble hallway, and try to remember where the King's quarters are. A servant presses herself up against the wall as I pass. Skidding to a stop, turning, "Where is the King?" I shout.

"Ah..."

"Now, Woman! I don't have all day!"

She points down a hall to my left. "Dining room."

I run, harder, with everything I've got left in me. I push the doors open and hear them crash against the wall.

King Gabriel sputters, liquid spraying out of his mouth, across the huge dining table. "How the hell did you get here?" he asks, standing and wiping his mouth with the back of his hand.

"Your daughter." I bend, trying to catch my breath, a breath I feel as wavering. Her magic is wearing off. I don't have much time.

"Where is she?" He leans to look behind me. "You were supposed to bring her home."

"Marcus is about to get her killed. Sent her into the burning caves, alone. I couldn't talk her out of it."

He slams his fist on the table, cracking it. "Little prick! Knew I couldn't trust him. Sonofabitch!"

"I need help." As much as I don't want to admit it, I've failed, again. "I can't do this alone."

Gabriel hollers to the servants near the door. "You! Gather my gear. And Sparrow's, from his... er... crypt."

"That's nice," I mutter. "Banish me but still allow me a holy crypt."

"Didn't want it to happen. Damn sad that it did. But rules are rules. The Council decided. My hands were tied." His eyes narrow on the newly cracked table. "Let's get this done, Sparrow, fulfill your redemption. Hasn't been right here since you left us."

The tingles that have been running through my body since I tasted Meg's blood lessen. "I have to go," I warn him. "The power... it's going away. I have to go back now."

Gabriel nods, waves his hand. "Go. I'll bring reinforcements." He palms his fist, cracks the knuckles. "Been a while since I've been in a good fight!"

I turn and run for the portal, praying to God that I make it through before whatever magic it is that Meg possesses leaves my system and what's left of my soul and goes... somewhere.

.....

CHAINS AND CHAINS

TWISTING my wrists in my new shackles, I inadvertently break the skin and fresh blood seeps out.

"Keep that up," Jim warns from across the room. "I won't stop them from draining you. It might be worth it to watch again."

"You're fucked in the head," I mutter.

"Probably." He turns back to his planning.

I look up to find seven sets of eyes on me, empty and hungry. My stomach churns. Fuck! This is taking too long. I can't remember those words to poof out of here. I'm stuck, trapped, waiting for help that's taking too long.

I shake my head, knocking the feather loose from behind my ear where Sparrow put it before the fight. It flutters to the ground in front of me. My eyes focus, it's a loon feather. Oh jeez, my heart cracks a little. Sparrow gave me the feather from my favorite bird. Picking it up, I press my finger to the quill. It's hardened from the glue, solid. Good thing Noah taught me how to pick a lock when we were dating.

I twist my arms, press the hardened quill into the

keyhole of the shackles, pull my legs up and try to hide what I'm doing. Digging with the tip of the quill, I hit the locking mechanism. I push, waiting to feel the lock click open. It doesn't happen. The quill starts to bend. I stop, take a deep breath, get ready to try again from a different angle.

There is a knock on the door.

"What the hell is it?" Jim shouts.

He moves to the door and opens it. There's nothing but a pile of feathers that mess the hallway, like a chicken wandered into the burning caves and exploded. A colorful chicken.

Jim bends, picks up a handful of feathers. "Motherfuck-er!" he shouts, but before he can turn or move away, his body slumps to the ground. The Hellions run for the door, two stay behind, eyeing me from the other side of the room. I press my knees to the handcuffs, holding them in place, hiding the feather in my hand.

A thick smoke invades from the hallway. Flames dance on the feathers, enveloping Jim's body–his headless body.

My heart leaps in my chest! There are footsteps, running, the sound of metal on metal, men grunting and groaning. Two more bodies fall on the burning pile of feathers.

The Hellions remaining in the room start to make their way to me, only to be interrupted by two figures rushing into the room. I recognize them as Sparrow and... my father, my real father.

"Don't think so, jackholes!" The two fly across the room with the wave of the King's long arm.

Sparrow runs for me. I stand, holding up my shackled wrists to him. "What took you so long?" I ask.

Sparrow stops, his fingers reaching toward the chain connecting my wrists. "Did they hurt you?"

I shake my head, trying to control the emotion swelling in my chest.

"Can you walk?" he asks.

I nod.

"Can you run?"

"I can try."

"Good, because I'm pretty sure your father is going to kick some ass and as much as I'd like to watch, I have to get you out of here."

We run for the door, Sparrow pushing me to jump around the burning bodies. I turn back to see at least a dozen winged warriors fighting in the hall.

"Who are they?" I ask, trying not to slow down.

"The Legion."

We exit the cave, a full moon illuminating the broken ground, the bodies of the walking dead strewn about, sleeping. Sparrow stops near the tree they left me in and grabs his coat off the ground.

I step toward him. "Oh God, I was afraid I'd never get to see you again. I'd never get to kiss you again." As I reach for his face, the shackles jangle.

Sparrow smiles his perfect smile, reaches for the metal at my wrists. He mumbles some words, his fingers pressed to the metal, and without a key, they click open.

"How did you do that?" I ask as the shackles drop to the ground.

"You going to show her all our secrets now?" I hear a deep voice from behind me.

Sparrow grabs my arms and forces me behind him, but not before I get a good look at Marcus walking to us.

"She's one of us. She'll learn of these things." Sparrow pauses, tips his head. "Nice wings." He smiles.

I look around Sparrow, find Marcus and see that his wings are bare. The beautiful white feathers are gone. The only thing left is a bony scaffold, just like Sparrow had before I glued it full of feathers.

"I told you what the King would do to you would be worse," Sparrow replies.

"At least he left me my memories," Marcus sneers. "That's more than he did for you."

"Good luck with those," Sparrow replies with a tone that's as flat as shit.

The figures of the warriors exit the burning caves and head toward us. Marcus looks their way, his face twists, he spits on the ground. "I won't forget what you've done to me." He jabs a finger at Sparrow.

"You did this to yourself," Sparrow says as Marcus backs up into the shadows. "Enjoy your time down here."

Marcus turns and runs.

Sparrow turns to me. "Where were we?" He draws me tight against his side. "Oh, yes, I plan on kissing you every day of my life." He presses his lips to mine. "Now, imagine heaven and *poof* us the hell out of this place."

"I can't. I can't remember those words." I look away, embarrassed—I think for the first time in my life.

"*Angele Dei, illumina, custodi, rege et guberna,*" Sparrow whispers, his fingers pressed against my leg.

...

"IT'S ABOUT GODDAMNED TIME," a familiar voice bellows.

My eyes flutter open and I find myself standing in a well-lit room. Someone grips my hand and when I turn I see Sparrow, now with perfect white-feathered wings on his back.

"Thought you kids were going to drag this out for all of eternity," the voice continues. I immediately recognize the large man in front of me. I recognize him from the zoo and the burning caves. My father. He stands from his seat, takes a few long strides to me, and wraps his arms around me.

"I've been waiting to do this for twenty-five years," he whispers in my ear. "I'm so glad that you're finally home. Just where you belong." He straightens himself and turns to Sparrow. "You!" He flicks his index finger off his thumb and plucks Sparrow hard in the forehead. "Jesus Christ, boy! You goddamn near took all of eternity to figure this shit out. We still have to worry about that asshole John. And I'm sure Marcus will be getting into trouble soon. Oh, and the King of Hell's top demon is gonna be pissed when he finds out we decapitated his only son and burned him up like a campfire marshmallow." The man turns and walks away from us, returning to his seat... no, his throne before us. "Christ, we can worry about that shit another day. My daughter is home!"

"That's my father?" I whisper to Sparrow.

"Yeah. King Gabriel. Can you see the resemblance?"

"Is it our eyes?" I recognize his have the same blue hue as mine. "Our hair?"

"No, your foul language," Sparrow replies, the corner of his lip tipping up.

"Now!" My father, my real father, rubs his hand over his chin. "Welcome home, Meg. What's mine will be yours once my time is done. And..." His eyes flick around the room as though he's lost his train of thought. He slaps his knee, focus renewed. "Mother of pearl you're feisty girl! Just like your mother. Been watching you for a while now. You'll do good here. Don't think the Council will like your attitude though. Well then." He clears his throat and narrows his eyes on Sparrow. "You, boy, better get to courting my daughter properly. We need heirs to the throne. Don't want her taking off like her mother and leaving you behind." My father looks at his feet and a sadness spreads over his face. "Well now, I guess I should save that conversation for another day..."

I get the feeling that twenty-five years without the woman he loved by his side must be hard. As hard as it was to look at Sparrow on that cavern floor and realize I'd never see him again.

"Oh," escapes my lips. Something runs through me, some feeling of relief of finding something I had lost. I turn to Sparrow, look into his green eyes, his handsome face.

"Are you okay?" Sparrow asks, his brow creased with worry.

"I'm fine. This is just so much." I walk to him and stretch my arms behind his neck.

"Oh, for Christ's sake, get a room," my father bellows and raises his hand. The doors on the far end of the room fly open. "Go! Before I puke."

Sparrow pulls my hand from behind his neck and leads me out the doors.

...

WE STEP out of the building into the bright sunshine and walk down a set of stone steps. I look around, taking in the brightness, the green trees and grass. There are fountains and walkways and mountains in the distance. It all seems to sparkle and shimmer so bright I wish I had sunglasses.

"Is this real?" I ask.

"Very. From here we watch over the human realm, we guide and protect. Participate in wars when it's warranted.

Keep the demons from Hell in check." Sparrow looks off in the distance.

I glance around us. "How do you leave here? How did you make it to earth and Hell?"

"Normally, we use the portal." He points across a courtyard to our left where there is a large arched building with winged guards standing as still as statues. "But you." He runs his finger down my arm. "You do that *poof* thing. No one has ever been able to do that before."

"Would you like me to take you to your living quarters?" I startle as a woman appears next to us. It's Teari. "Welcome home, Meg." She smiles.

"Sure, Teari," Sparrow tells her.

"What are you doing here?" I ask.

"This is my home and since I am the King's personal healer, he sent me to check on you and show you to your room. You look good, Meg. It's amazing what five minutes of Sparrow leaving his pants on can accomplish." She gives Sparrow an annoyed look.

I feel my face flush.

We follow Teari through a courtyard, up a set of stairs, toward another entrance at the side of the towering castle, and down a stark stone hallway where she stops in front of a large wooden door. Sparrow reaches for the door handle and pushes it open.

"Make sure she gets some rest." I hear Teari's voice, then her footsteps echo, as she walks down the hall, away from us. "Servants will send food."

Sparrow leads me into the room. "Wow." He circles the room before closing the door. I stand still, taking in the large room. There are floor to ceiling windows, a sitting area, large fireplace and massive four-poster bed covered in golden linens.

"What do you think?" Sparrow stands behind me and

wraps his arms around my waist. "This is way nicer than my place."

"Really?"

He shrugs. "I think so."

Noticing a door near the fireplace, I head toward it. Sparrow follows. Pushing the door open, we walk into a huge bathroom decorated in gold and tiny glass tiles of every color imaginable. There is a sunken tub in the middle of the room, a large vanity with double sink, gigantic gilded mirrors, and a glass door, which I can only imagine leads to a shower.

I head for the shower door. Wrapping my fingers around the golden handle I pull. "Dear God."

"What's wrong?" Sparrow asks.

Before me is the most luxurious shower I've ever set my eyes on. More glass tiles, multiple showerheads, and fluffy towels hang on a golden rod. I turn the shower on, adjust the dial, and watch as there is an explosion of water. Steamy mist surrounds us and, it seems, even the water in this place glistens. It's like diamonds are shooting out of the showerheads.

"We are definitely in heaven," I whisper.

I kick off my boots and reach for the hem of my shirt. There is a loud knock on the door. Sparrow hesitates for a moment before turning and leaving the bathroom. Stripping off the rest of my clothes, I hear the murmur of voices, followed by the scent of something amazing. Sparrow walks into the bathroom again.

"Food's here," he says, stopping near the sinks. "What do you want to do first, eat or shower?"

Toughest. Decision. Ever.

My stomach grumbles loudly. I wave the steam away from my face, bite my lip. Sparrow glances at the bedroom, then back at me. It seems neither of us knows which luxury to indulge in first.

A hint of mischief ignites in Sparrow's eye.

"What?" I ask.

"You're already naked."

I kick my clothes past the threshold of the shower. "It seems I am."

He toes off his shoes, pulls his shirt over his head in one swift movement, and as he moves at a near running pace, removing his pants on the way, he says hurriedly, "Food can wait."

...

SMELLING FRESHER than I have in my entire life and wrapped in the largest, softest towel I've ever seen, Sparrow and I stand next to a small table tucked in the corner of the room, near a balcony. Next to us are carts of food holding an array of platters of meats, cheeses, breads, vegetables, and pitchers of water and sweet wine. I load my plate with roasted chicken, creamy rice, tiny ears of corn, steaming peas, warm rolls and a generous slab of soft butter. Sitting down, I wait for Sparrow and drink a glass of water. He sits across from me, pours two goblets of wine, and pushes one toward me.

We eat, both of us so focused on filling our empty stomachs that neither of us able to speak a word.

There is a knock on the door. It swings open and Teari walks into the room. She gives us a half-approving look. "Seems you both found the shower and the food." She walks to us. "Feeling any better?" she asks me.

Mouth full and stomach about to explode, I nod, chewing slowly.

"You're going to make yourselves sick eating like this." She glances at the nearly empty buffet.

"Haven't had real food in weeks," I remind her between mouthfuls. And I haven't felt full in weeks. This is the first time the hunger slows and the fullness sticks around.

"Yes, well..." She blows out a breath of air, her eyes settling on my naked shoulders, then Sparrow's naked chest. "You know they stocked the closets for you both? There are actually clothes in there that will fit both of you."

Sparrow's hands stop just before he fills his mouth with a large cut of steak. "Clothes can wait." He shovels the beef in his mouth, leans back and moans. "Oh," he mumbles, "you have to try this, Meg." Cutting a large slab of beef, he moves half of it to my plate using his fingers.

"Seriously, Sparrow." Teari places her hands on her hips. "Have you forgotten all of your manners? You're not some wild human–" she stops short, glances at me.

I shrug. "Did you just stop by to pester us?" I ask, stabbing the beef with my fork and cutting it roughly, annoyed.

"No. I actually came to let you know that King Gabriel is planning festivities tomorrow. In celebration of your return."

Apprehensive about attending some fancy angel party, I look to Sparrow and try to gauge his feeling about the situation. But just like when we were standing at the Canadian border and he was watching the birds in the trees, he now shovels food into his mouth with the same distracted look on his face.

"It will be fine." Teari waves a hand at me. "Just don't make yourselves sick on the food." She turns and heads toward the door. "Sparrow," she turns just before leaving, he pauses mid chew. "I know it's been a while since you got to experience the joys of life, but make sure Princess Meg gets some rest. Don't want her looking like crap at her debut party." With that, Teari closes the door.

We both stop chewing and look at each other. Sparrow's lip twitches, and for some reason, a laughter bubbles up from deep inside me. Food sprays out of my mouth and I lean back in my chair, clutching my distended stomach, laughing.

Sparrow tips his head to the side, chewing calmly and swallowing. "Are you okay?" he asks.

Trying to stop the laughter, I sit up, take a few deep breaths. "She just called me Princess Meg."

Sparrow looks longingly at his nearly finished plate of food and back to the buffet. He takes a swig of his wine, wipes his mouth across the back of his hand and replies, "That's who you are."

"Oh, no no no. I'm not a princess. Just a little piece of North Country trash, raised by a fucking demon. I killed my mother the day I was born, got the shit beat out of me, and now... and now..." Confusion twisting my insides, I stand abruptly, tipping my chair over.

"Meg?" Sparrow's brow wrinkles in concern.

I head for the closet door and open it. There are rows of clothes, every color and every fabric imaginable. I reach for a pair of soft looking pants. Sparrow's hand lands on mine, stopping me.

"Let's wait on those," he says softly, wrapping his hand around my wrist and pulling me close, pressing his lips to mine.

When he breaks the kiss, I let out a sigh of frustration. "What did Teari mean, when she said it's been a while since you enjoyed the joys of life?"

He moves his free hand behind my neck, his fingers running through my short hair. "With banishment for losing King Gabriel's last born daughter, came the punishment of death."

"Death? But... you seemed so alive there. We spent weeks together and never once did I recognize you as being dead."

"That's how our kind exists in Hell."

"Why?"

"Because we don't belong there."

"Oh." I try to step away from him, but his hand behind my neck just draws me closer, until the towel stretched across my chest presses against him. "And now you're alive?"

"King Gabriel, your father, he can do that sort of thing."

"Oh Jesus..."

"What?"

"I had sex with a ghost." I look at him, slightly horrified.

He chuckles. "Well, I wasn't really a ghost. Don't think too much about it. It was good–no, great. Leave it at that."

"This is all too much." I shake my head. "Will they know what happened to me? Does this entire kingdom know that I almost birthed a child to the son of a demon? And what those Hellions did to me? I don't want them... I can't stand them looking at me the way those doctors did when I woke up from that coma."

"Don't know." Sparrow draws me closer, presses his lips to my forehead. "Give yourself time. Slow down."

"Oh," I mouth, taking it all in. "This is so fucked up. All of it." Taking a calming breath to settle my nerves, I reach up on my toes and press my lips to his. As I lean back, Sparrow's eyes turn to pools of emotion. "You have your wings back." I reach out and run my finger over the downy white feathers on is back.

He runs his palms over my shoulder blades. "You should too." He moves his hands to my hips. "You'll have to ask your father how to call on them."

I shake my head. Remembering what he, my father, the King, said to me. "He wants heirs to the throne?"

Sparrow nods.

"I can't..." Remembering the loss of the child I once carried, I find myself unable to finish the sentence. "Doesn't he know what they did to me?"

"When Teari healed you, she healed all of you. Even what you lost." His hand travels over my towel-covered stomach and stops at my lower abdomen. "But that's not important." He tightens his arm across my back, pressing me to him. "You're safe, you're home, and I'm never taking my eyes off you again. If there is one thing I learned from my twenty-five years of death, it's that I cannot live one second without you." Sparrow dips his head, presses his lips to mine. That emotion I felt in the burning caves, when Sparrow ran into the room to rescue me comes flooding back, flooring me. Finally, for the first time in my life, I have someone who really cares for me.

"I love you," Sparrow whispers on my lips between kisses.

"You promise?" I ask, running my fingers over his chest and across his shoulders, pulling him closer.

He stretches his arm behind his back and pulls one of the downy white feathers out of his newly replaced wings. Holding it between us, I take the feather from his fingers.

"No one has ever given me a feather before." I stare at it, run my fingers over the velvety softness, the memories of all our time spent searching for feathers flashing through my mind.

"I would give them all to you," Sparrow says. "Every single one."

"You promise?" I ask.

"I promise."

"That's kinda weird, you know. Offering to mutilate yourself for me."

"Doesn't matter. A promise is a promise." His hand moves down the towel covering me, sliding between the part of it.

"What are you doing?"

"A promise is a promise, and you swore just a few minutes ago."

An involuntary shiver runs through me as he touches my bare hip. "Seems I did," I whisper as he bends, presses his lips to mine.

"Ah, Meg," he whispers on my lips as his hand dips lower, pushing my legs apart. "I can't seem to get enough of you." My hands move to his chest and around his neck, gripping onto him. "You're so perfect, for me, just for me." His hand slides across my abdomen, stopping at my belly button before sliding lower. I tilt my hips, showing him exactly where I want his hand to be and a moan escapes my throat as his fingers taunt and torment me in places no one else ever has. Sparrow whispers sweet words, snowy owl words. And they make me forget that I ever felt wrong here, at least for this moment.

...

Unable to sleep, possibly from so many nights spent running, I lay in bed, wide awake with Sparrow's arm and leg draped over me, his face buried into the crook of my neck. I untangle myself from him, slide across the mattress—the best mattress ever—and head for the closet. Pulling out the soft pants I found earlier, and a plain black shirt, I dress myself. When I'm done, I turn and watch Sparrow as he sleeps, his face slack, hair tousled and body limp. He sleeps soundly for the first time in twenty-five years, I imagine.

Walking to the balcony and grabbing a roll off one of the carts as I pass, I step outside, breathe in the fresh air, turn and look up. A castle, a fucking castle. I move my focus across the grounds. Everything still seems to twinkle and glow, even at night. It's strange, different and more beautiful than anything I've ever seen in my pathetic life.

Feeling slightly recovered from my pity party earlier, I still sense a nagging in my gut. And since I'm not able to figure out exactly what it is, I do something that I know I shouldn't, but I just have to at this moment. There is something I need to see.

Envisioning my little house, picket fence and all, I repeat those words Sparrow told me, *"Angele Dei, illumina, custodi, rege et guberna."* And faster than I can blink, I'm out of the castle and standing on the sidewalk in front of my house.

Well, my old house. In the human realm. Let's see if certain items exist in both places.

It's dark, a slight breeze blows and there is a creaking noise. I turn to find a *For Sale* sign swaying in the front yard.

The roll is still in my hand. Shoving it in my mouth, I walk up onto the porch and look in the front windows. The living room is empty. Knowing that no one ever locks their doors in Gouverneur, I try the front door, and when the handle turns, I push the door open and walk inside. Figures. At least there are no stray cats here. I wander the empty living room and kitchen before heading for the stairs. Stopping on the landing, I swallow hard, break out in a sweat, and I am reminded that you never go back to the scene of the crime.

The carpet is gone. The rest of the stairwell and the upstairs hallway are stripped. But the old wood is still there, parts of it stained a deep brown. Blood. With one bare foot, I use my toe to open the hidden compartment in the first step above the landing. It's empty. The gun that saved my life is gone.

I make my way up the stairs, take a right and push open my old bedroom door. It seems they haven't started renovations in here. The sweating gets worse. Stepping over the stains in the carpet, I head for the corner near Jim's side of the bed, where Sparrow found the lock-box. Flicking the light on, I search the nightstand, under the bed, the entire area, until I find it tucked behind the nightstand in a tiny space cut in the wall.

"What a dick," I mumble to myself, twisting the hook and opening the metal box. It's filled with papers, the same letters from the banks and the lawyers that were there when Sparrow found it. I dig through the things until I find what I'm looking for: the blurred picture of my mother. It seems strange to me that these same things can exist in both realms. Something I'll have to ask Sparrow about.

There is the sudden pounding of footsteps running through the house and up the stairs. As I jump to my feet, a figure arrives, standing in the doorway of my bedroom. I recognize him instantly. Officer Sullivan, Jim's father, his Watcher as Sparrow explained, from the human realm.

"You." He reaches for the gun at his hip, takes a step into the room. "Figured you couldn't stay out of trouble for five minutes, dumb shit. You're going to pay for your little band of fucking fairy men killing Jim. His real dad is pissed." Officer Sullivan takes two more steps toward me.

Mumbling to myself, I *poof* the hell out of there without saying a word to him and find myself on the balcony of the castle, before I can bat an eyelash at Officer Dickweed-Sullivan. With my heart beating from the adrenaline rush of seeing Jim's Watcher, I catch my breath for two minutes before heading inside the castle.

Moving into the room, I take another roll off the buffet and stop to take a swig of the wine before heading to the closet. I tuck the lockbox along the wall in the back.

Returning to my side of the bed, I slide under the covers and next to Sparrow. Propped up on one elbow, I watch him, just as I watched him in that field and unbuttoned his coat while he slept. This time he doesn't wear a coat. I know he wears nothing under these blankets. I pull them back, revealing him in all of his fabulous manliness. A muscle along his ribcage flexes, another along his thigh. Leaning forward, I inspect the downy wings on his back. They seem to flex and fold, molding to his body as though they were another set of arms. Reaching out, I run my finger along the feathers closest to me.

"You smell like humans." Sparrow's voice startles me.

Pulling my hand back, I reply, "I am human."

He reaches for me, pulling me tightly to him as a child would their favorite stuffed animal, pressing his face into the crook of my neck and breathing in deeply. "No, you're not. Did you find what you were looking for?" he asks.

"I..." He squeezes me tighter. "I'm not sure."

...

Waking up, it's hard to tell if it's morning or later, since it always seems so bright here. There is a knock on the door. The handle jiggles before the door opens. Teari walks in. Sparrow shifts, propping himself up on an elbow and running his free hand up my back.

"Seriously, you two are still in bed?" Teari asks as she

carries two large garment bags to the closet and hangs them on the hooks of the closet doors. "Get up and get showered." She turns to look straight at me. "You have less than an hour before your debut Ball begins."

Sparrow throws back the covers and stands, naked as a baby. Teari makes a huffing noise, reaches into the closet and throws something behind her back. It lands at Sparrow's feet and as he lifts it, I see that it's a white robe. Teari throws another one at me.

"Let's go. Let's go. Let's go!"

"What about breakfast?" Sparrow asks, pulling on the robe.

"You've missed breakfast. And lunch. There will be food at the Ball." Teari unzips the garment bags, revealing a creamy white suit and a sparkling golden dress. She turns swiftly, walking out of the room. Before she closes the door, she shouts, "You have twelve minutes before I return and you both better be showered and dressed by then."

When Sparrow and I exit the bathroom, both refreshed and awake, we get dressed. Since my hair is too short to do anything with, I simply leave it as it dries. Both done, we turn to face each other. I gasp. Sparrow wears the white suit, a stark contrast to his brown hair that is now combed, parted and styled. Under the suit jacket he wears an emerald satin shirt, which makes his eyes seem an even brighter green.

When he says nothing to me, just stares, eyes wide and mouth slack, I turn to face the mirror. The dress is a fitted, sparkly gold sheath stopping just below my knees, the straps across the shoulders show the feather tattoo across my collarbone. The scar in the center of my chest, where Jim stabbed me, is now completely healed and invisible.

"Is this how you people always dress?" I ask.

Sparrow clears his throat. "Definitely not." He takes two

steps to me, but before he gets too close, there is a sharp rap on the door and Teari steps in wearing a gown like mine, but in shimmering white.

"Why are you guys wearing white and I'm wearing gold?" I ask.

"Because, Princess," Teari replies. "This is your Debut. You will be the only one wearing color."

"Oh."

She thrusts a pair of shoes toward me. They're not Keds, which I would normally wear when dressing up, in a jean-skirt and tank-top. They're towering heels which I am sure I will break my neck wearing.

"No, Sparrow, I do not have food for you." Teari snaps. "There will be a buffet, so stop looking at me like that." She walks close to Sparrow, tucking something into his breast pocket and when she steps away I see that it is a peacock feather in bright green and blue. Teari pats his shoulder. "All set, Legion Commander, Sir. We're glad to have you back."

The corner of Sparrow's lip twitches up.

Teari inspects me, now that I'm wearing shoes. She fans her hands over me and nods. "Good. You did get some rest." She pauses. "You know, I can heal your skin too, Meg. Make those tattoos go away."

"No," I respond firmly. "They are part of me and who I am."

"Yes," she settles her finger on her chin, "about that. You are royalty here, there are things that are expected of you. King Gabriel has let the rules slide because of your... back-ground. But this is the last night of it. We can't have you living in sin within the Seven Kingdoms of Heaven. That's blasphemous. Sparrow will return to his home tonight and court you like a true gentleman."

"You're not the King, Teari," Sparrow says.

"No. But I am his personal healer, and he listens to the

words that I say." She nods swiftly, snaps her fingers. "Let's go. We can't be late."

...

When Teari said that everyone would be wearing white, I guess I didn't understand how many people would be wearing white. It's like a reverse wedding.

My father moves toward us. What's even more intimidating than his size are the giant, multihued and gold colored wings that have seemed to sprout from his back. He holds out an elbow for me to take, motioning for Sparrow to step aside. I hesitate. The old habit of avoiding the touch of others is hard to break. As I look up to his face, which is oddly reminiscent of my own, he smiles, a soft, warm smile that breaks my uncertainty. He's so tall I have to reach up, uncomfortably. All noise in the cavernous room stops.

With a booming voice he announces, "I would like to introduce my youngest daughter, Meg."

His announcement is followed by a lot of clapping. He takes my elbow, leads me down the small landing that we stand on, into a sea of people–no, angels. They chatter amongst themselves.

I look back at Sparrow one last time before the crowd surrounds us and I can no longer see him.

"Ah," my father tugs on my elbow. "Here we have the remaining six council members."

We stop in front of six large men, just as tall as my father, who have elegant wings and wear unpleasant looks on their faces. He waves at them and walks away without a word.

"Um... aren't you going to introduce me?" I whisper.

He pats my hand that's resting in the crook of his arm. "No, no. Not today. They're assholes. Besides, Raphael is still pissed that his daughter chose my kingdom over his."

"Which daughter?"

"Teari."

"So she's a princess too?"

He shakes his head, his long, dark hair brushing his shoulders. "Not in my kingdom. If she had chosen to stay in Raphael's kingdom, then she would have been."

I nod at a few of the people that move out of the way for us, plaster a smile on my face. "So, I don't understand all of this, realms and kingdoms and shit."

He clears his throat. "I forget how much you've missed, not having your mother and all. Bless her soul." He slows his pace. "There are the Seven Kingdoms of Heaven, each of the original Archangels were appointed as ruler of one. Then we have Lucifer, the fallen, ruling over the realm of Hell." The commotion in the room dies down to a whisper.

"What about the human realm? The earthen plane?"

"Ah, yes, that is God's land. The Seven Kingdoms watch over the humans and keep Lucifer's demons in check."

"Sparrow said you would show me how to call on my wings?"

"You may have the Archangel lineage and your gift of *poofing*, however, you lack faith and you will not be gifted with your celestial wings until you find that faith."

Glancing around the room, I ask "How do you know I don't believe?"

He looks me up and down and frowns.

"That easy, huh?"

"Not only is that easy to see, it's also easy to see that you lack faith in yourself."

Waving my hand at him, I reply, "I don't want to hear

about me. Tell me something else. What happened to my mother? Why did she leave this place?"

"Our union was forbidden, by her father–"

"Who's her father?" I interrupt.

He clears his throat, dips his head and whispers so quietly in my ear. "Lucifer."

Every eye in the room is on us, all commotion ceases. I stop, my back straightens, muscles stiffen. It's two seconds until the partygoers resume whatever they were doing before Gabriel uttered the name Lucifer.

"You see, child, things are not perfect, not even in heaven. Your mother fled to the human realm to hide you. And I sent my best Legion Commander to watch over you both. And, well, you know the rest." He pats my hand. "Don't worry about Sparrow. I forgive him. I had to banish him down there because Lucifer demanded it for the death of his daughter. Now you're here, things are right, and it's about time one of us had a child with some... edge. It's probably the darkness of your grandfather inside you. You will fight it your entire life, no doubt. But you will choose to do what is right. I can tell this. You may not have faith in yourself, Meg, but I have good faith in you."

And then it clicks, the reason why I feel so odd here, why I've had the inclination to do so many bad things in my life. I blamed the father that raised me, the lack of a mother, my trailer-park roots, but all the time it's been an inherent darkness.

He tugs me along and I stumble in the high heels. Gabriel rights me with one hand. "Ah, here we go. The buffet."

We stop in front of a long table filled with food. There are crystal trays and platters holding fruits and vegetables, steaming breads, meats cooked several different ways. King Gabriel hands me a crystal plate. Following behind him, I load my plate, my stomach growling the entire time. It seems I may never eat my fill.

"You should try the quail," Sparrow's familiar voice whispers in my ear.

Turning, I find him following behind me, two plates gripped in his hands, loaded with mountains of food.

"Are you seriously going to eat all that?" I ask.

"Absolutely."

I follow Gabriel to a table in the front of the room. He gestures for me to sit next to him. Sparrow sits in the seat on the other side of me.

Before King Gabriel sits, he raises his arms in the air and bellows. "A prayer before we begin."

A hundred hushed voices whisper throughout the room, the words too quiet for me to hear. I notice Sparrow does the same.

I sit awkwardly, waiting for them to finish. After a moment passes, the clanging of silverware and roar of voices resumes as the room filled with angels eats their fill.

Pushing a carrot around on my plate, I spear it and bring it to my mouth. Chewing, I know it should taste wonderful, just like the meal we shared last night, but it seems my taste buds are not working with the news of my mother being the daughter of Lucifer so fresh in my mind.

Sparrow cleans both plates in record time. Wiping his mouth, he leans closer and asks, "What's wrong?"

I simply stare at him, unable to get any words out of my mouth.

King Gabriel clears his throat and leans to my other side. "Perhaps, Sparrow, you should begin your courting and ask my daughter to dance."

Sparrow's lip tips up in a half smile. "Meg?" He holds out a hand.

"There's no music," I reply.

"Oh, there is," Gabriel chirps in. "You just have to listen for it."

Tipping my head, focusing over the dull roar of the hundreds of voices talking, I start to hear the flowing soft notes of a harp.

"Meg?" Sparrow stands and curls his fingers, beckoning me.

As I stand, I catch the familiar image of Teari sitting on the other end of our table, her beautiful face set quite grimly.

Sparrow leads me to a small dance floor to the left of the tables. The commotion of the partygoers never ceases. It seems even though this is my debut ball, my presence here is nothing special. Something throbs in my gut. I feel wrong.

Sparrow stops, spins, and pulls me into his arms. I catch him staring at the feather tattoo that's across my collarbone. The harp music suddenly seems louder, a flowing waltz tune. Sparrow leads me into a smooth, sway of a dance.

Unable to ignore how I'm feeling, I say, "This is all too strange."

"How so?" Sparrow asks.

"I'm not used to all this shine. I've been in the dark for so long. I'm darker than all this." I sigh, fighting with getting the words out of my head. "King Gabriel just confirmed it."

"Unpossible."

"Stop making up words."

"I won't."

"You have to. Unpossible isn't a real word."

"Don't care. Who's going to stop me? I can say what I want."

"This feels wrong." I start to pull away, but Sparrow holds me tighter, turning and waltzing until we have left the dance floor and stand alone on another balcony.

"Better?" he whispers in my ear.

"A little. How many balconies do they have in this place?"

"Hundreds."

"Oh."

"What's wrong?"

"I don't fit in here, Sparrow. This is worse than anything, ever."

"You fit here, in my arms, therefore you belong." He rests his head against mine and starts to hum *Take me Home Tonight*.

"Sparrow?" I interrupt him.

"Yeah."

"Why are you singing an Eddie Money song?"

"I just remembered I like him too."

"Oh... Sparrow?"

"Um hmm."

"I need a beer. And..."

"And?"

"Nachos."

A deep laughter erupts from his chest. He pulls away from me and tips his head, his green eyes gleaming with amusement. "Okay."

"Okay?"

"Let's go."

"Anywhere?"

"Sure."

"Dressed like this?" I motion to my dress and his suit.

"Yeah. It will be fun. In the morning I have to return to my duties as Legion Commander, so this is my last night for fun."

"Okay."

"So, your choice, where are you taking me?" His hand

lowers and I feel his thumb rub across that birthmark on my leg.

Thinking of this college bar I used to hang out at, before I met Jim and let him try to kill me, I whisk us there in a heartbeat.

...

Chubby's. That's what the neon sign says in red, lighting up the sidewalk. The sound of drunken college kid laughter and hooting fills the air. I turn to Sparrow and find him looking completely normal. No wings.

"Where are they?" I ask and point to his shoulder.

He smirks. "Invisible here. Don't want to freak out the humans. So, this place?" Sparrow asks, gesturing to the sign.

"Best nachos. Ever." I head for the steps and feeling the closeness of Sparrow behind me, I pull the door open with a confidence like never before. All noise ceases in the bar.

"Maybe we should have changed clothes." I murmur to Sparrow.

"Nah. We look too amazing." He presses a large hand to the small of my back and leads me to a corner table.

A waitress is there in an instant. And I'm pretty sure I'm invisible because all she does is stare at Sparrow when he says, "Large nachos and two beers, please."

She smiles at him when she returns with our order and still doesn't acknowledge my existence.

We eat in silence and wait for the rest of the bar to forget about the overly dressed couple in the corner booth. I sip my beer, shove a largely topped nacho in my mouth.

"What's wrong?" Sparrow finally asks.

I shake my head. "This was a heck of a lot easier when both of us couldn't remember shit."

"Yeah." Sparrow waves his hand and motions to his beer. The waitress brings another. Sparrow starts to peel the label on his empty bottle. "What are you looking for, Meg?"

I stop halfway before delivering another loaded nacho into my mouth. Dropping it back onto the plate, I lean back and take a long swig of my beer. "I don't know."

Sparrow blinks, tips his head to the side, twirls his beer before drinking from it. "Tell me," he demands. "Just tell me."

I exhale out a breath of frustration. "Okay. I just..." My eyes settle on my beer. I can't believe I'm such a coward that I can't even look at him. "I just... You remember when we were wandering through Hell?" He nods. "I felt normal there. I felt fine. Even forgetting everything that happened with Jim and learning about my mother. I feel strange up there, different. And, I still feel like... like there's something I need to know. Some question I need answered."

"You think you need to go back."

I nod.

Sparrow reaches forward so quickly I barely see him move, I just suddenly feel his hand on my cheek, my neck, centered over my heart where Jim stabbed me. "Promise me you won't go alone."

I know that I'm staring at him, wide eyed.

"Promise, Meg."

My heart starts to beat faster.

"Promise. Now." His green eyes blaze into mine.

"Fine." My heart begins a rapid flutter. Sparrow tips his head, studying me. He knows I'm lying. "I'm a sinner," I warn him. "You know this."

"Yeah, you're bad to the bone." His hand moves to my cheek again, his fingers brush the short hair away from my face. "But I'm batshit crazy. Don't you think for one second that those Hellions have forgotten about you. Your blood is gold down there, rubies and jewels to those who are damned. You're worth even more to me." His fingers press down my spine, his thumb rubs across the feather tattoo on my collarbone.

"You're acting weird again, Sparrow," I warn him.

He smiles, a soft toothy grin so much like the one he gave me when we were standing at the Canadian border. "I told you, Meg. You and me, we're invincible together. Just wait and see. Don't go alone." His fingers slip under the strap of my sparkly dress, eliciting a shiver from me. "Let's go."

Sparrow stands, takes my hand and pulls me to my feet. We walk out of the bar and around the corner into the shadows where no one can see us. I deliver us to the grounds outside the castle. Sparrow pulls me close, presses his hot lips to mine in a demanding kiss. He tastes like beer and smells a little bit like the smoke of the bar. It makes my trailer-park roots tingle. And as I push my fingers into his hair, a deep sound rumbles in his chest.

Pulling back, I ask, "Did you just growl?"

"Yes."

"Why?"

"Because if I did what I really wanted to... what I want to do right now. I'm sure King Gabriel will send me away." I press myself closer to him. Sparrow groans, pushes me away until I'm at arm's length. "I have to go."

"Where?"

"To my place."

"Can I come?"

Sparrow looks up at the castle walls before he looks at my face. "No. Gabriel's going to kick my ass."

Looking up at the castle I notice a curtain flutter.

Sparrow lets go of my arms, flexes his wings and thrusts himself into the night sky. He starts flying to the left, pauses, turns and heads for the right. He smirks down at me. "Wrong direction."

"Do you even know where you live?" I ask.

"Think so." With another thrust of his wings, he speeds off into the night.

Sighing, I turn and head up the castle steps. Walking down the long empty hallway, I find my room and head inside.

Closing the bedroom door, I push a chair in front of it, positioning it under the door handle to stop anyone from entering. Then, stripping off the sparkly dress, I head for the shower that shoots out steaming, glittering water.

Clean, wrapped in a towel and staring at the closet before me, I run my fingers over the racks of clothes. Never before in my life have I ever had so many to claim as my own. Never before have I ever had such soft fabrics or so many underwear and socks. I choose underwear, a pair of fitted yoga pants and a wide necked sweatshirt. Then I run and leap onto the giant bed I shared with Sparrow last night. I run my fingers over the soft sheets. Sitting, I pull the heavy comforter up to my chin and lay back on the overstuffed pillows. And then, I stare at the ceiling, wide-awake and alone.

It's not long before I become antsy. I throw the covers back, return to the closet and reach to the back to retrieve the lockbox I hid there. I remove the picture of my mother and head back to the bed.

Staring at her image, remembering those words that John Lewis told me every morning, *you killed her and don't you forget it*, I wonder what she would have been like had I not killed her.

"I'm sorry I killed you," I whisper to the picture.

Somehow, staring at her for longer than I ever have in my life, I fall asleep.

...

FEELING a sudden presence in the room, my eyes flutter open and I scream at the dark figure looming over me. All I can think is, Shit, one of the Hellions has found me! I scream so loud that the back of my throat hurts. Moving to get away, a hand clamps down on my leg. I kick and scratch and scream louder. Backing up, I fall off the other side of the bed. As the stars clear from my vision, the figure moves and offers a hand.

"Meg?"

Oh, it's Sparrow's voice.

"Oh my God, Sparrow, you scared the shit out of me!"

"Why is there a chair in front of your door?" I take Sparrow's hand and he pulls me to my feet. He's wearing dark cargo pants, boots, and a black shirt. There are pockets and clips and straps attached to him with strange weapons that make him look like he's headed to war. "Teari tried to wake you and couldn't get in."

"Oh, I just wanted some privacy." I shrug.

Sparrow crosses the room and removes the chair from under the door handle. "No one will hurt you here, Meg. You're within the Seven Kingdoms of Heaven."

Teari pushes the door open and by the look on her face she's furious. "Uncalled for. Locking the door." She walks right up to me, nose to chest. I can't get over how tall these people are. "You could have been injured, you could have been... Let me see what's wrong with you." She reaches out a hand to touch me. I slap it away and back up.

"Don't touch me."

Teari frowns. "What's wrong with you? What have you been up to? Don't think we don't know you've been sneaking around." Teari's eyes snap around the room, stopping near the bed. The picture of my mother rests there. It must have dropped when I fell.

Five quick steps and I snatch up the picture.

Teari holds her hand out. "Who is that?"

"None of your business," I reply.

She walks toward me, reaching out, demanding.

"Teari," Sparrow warns from the doorway. "Maybe you should wait outside while Meg gets ready for the day."

Looking down her perfect nose at me, Teari turns sharply, the tips of her folded wings dragging on the floor as she leaves. Sparrow kicks the door closed with one booted foot. I glare at him. He shakes his head. "I told you, we don't win the wars of Heaven and Hell by trusting everyone."

"I don't give a fuck who Teari trusts." Stomping to the closet, I pull out a pair of jeans and a pair of leather boots. I remove the yoga pants I was sleeping in, pull on the jeans and boots and shove the picture of my mother in my back pocket. I leave on the sweatshirt.

Sparrow stands in the middle of the room now, arms crossed, looking very imposing.

"What?" I snap at him.

His shoulders tense. "I don't like sleeping at my place, alone."

"Yeah, well I don't like having the shit scared out of me and getting yelled at first thing in the morning."

His eyes flit to the open balcony doors, which I'm assuming he came in through. "I have training today."

"Sorry for you."

"What will you do today?"

I shrug. "Don't know. Maybe speak with Gabriel. I have questions for him."

"Will you come see me? I'll be at the barracks behind the castle."

"Don't they have rules against visitors showing up while you're working?" I ask.

"Don't care." He walks to me in a few long strides, bends, and places a quick kiss on my cheek before heading for the balcony. He gives a grin. "Stay out of trouble, Meg." And with one powerful thrust that sends the curtains billowing in the air, he flies away.

Opening the door, my eyes immediately focus on Teari standing in the hallway, pacing. She turns and before she can say one word I tell her, "Take me to Gabriel."

"Very well. Follow me."

She leads me down long hallways with towering windows that let in the bright light of this place. I shield my eyes with my hand.

...

KING GABRIEL SITS at a dining room chair, his chin thoughtfully resting on the curve of his fingers, his shoulders curved and stiff. Rodin's *Thinker* in the flesh. As Teari lets the door slam closed behind us, he startles.

"Ah," Gabriel stands, his dark blue robes billowing about him. "Meg." And as if he senses something is off, he frowns, waves Teari out of the room and asks, "What's wrong?"

"The darkness," I step closer to Gabriel, my hand on my chest. "I feel wrong here."

Gabriel nods, crosses the room and takes both of my

hands in his, "Your soul seeks answers, closure. That is all." He looks me over. "Tell me, Meg, who raised you?"

"A man named John Lewis." I find it hard to control the shudder that runs through me at the mentioning of his name. "He turned into a demon when he died."

Gabriel sighs. "I wish I could have done things differently. Clea would still be alive."

"Clea, that was her name?"

He nods.

Clea... the name rolls around in my head and brings forth an image of dandelions and warm sunshine. I never had the courage to ask John Lewis what her name was. Remembering that I met John in Hell when he died, I ask, "If my mother died, where did she go?"

"What do you mean, child?"

"This is Heaven, she was an angel, where did she go?"

He shakes his head slowly. "She was a different kind of angel. Her soul was never released from the earthen planes. Somewhere, down there, she rests. Wherever John Lewis hid her."

I pull the picture out of my back pocket; stare at it for a second before showing it to Gabriel. "Is this her?"

He smiles warmly. "Yes." He runs one large finger across the picture, clears his throat, and looks down at me. "You must find her. You must set things right. Only then will you quell that feeling of loss for her."

"I can go? Just like that?"

"You don't need my permission." Gabriel walks back to his chair and sits.

"But Teari–"

He waves one large hand, dismissing my words. "Teari has a big head sometimes. Go whenever you like. But I would recommend taking Sparrow with you."

"Yeah... suppose I should." I turn to leave, but stop. "Gabriel?"

"Yes."

"Where can I get a pair of sunglasses?"

"Sunglasses?"

"This place, it's too bright. Hurts my eyes."

He snaps his fingers and a pair of dark glasses appear on the table.

I reach for them. "Thanks," I say as I leave the room.

Wandering the castle, it takes far too long for me to finally find the front door and follow the glistening sidewalks around the back to the barracks.

...

ROUNDING the castle takes approximately fifteen minutes of walking. I descend what seems like one-thousand stone steps toward the barracks. It looks like a football field, all green shimmering grass, wooden stands and a large stone building. There is a group of men standing around and as I walk I pick Sparrow out of the bunch. He's the tallest and his disheveled brown hair seems to glisten in the light of this place.

One long arm reaches up and waves at me. The men split into groups of two, a horn sounds, and then it's dirt clouding the air, mixed with feathers and grunts and groans. They're all fighting.

I run down the rest of the steps, to the sideline. A horn sounds, they stop. A loud voice yells, "Break."

A figure jogs toward me. I recognize Sparrow. He's covered in scrapes, bruises and there's a tear in his shirt.

"Hey." He smiles at me.

"This is your job?" I ask. "Wrestling in the dirt?"

He shrugs. "Training. You have to practice with the best to learn how to fight the worst." He presses his fingers to a cut on his cheek. "Come on," he tugs at my hand. "I have a short break. I'll show you my place."

"So you found your house?" I ask.

He grins. "Yeah, on the second try. Someone wasn't very happy with me last night."

We walk behind the barracks to a winding path, past a few small houses and into the forest. He leads me up the front steps of a stone house and opens the door.

"You live here?" I ask.

"Yeah."

It's no bigger than an apartment. Sparsely decorated and surprisingly clean. Sparrow heads for the sink, turns the water on and washes his hands before reaching for a towel and cleaning the dirt off his face.

"What do you think?" he asks, turning to me.

"It's not a castle but it will do," I tease him.

Sparrow laughs, reaches out and pulls me to him, pressing his lips to mine, his hands running up the back of my shirt and pressing me closer to him. And, like always, I melt into him like I never have with another man.

Abruptly, he pushes me away and inhales a deep breath. "We have to stop," Sparrow groans, adjusting my shirt.

"Why?"

"Gabriel sees everything in his Kingdom." He steps back and adjusts his pants.

"He can see through walls?"

"Something like that."

"He gave me permission to leave and find my mother. Come with me."

"Now?" he asks.

"Yes. I have to figure this out."

"Meg, I can't go now. I have the rest of the day to train and test. I have to go back to the barracks. Let's wait until tomorrow."

"I can't wait until tomorrow."

"I asked you not to go without me."

"You give me no choice. I'll be back soon."

"Wait! You can't go without me. We have to go together."

"I've done this whole thing, this life and living thing, I've done it alone for this long."

"And that's exactly why you need to wait for me."

"Be back soon." Leaning forward, I kiss his chin. "I promise."

In a flash, I'm gone.

...

IN MY MIND'S eye I follow her image, moving quickly from place to place. I focus, *poof*. It seems everywhere I go she is never there, earth and Hell and Heaven. I find just bits and pieces, a whisper of smoke of who she was. Tiny shards of her essence. I follow them, an internal pull bringing me closer to the parts that are stronger. I hear a gasp in one place, a thud in another, a scream in yet another. Having no idea where I emerge, keeping my eyes closed, I connect the dots of who she was in every place that she's ever been. The feeling of her gets stronger and stronger, tugging at the soul within me until I stop, open my eyes, focus on the patch of grass in front of me, the broken down trailer to my left, the sound of an airplane flying overhead. I am home, the broken down trailer I shared with John Lewis. The brightness lets me know I am in the human realm.

Standing in the backyard, something is calling me, deep from under that dirt. Something is calling me to dig.

I run for the shed, push the old rusted yard tools around until I find a shovel. Returning to that spot in the yard, I dig.

There is the fresh scent of broken grass, the metallic earthy smell of the soil as I dig and toss it into a pile. I dig and dig, that feeling in my center growing stronger. Placing my foot on the spade, pushing down with every muscle in my body, the shovel hits something. I move the dirt, drop to my hands and knees, press my fingers into the moist soil and find a fabric buried under there. Pulling, brushing the soil away, tugging with all my strength, the earth releases whatever treasure it was trying to hide.

I fall back. Soil sprays over me. A sack lands near the hole I've dug. Sitting up, I reach for the old burlap and untie the twine at the top. Opening the bag, I reach in and pull out a skull. There are other bones in there, long ones, tiny ones, broken ribs and vertebrae. It is a skeleton in a bag.

I hold the skull in front of my face and whisper, "I found you, mother. Now I will return you home."

Leaving the hole in the yard, *poof*, I return to Gabriel's Kingdom.

...

KING GABRIEL SITS at a dining room chair, still Rodin's *Thinker*.

He turns as I appear and holding the dusty bag out to him, I say, "I found her! Clea, my mother. I found her! I brought her back so you can bring her back to life." As I advance toward him, dirt falls off my clothes and out of my hair.

Gabriel frowns. "I cannot bring her back."

"But you did with Sparrow. You brought him back. Made him alive again."

"Yes, but she did not originate here." He motions to the soil-covered sack with a sorrow I cannot ignore.

"Then where do I bring her? How do I make this right? I have to free her soul. I have to see her. I have to tell her I'm sorry. It was my fault that she died!"

As Gabriel stares at me, he tips his chin, his blue eyes blazing into mine. "It was the greed of the damned that killed her. Not you. But... Hell. The Burning Caves..."

I gasp. "Her father–"

"Lucifer." Gabriel finishes my thought.

In an instant I know where I have to go, what I have to do. *Poofing* to Sparrow's house, I let myself in to collect him and bring him with me.

"Sparrow?" I ask and hear the sound of quiet words being spoken.

"She left you," a soft voice says.

"No, she didn't," Sparrow replies.

"Looks to me like she did."

Walking toward the sound, I reach the threshold of his bedroom. Sparrow stands facing a window, shoulders sagging. There is a large gash across his back, glistening with blood.

"She knows you can't follow her, and her type. This is why we don't get involved with humans. They're not like us. They break hearts. She ruined you once already."

Teari lays her hand on his bare shoulder. She bends, pressing her lips to his neck.

My heart stops beating.

It is very hard for me not to punch her in her beautiful

face right now. Forget the fact that she towers over me by almost a foot. If she were standing closer to me, I would have tried. But instead, *poof*, I take my broken heart and return to Hell and the tree I sat in and waited for Jim to retrieve me from not so long ago.

Stupid of me to think that things could have been different, that I could have deserved different. It seems Sparrow lied to me. There are things that can hurt me very much from within the Seven Kingdoms of Heaven.

......

SPARROW

"You shouldn't have done that." I push Teari away from me.

The front door slams and the house is filled with the sounds of one very angry person headed my way. Teari's eyes widen and we both turn to watch a flaming mad King Gabriel storm into the room.

"What the hell!" Gabriel leers over me. "Where are your fucking clothes?"

Lifting my hand, I wave the shirt at him. He spins, pointing one very large index finger at Teari. "She saw you. Both of you. And whatever the hell you were doing here." Leaning close to me, he pinches his finger and thumb together. "I am *thisclose* to sending you back to Hell." He spins. "And you! You want to go back to your Father's Kingdom? I gave you refuge here. I protected you. And I forbid you from going near Sparrow. Your actions are forbidden, you know this."

"He was injured," Teari retorts.

"I don't give a crap! You two are in deep shit. And I swear to God you both better fix it! She came for your help,

Sparrow, just like I told her. Just like you asked her. And she walked in on this... whatever the hell you two are doing. Now, Meg is sitting outside the Burning Caves, alone."

My gut drops in that second. She barely survived her first visit to the Burning Caves. And it's been a few days, Jim's father will have recruited new Hellions to replace the ones we killed, he'll want revenge. And what better revenge than a child for a child.

......

WOODSMOKE AND PINE AND TRUE BLOOD

As I sit in the tree contemplating my first move, it's not long before the small hairs on the back of my neck start to rise, sending a tingling sensation down my spine. Turning, I see the half burned face of Jim watching me.

"You're dead," I tell Jim.

He smiles, lopsided, half of his face looking like it's melting off. "Not quite." Just as he speaks, seven forms step out of the shadows.

Oh shit, Hellions.

"But the Legion, they killed you all." I start to move higher into the tree to get away from them.

"Ah, Meg," Jim starts, "Something they forgot to tell you about. We have a Treaty. One realm is not allowed to fully decimate another realm's policing force. They didn't kill us all. No matter how much bad we do, they can't take us all. And lucky for you, I always have a stash of Hellions waiting for their turn at the action."

As I climb, the bones rattle in the burlap sack. Jim tips his head, focusing on the bag.

"What have you got there, Meg?"

Ignoring him, I climb higher.

"Oh, Meg," he starts in a sing-song voice. "Dear, sweet, little, Meg. What have you got in that bag?"

Gripping the top branch, holding tight, I watch in dread as Jim runs, kicks his feet out sideways and rams into the tree trunk. The entire tree jolts. I try to remember the words Sparrow taught me, so I can poof out of here, back to someplace safe. But I can't focus. My heart is beating too fast, my arms shaking.

"Get her down, boys!" Jim shouts.

And then the tree is jerking and swaying. I twist the twine that holds the sack closed around my wrist, just as one of the largest Hellions runs full force into the aging tree. With a horrible cracking sound, the tree begins to tip. I scratch at the branches, try to hold on, but, I fall.

The feeling of weightlessness lasts only a second before the gravity of Hell smacks me hard against the ground. And then all I feel is the breath rushing from my lungs, an ache in my head, and hands grabbing onto me. They grab my arms, my legs, start dragging me.

"NO!" I scream, tasting blood in my mouth. "NO! NO! NO!" I try to kick, but my legs don't seem to be working as well as they did before the fall. Turning my head, I search for the bag containing my mother's bones, relieved when I find them still tied to my wrist.

"Got someone who wants a word with you," Jim says.

Trying to look between the large legs of the Hellions, I see his form behind us, following. Jesus, I should have waited for Sparrow, even if he was screwing around with Teari. At least I could have had some help down here. Struggling, trying to pull my arms out of their hands, they enter the burning cave.

Woodsmoke and pine. I don't think I will ever get over the fact that the caves of Hell smell so pleasant. I don't get to experience the scent for long. Ripping my arms out of their grasp, my shoulders hit the floor, and then my head. A darkness clouds my vision, the shouts of Jim fill my ears before a harsh ringing takes over and then... nothing.

...

As I open my eyes, I find a large man staring down at me with black as night eyes and matching hair. He's wearing what looks like a leather vest and matching pants, and the wings that rise from behind his shoulders are darker than the shadows at night. The room is cavernous with a large fireplace in the corner, bookshelves, altar, and a large leather chair with a coffee table.

Clenching the bag tight in my fist, I start to whisper, "*Angele Dei, illumina, custodi–*"

The man smiles. "You know Latin, granddaughter?" His voice is so deep it rumbles in *my* chest.

Granddaughter? Oh, Lucifer, in the flesh. I shake my head; stop when I feel a sharp throb. "No."

"Those words you speak, where did you learn them?"

"From a friend. It's nothing."

"Sounded like something. Sounded like you were about to do something spectacular!" He takes an intimidating step closer to me. "Would you like to see what happens when I speak those words? Would you like to see what happens when I pray to the Lord in Heaven?"

Scrambling to my feet, I take two steps back. "No."

He stops moving, his focus moves to the vee of my legs. His head tips. Brow furrows for just an instant. "You have the ouroboros."

"No." I shake my head.

"Yes." He points to my thigh. "Little circular mark, uneven, looks like a snake eating its own tail."

My head tips, mirroring him, as I recall what the birthmark looks like. There is a mark, a small break in the circle of the mark, a V tipped on its side, it could very well be a mouth.

"Haha!" he laughs, claps his hands loudly and his dark wings spread wide, taking up the width of the room.

"Stop it, please. I've only come to find my mother. Gabriel said you could help." I thrust the bag of bones forward and shake them. Dust clouds away from the bag and the bones clank hollowly against each other. He stops, focuses on the bag in my hand. "He said you could help me," I whisper.

Lucifer stands straight, his wings tucked behind him so they are barely visible. "Take out the bones," he demands.

Crouching, I untie the sack and pour the dry bones out onto the aged tile floor.

"Clea," Lucifer whispers. He inhales a deep breath and blows a steady stream of air over the bones. A great wind whips about the room. I shield my eyes, step back, feel my clothes pull in every direction. The bones rattle, clank, dust fills the air like a tornado in the room. I can taste the salt, the grit on my lips from the cave. The wind whips so hard I can't take a breath.

Stumbling backward, large hands grip my upper arms to stop me from falling. What feels like rock presses against my back, keeping me in place as I struggle to get free. The wind dies down. I get my footing and pull my shoulders away from whoever is holding me. There is hot breath in my ear, my hair tickles the side of my face, and a voice says, "I have not forgiven you for trying to kill my son."

"Let her go, Vine," Lucifer bellows. "I forbid you from laying a hand on my own flesh and blood."

The hands push me forward, toward the new figure in the room. She turns. I pull the picture from my pocket and hold it up, they are the same. Her hair is dark as night, her eyes too. But her skin is ghostly porcelain white like I've never seen before. She stands just a few inches taller than me, slender and fine boned. She could be my twin, my dark twin.

"Oh, child," the figure whispers.

"Mom…"

She reaches out a hand, touches my face. She's cold. "You're not alive," I whisper to myself, reminding myself.

"I have enough life left in me to be able to appreciate seeing you." She smiles, her red lips tipping up.

A hot tear I didn't know I was holding in slides down my face and over her hand.

She frowns, moves her free hand to the other side of my face. "Don't cry."

I wish I could stop, but the tears stream out of my eyes, down my face, soaking the neck of my shirt. "I'm sorry. I'm so sorry I killed you." I take a shuddering breath and move to wipe my face.

"Oh," her cold arms surround me, "you didn't kill me, child."

"Yes, John… John Lewis told me so." I release a hard shudder and swallow down the remaining tears that are threatening to stream down my face. "He said I killed you on the day I was born. It was my fault, all my fault. If I were never born, you'd still be alive."

She turns and gives Lucifer a look before she says, "John Lewis' words are no better than the pond of scum he was formed from. Don't listen to him."

"He's going to die," I tell her flatly. "The Legion is going to kill him."

The warmth of the burning caves surrounds me as she pulls away. She gives a sharp nod. "Good."

"But, you're dead."

"We don't really ever die. Creatures like us. Just… our souls go where they belong."

"But you can't belong down here."

She shrugs, her image wavering. "I did things, broke rules, birthed an ethereal child in a realm where she didn't belong. You could stay here with me. We have all the time we need now."

I catch Jim's half-melted face out of the corner of my eye, watching me intensely. He still wants my blood. I will never be safe down here. "I don't think I can stay here."

"Where will you go?"

"I'm not sure."

She smiles. "It's what I wanted for you, the ability to make the choice freely." She glances at Lucifer before taking my hand. "Come, I'll walk you out of this place.

I would like to try and *poof* out of there, but after the fight with the Hellions and Jim I'm too weak. "Will you let me leave?" I ask Lucifer.

He gives a nod. "You returned my daughter to me. And for this I will allow you safe passage and one favor."

"One favor?"

"You never know when you might need a favor from the King of Hell."

He holds out a weapon, similar to the one Sparrow carries, but smaller. It hums and glows as I wrap my fingers around it. "What's this?" I ask.

"Your weapon. Forged in the fires of Hell. It will only come alive for you. It will protect you. Give you safe passage to the portal."

Twisting my wrist, gripping the weapon harder, I say, "Sparrow has one of these."

"His was forged in the light of the Heavens. Yours is very different."

"Thanks," I reply as my mother pulls me closer to the door.

The Hellions and Jim fidget in the shadows as my mother opens the door to a cavern hallway that's barely lit. Out of the corner of my eye I see Lucifer give a stern shake of his head to the others in the room. I hope it's an order not to follow me.

As we walk, my footsteps are the only ones making a hollow sound on the stone floor. My mother seems to float as she tugs at my hand, weaving down dimly lit hallways, past closed doors. Every so often the sound of metal squealing breaks the silence; things peek through cracked doors at us. And when I can see the light at the end of the tunnel, she finally speaks again.

"You came alone?" my mother asks.

"I wasn't going to. It's just... something came up." I decide not to tell her about finding Sparrow with Teari's perfect lips pressed to his skin.

She stops at the threshold to the Burning Caves. Turning, I find that I can almost see through her pale skin in the light.

"I can't be out here in the daytime," I warn her. "The dead walk, they'll come after me."

She shakes her head from side-to-side, her dark hair brushing against her shoulders. "Not while I'm with you, child." She begins moving, floating over the dusty earth, past the fallen tree that the Hellions knocked me out of, past the scuffle marks from Sparrow and Marcus' staged fight. We head north on the same road that I came to this place on with Sparrow and Teari and Marcus. It's not long before the shuffling starts, the moaning, the thud of bodies knocking into each other as they race at a snail's pace in our direction.

"Here they come," I warn her.

With the flick of her hair over her shoulder, "And there they wait," she replies.

Turning, I see that they wait behind us, never getting any closer until we are ten more steps ahead of them. Attaching my new weapon to my belt loop, I shove my hands in my pockets, unsure of what else to do with them.

"Tell me," my mother says, "tell me about your childhood."

Shaking my head, I reply, "I don't think the childhood I had was one a mother wishes for her child."

She stops walking. "Was Sparrow not there?"

"Sparrow was not there."

"But he was ordered to stay. To protect you, and for more, for your future. I handpicked him. Saw in the stars what you two would become."

"You chose him for me?"

"Yes. He was... he is–"

"He was banished to Hell for losing us, for your death."

She paces in a small circle. "Well that's, that's unfortunate. But you found him? You met him. How?"

Walking again, I tell her, "I was in a coma. Jim tried to kill me. And I guess, I guess I was here, somehow. Sparrow found me here while my soul was teetering on edge."

She spins in a circle around me, ruffling my clothes. "So it was fate. I was right." The feeling of her cold hands on my cheeks stops me in my tracks. "Together, you both, you will be invincible."

"That's what he said."

My mother giggles, a light and beautiful sound emanating from her throat. "Has he told you–"

"Has he told you what a dick he is?" A deep voice interrupts us.

I turn sharply, searching the forest edge. A dark figure emerges. Olive skin, imposing, dressed in the same dark combat gear that I last saw him in and featherless wings. Marcus.

As he advances, I look to my mother. "I cannot control him. He is not one of the walking dead."

"What the hell." Reaching for the weapon on my hip, I grip its handle and hold it in front of me as Marcus gets closer.

"Where is he?" Marcus asks, slowing once his chest nears the tip of my blade.

"Not here. He's not here," I reply.

"You came without the Sparrow Man?"

I nod.

"Stupid." He steps forward, the blade pressing into his chest. I take a step back. "I know what your blood can do. And it's just what I need to get out of here."

He takes two steps, one large hand slaps my arms, sending my weapon sliding across the road. Marcus moves so fast, grabbing the front of my shirt in his fist, lifting me off the ground. I kick my feet, shift my hips, and kick him in the thigh, the groin, the lower part of his stomach.

Marcus drops me, reaches for the blade Lucifer gave me. I scramble to reach it first. Marcus grasps the blade, kicks me in the ribs. As I roll his boot comes down on my chest, the tip of the blade against my neck.

"Just a little blood," he whispers. "Just enough to get me out of here."

He pushes, I feel the tip next to the pulse in my neck, he pushes harder, but nothing happens.

"What the fuck!" His livid eyes zero in on the weapon.

Unable to stop the laugh that escapes my throat, I tell him, "It doesn't like you, Marcus."

The blade clangs to the pavement. Marcus reaches for

me. "Don't need it anyway. I have other methods of making you bleed."

Reaching down, I grasp the hilt of the weapon at the same time as Marcus grips the front of my shirt and pulls me to my feet. Marcus lifts me into the air, my feet dangling. He pulls back his free arm, forms a fist. I wrap my fingers around the grip; catch my mother's face behind his shoulder. She nods. Lifting my arm with one swift movement, I aim for his neck and slice.

Marcus drops me. The taut muscles that kept him so tall and intimidating go limp. His head slides off his shoulders and lands on the pavement with a wet *thwacking* sound.

It concerns me, the ease as to what I just did, and how little I feel about it. Yes, something dark must loom in my soul to do that and feel nothing.

"Very good, child." My mother snaps her fingers and Marcus' body goes up in flames. "Now, where was I before he interrupted me? Oh, yes, has Sparrow told you about his wings?"

I shake my head. "They were featherless when I first met him. And, well, he's never brought it up."

She rubs her cold hand across my shoulder. "He'll tell you. I'm sure. Now, we have a flight to catch."

A wisp of smoke and a strong wind blows over us as she transforms into a giant bird. Some mix between a vulture and a crow and as massive as a dinosaur.

"Argentavis," she says, answering my unasked question of what the hell she is.

"What?"

"Argentavis," she says again, "largest bird to fly."

"Sparrow would be so jealous right now."

She blinks her beady eyes at me. "Damn right he would be. Get on."

She lowers her large body to the ground, allowing me to

climb on her back. Bouncing a few times on her nimble feet, she jumps, spreads her giant wings and lifts us into the air.

"I have someone that you need to meet," she says.

She turns, flying faster, just above the treetops. If I reached out, I could fill my hands with leaves. Instead, I grip the feathers on the back of her neck and tighten my knees against her sides as she flies faster. I close my eyes as the wind *whooshes* by my ears. A blast of air hits my face. She slows, glides, tilts her body and lands.

Opening my eyes, looking around in the pale moonlight, I recognize the field, the nearby forest, the old barn in front of us. I slide off her back and she resumes the form of my mother again. We are at the barn, on Route 37, the barn with the snowy owl. Sparrow's snowy owl.

My mother speaks. "I could tell by the sadness in your soul that you have lost a child."

I nod.

"Was it a boy or a girl?"

"Girl." I swallow the lump in my throat.

"And did you have a name for her?"

Jim didn't know, but I had a name ready, picked out weeks before he tried to kill me. The lump grows, becomes too hard to hold down as I choke out the name, "Elise."

Movement at the top window of the barn causes me to look up. There is a white head, a white body speckled with brown. Before I can comprehend what is happening the owl flaps its wings, takes off into the air, circles once over my head and descends. I hold my arm out like I did when Sparrow was last here with me. The owl lands, tips its head to the side and looks into my eyes. Staring into the golden pools of the snowy owl's eyes, I exhale as it blinks twice, leans forward, and presses the front of its forehead to mine.

We stand like this, bird and human, in the moonlight,

for far too long until the owl straightens herself and lifts into the night sky, disappearing into the forest treetops.

Finding my mother watching, I ask, "What was that?"

She smiles, shrugs her shoulders.

"Her name is Elise?" I ask. "The owl... she... she's my... what is she doing here?"

"She is two-thirds darkness, one-third light. She is where she belongs. The brightest light in the darkest of places. But you've met her already, haven't you?"

With a shaky voice I respond, "Yes, with Sparrow. He wanted two of her feathers."

"And did he get them?"

"Yes."

She smiles again. "Lucky man. She doesn't give her feathers to just anyone." My mother walks closer, places her hands on my shoulders. How I wish I could feel them warm, instead of their icy coolness. "Are you ready for me to take you to the portal?"

I shake my head. "No. I can't go back there. I'm not ready to see him, not yet. I need some time. I need to think about all of this."

"Very well."

A shudder runs up my back, a sense that someone or some things are near. "I think the Hellions are close. I can feel them."

In a wisp of smoke she returns to the figure of the Argentavis. "Let's go. They can't harm you for the time that you're here. This time. But there's no need to give them any opportunities. Where do you want to go?"

I whisper the place in her ear.

...

Clea lands next to the small castle on Wellesley Island where Sparrow and I spent the night after returning from Canada. She transforms into her human figure.

"Meg, you are strong enough to return on your own."

I nod my head.

She wraps her cold arms around me, kisses my forehead. And when she pulls away, she's holding up her fist with three large, black feathers in it.

"What are those?"

"For you, for Sparrow, for Gabriel. Tell him I love him. Could you do that for me, child?"

"Yes."

She pushes the feathers into my shaking hands. "It's been so good to finally meet you. You have become so much more than I could have ever hoped for." She steps back, turns back into the Argentavis, lifts herself into the night and disappears.

...

Sitting on the pier by the lake, far too close to the morning to avoid the walking dead, I hear the plop of seagull poop fall dangerously close to my shoulder. Inching over, I run my fingers over the feathers given to me by my mother. The eerie tremolo of the loon breaks the morning quiet. Looking down at the small pier, I wish I had a steaming cup of coffee to enjoy the loon calls with. The pier moves, I lift my eyes to find a tall figure standing in front of me, dressed in the same combat gear as I last saw him in, his downy, white wings spread wide.

"Impressive wingspan," I say. "You know what they say, big wingspan, big–"

He pulls the wings in until they disappear behind his back and I can only see the curve of them peeking over his broad shoulders. "Meg, I didn't come here to joke."

I throw a rock, much harder than I need to, into the lake. The loon calls again.

"Want to go pluck some feathers?" I ask him. "Relive the old days?"

"Don't need to. I know who I am now."

"Oh yeah, I do too. You're Teari's boyfriend." I stand and turn to leave, but I stop short, finding Teari standing behind me. "I have no words for you." I walk around her.

"I'm sorry, Meg." She reaches out and grabs my arm. I pull away from her. "It was wrong of me. I seek forgiveness. From you."

"Forgiveness?" I scoff.

"I'm serious," she replies. "What you saw with me and Sparrow. It was nothing. Actually, it was unwanted on his part."

Sparrow moves his mouth into a thin pressed line and scowls. Seems he doesn't have fond memories of that moment either.

"Fine. I forgive you." I cross my arms and glare at her.

"He is special to you, only you. See you at home." Teari gives Sparrow a quick nod before lifting into the sky and heading in the direction of the portal to cross realms.

Turning, Sparrow advances toward me from the end of the pier where he has been waiting.

"I asked you to wait for me," he scolds.

"I'm sure you can figure out why I was eager to leave." I tip my head, and Sparrow shakes his.

"I don't know what got into her." Sparrow reaches for me, his hands settling on my arms. "I was injured." He shakes his head again. "What have you been doing here?"

"I met my mother," I tell him.

"You did? That's, well, that's great." Sparrow smiles.

"She can turn into a giant fucking bird. An Argentavis."

Sparrow's eyes twinkle in the morning light. "Awesome."

"Here." I hold out the feather she gave me. "She wanted me to give this to you. Her name was, her name *is* Clea, daughter of Lucifer, lover of Gabriel, mother to... me."

Sparrow reaches for the feather and just as his finger pinch the shaft, a zap of static arcs toward his fingers. His eyes widen, bright green with pin-point pupils before returning to their normal state and focusing on me.

"What was that?" I ask.

"N... nothing."

"That wasn't nothing. What just happened? Tell me."

"We must go. Now, Meg." Sparrow grasps my hand.

I pull away from him. "What did you see?" I demand.

"Remember when I told you we're invincible together?" he asks.

"Yes, and Clea said the same thing."

"I saw a dark future, one where we are separate." He closes the space between us and takes my hand again. "She showed me, Clea showed me." He squeezes my hand tightly, runs his thumb over that mark on my leg, starts to say the words but nothing happens.

"Shit," I mumble. "I hit my head earlier."

He nods. "This won't be good."

We turn to find the seven Hellions and half-melted Jim advancing.

"Stop!" I hold my hand out to them. "Lucifer forbade you from touching me. He promised safe passage out of this place."

The largest Hellion, the one with the scar down his face, laughs. "We can't touch the granddaughter of Lucifer, for now. But we can touch the bird-man. We owe him. Look what he did to Jim's pretty face."

Pulling the weapon from my belt, I hold it in front of me, step in front of Sparrow. "If you would like my feathered friend here, you will have to go through me first."

They advance. One grabs my free arm, tries to tug me away from Sparrow, but Sparrow wraps his arm around my waist, holding me tightly to him. They chuckle, an arm rises, something flies through the air. Sparrow coughs, groans. And then, something so strange happens, the feathers burst from his wings, surrounding us in a flurry of white, a storm, a blinding fog. The feathers slide across my skin, soft and sleek. Yet, elsewhere, everything they touch echoes with the sound of a million razorblades clanging to the ground. The Hellions scream. Sparrow slumps to the ground, knife sticking out of his side, his scaffold of featherless wings returned.

"Jesus, Sparrow." I reach for him.

"Now, Meg," he coughs, bright red blood filling his mouth. "Take me back to Gabriel. He can fix this."

Feeling the strength inside me, *poof*, we are gone.

...

GABRIEL SPUTTERS on his dinner as we drop into the dining room.

"What the–" Gabriel starts.

"Fix him!" If his featherless wings weren't enough to indicate a problem, I roll Sparrow's body to reveal the knife sticking out of his side.

"Ah, knife in the ribs." Gabriel's fork clangs on his dinner plate as he stands. "Not usually a life ender for our kind but... What the shit, Sparrow, you've gone and lost your feathers again. You look like a boiled goose."

"Gabriel! Help him, please."

Gabriel turns his focus on me. "What happened? You went to the Burning Caves alone. Sparrow was supposed to sweep in like a knight in shining armor and save you."

I shake my head from side to side and remembering the feathers from my mother, I pull one out of my pocket and hold it out. "Clea says she loves you."

Gabriel's fingers pinch the feather's shaft. And just like with Sparrow, a tiny arc of static connects with his fingers, his eyes widen, a bright blue sea with pin-point pupils before returning to normal and focusing on me.

"Fuck," Gabriel says.

"What?"

Sparrow groans on the floor.

"I will help him," Gabriel replies. "But only on one condition."

"What's that?" I ask.

"You promise never to leave the Seven Kingdoms of Heaven, ever."

"Why? What did you see?"

"Promise, Meg. Promise me. Promise on Sparrow's life." He crosses his arms. "Promise now or I let him die."

"Why?"

"Promise."

"What did you see? Sparrow saw something too. What?"

"Promise."

"Why?"

"Promise."

"I can't–"

"Promise."

"Gabriel–"

"Now, or he dies."

"Wh–"

"Now."

"Fine!"

"Is that a yes?"

"YES!" I scream.

"Say it."

"I promise never to leave the Seven Kingdoms of Heaven!"

"Good. Close your eyes."

Dropping to my knees, pressing the heels of my hands against my eyes, I shut them tight. Still, I can feel heat, sense a brightness in the room, hear the groan of Sparrow, the sliding of a chair, the whispering of words.

Warm arms wrap around my back and lift me to my feet. "It's okay," Sparrow's voice whispers in my ear.

Burying my face in his neck, I ask, "What did you see?"

"Later," he promises, rubbing my shoulders, my arms, my back, pressing his lips to my temple.

"Get a room," Gabriel grumbles before he leaves the room, slamming the door on his way out.

...

LISTENING to Sparrow in the shower that shoots diamond-glistening water, I move a chair under the bedroom door handle so no one can get in. Pulling the last Argentavis feather from my pocket, I twirl it in my fingers and switch it from hand to hand.

"What did you show them, mother?" I whisper to the feather.

There is an arc of static electricity, my fingertips tingle, my eyes widen and... I see... I *see*.

Wars. Blood and death. Good and evil. A dead Sparrow. A motherless child and a fatherless child. Light and dark. The earthen plane and the ethereal realms. A burst of bright light. An explosion. Fear and pain. Emptiness. A dark, never-ending vat of emptiness that would suck every joyful moment right out of me.

I drop the feather, run to the bathroom, pull the door open and run into the huge shower stall fully clothed. Reaching for Sparrow, I grip his arms, shoulders, neck, face, just to make sure he's real, he's alive.

"Meg?" he asks. "What's wrong?"

"I saw," I tell him. "I saw… the feather… Clea. I saw."

"Oh, Meg." He pulls me to him, locks me in a tight embrace.

"What does it mean?"

"I'm not sure of all of it. But just remember, we are invincible together."

Shuddering in his embrace, his words scorch me with their truth. I hold onto him tight, the water soaking through my clothes, afraid to lose the one person who has ever showed me love and caring and truth.

About the Author

M. R. Pritchard is a two-time Kindle Scout winning author and her short story "Glitch" has been featured in the 2017 winter edition of THE FIRST LINE literary journal. She holds degrees in Biochemistry and Nursing. She is a northern New Yorker transplanted to the Gulf Coast of Florida who enjoys coffee, cloudy days, and reading on the lanai.

Visit her website MRPritchard.com and join her newsletter to receive a monthly update on new releases, freebies, current projects, and daily shenanigans of an author's life.

Follow on Amazon to get alerts on new releases.

If you enjoyed *Sparrow Man*, please leave a review, tell a friend, or gift to a friend. These small acts keep authors writing. Thank you.

Also by & Social Links

Science Fiction/post-apocalyptic:
The Phoenix Project Series:
The Phoenix Project
The Reformation
Revelation
Inception
Origins
Resurrection
The Safest City on Earth
The Man Who Fell to Earth
Heartbeat
Asteroid Riders Series
Moon Lord
Collector of Space Junk and Rebellious Dreams

Steampunk:
Tick of a Clockwork Heart

Dark Fantasy:
Sparrow Man Series

Fantasy/Fairy Tale Love Story/Romance:
Muse
Forgotten Princess Duology
Midsummer Night's Dream: A Game of Thrones

Poetry/Short Stories

Consequence of Gravity

NIGHTINGALE GIRL
by M. R. Pritchard

TWISTED PARADISE

Restlessness prickles under my skin. It feels like one of those never-ending winter days when breathing kerosene heater fumes for hours on end starts getting on your last nerve. It's sad, really; all it took was one week for me to go trailer park crazy. I'm edgy and antsy. And to make it worse, Sparrow vowed to respect King Gabriel's wishes regarding sins of the flesh. That's what I get for swearing never to leave the Seven Kingdoms of Heaven.

"You know, if you focused on other things instead of what Sparrow's got hiding in his pants, you'd be doing this better." Teari's chipper voice breaks my concentration.

The gentle brush of her fingers flutters across the skin of my shoulders. I turn quick to face her. "Don't touch me," I warn.

She holds her hands out as though she were thinking about doing it again. "Wouldn't dream of it." She smiles sweetly.

"You're not supposed to be able to lie." I glare.

"I didn't lie, Meg. I just said I wouldn't dream of it. Because I wouldn't. You rarely enter my dreams."

I run to the mirror on the far end of the dining room to see what she did.

"Teari!" I yell when I see that my hair is three inches longer.

"What?" She shrugs and sits on a velvet-upholstered club chair, crosses her long legs, and admires her fingernails.

"I told you to stop doing that!" I pull my shirt up and check my skin. The tattoos are still there. The spattering of stars is still across my left shoulder, the anchor still on my rib cage. I pull out the waistband of my pants and check the heart—it's still there. Thank God. I pull the shoulder of my shirt down and check the tattoo of the black quill across my right collarbone. Disappointment hits me hard. It's faded.

"That is his favorite one!" I turn to Teari and clench my hands into fists. "You know how Sparrow likes feathers."

Teari stands quickly, her skin blanching when she gets a good look at how angry I am. "You're supposed to look like a princess."

"I don't give a crap what your fluttery Angel princesses are supposed to look like. Stop trying to change me." I grit my teeth and hold in a long stream of curse words. I don't care if the Archangel Gabriel is my father. I'm not going to pretend to be one of their princesses. He said he liked my spunk. It reminded him of my mother.

"I can't get this fixed up here in *Angel-land*. And I promised on Sparrow's life not to leave."

I would love to strangle Teari right now. I don't care if she towers a foot above my head. I think my hands would wrap nicely around her neck.

Teari fidgets with the waistband of her slacks. She looks like a damn supermodel standing in front of me. I want to claw her eyes out.

"It's fine," she says.

"It's not fine. It's faded!" I walk toward her, ready to attack. I point to my shoulder where the quill tattoo is. "And it's his favorite."

Teari steps back, her eyes widening. "I helped you," she reminds me. "When you were in Hell, I healed you. I made you whole again." Her perfect face begins to look worried.

True, she did heal me. Teari came to help me and Sparrow when we were trapped together in Hell. She healed my wounds after my a-hole of an ex strung me up like a turkey and stabbed me in the chest with a knife.

While strangling Teari might help me feel better, it would leave my father without his personal healer. I cross the room to get away from her.

"Stop screwing with my tattoos and hair," I warn her.

A few moments pass before I come to the conclusion that causing Teari physical harm is unladylike—something Sparrow's always nagging me about. I weave around her and leave the room, slamming the door closed behind me.

They want me to be on my best behavior here, but Teari is making it awfully difficult.

I walk down lengthy hallways with towering windows that let in the bright, heavenly light of this place. Shielding my eyes, I wish I had brought my sunglasses with me. I avoid the sunlit expanses and walk in the shadows along the wall. It's not long before I'm standing at the door to my room.

There's a plush mattress on a frame, a bathroom with a tub and shower, fluffy towels, clean sheets, fresh pillows, a balcony, and a closet full of clothing. None of this ever existed in the single-wide trailer I grew up in. I came close when I spent my inheritance on that little house with a white picket fence. Tried to pull my roots out of the North Country gutter, but while it seemed money could buy me a home, it couldn't hide me from my demons.

I open my door and step into my room. A warm breeze billows the curtains of the floor-to-ceiling windows. The golden linens on the giant four-poster are not the crumpled mess that I had left them in earlier. I look around and notice that my towel is no longer on the floor by the bathroom, either. Teari must've sent someone in here to clean up.

I walk past the bed and grab my sunglasses off the table in the sitting area. It's so bright here that it hurts my eyes, gives me a headache. Trying to control the darkness within me is hard enough; I can't stand constantly being illuminated by the sunshine of Heaven, as well. Even if it does sparkle prettily. Daylight hurts Hell-dark adjusted eyes.

I reach for the small machete-style weapon on my nightstand. Forged in the fires of Hell, it only cuts if I'm the one holding it. Lucifer gifted it to me after I delivered him the bag of bones that was my mother. He also promised me one favor that I have yet to use.

My thoughts turn to Sparrow and our time together down there.

Sparrow's an Angel, tall and handsome and a little peculiar. He's better than he used to be. When we were trapped in Hell, he was batshit crazy. The poor guy was nothing but a cracked nut when we found each other. We can blame my father for that, though. He banished Sparrow, stripping his wings and taking his memories, leaving him to wander the zombie-strewn wasteland of Hell. As fate would have it, that's where we found each other.

Sometimes I think that Sparrow is the best thing that's ever happened to me. Better than finding out what I truly was: more than North Country trash, the daughter of an Archangel, the child of forbidden love.

I secure the weapon in the thigh holster Sparrow made for me and put my sunglasses on. Leaving my room, I make my way to the door leading to the courtyard at the end of the hall. As soon as I step outside, my skin sizzles. It's bearable, almost.

I wonder if the sun is like this in the other Kingdoms of Heaven? Teari is supposed to teach me about them, but she's too busy working with the Legion, being my father's personal healer, and trying her damnedest to turn me into a princess. I've learned a few things, though: The earthen plane is God's land. The Seven Kingdoms of Heaven are ruled over by the Council of Seven Archangels. Hell has Lucifer.

I make my way past the sparkling stone fountain and down the marble steps set into the hillside. I stroll past the barracks where the Legion trains; the grounds are empty. They must be on break, which means Sparrow will be home. Good, I haven't gotten him alone in a few days. I pick up speed and head for the trail behind the barracks.

Thick forest shades the winding path to Sparrow's house. Having finally escaped the sun, I take off my sunglasses and hang them on the front of my shirt. Windows and doors close at the houses as I pass. There are some inhabitants of this place who are not happy about my presence here. They don't like the idea of me tainting their *goodness*. I am the blackened stain of my father's Kingdom.

Click here to read the rest of Nightingale Girl on Kindle